CHAPTER ONE

Zvi rolled over in his bed so he could look out his bedroom window. He couldn't sleep. His mind was troubled with a lot of unanswered questions. Questions he knew probably should be left alone. But that wasn't Zvi's nature. This wasn't the first sleepless night. He had been troubled for some time.

He lay on his stomach listening to the birds as they awoke to another day, singing their endless melodies. No one was up and about yet. He searched the streets and walkways. Still too early, except for the curious. He got out of bed, dressed and walked quietly outside, so not to disturb the rest of the family.

The sun wasn't up yet. But then in this land of Brahm's, the land of plenty, there was never complete darkness. The lights issuing forth from the mountain of lights filled the heavenly skies with pastels of blues, golds and pinks. And these colors mixing together as two clouds colliding together making an unbelievable array of colors. The streamers-or-light shooting out and beyond, engulfing everything. Reaching so far distant that the sun was even engulfed by its own brilliance.

Zvi walked peacefully through the gardens and across the lawn. The fragrant aroma from the many roses and orchids provided a perfumed atmosphere that flowed gently in the air behind him. The grass was wet with dew and bathed his feet as he strolled towards the shore of the endless ocean.

He paused for a moment and gazed out across the water. *Strange,* he thought to himself, *how this great endless body of water can be so calm and quiet now and then without any forewarning become an angry giant, ready to consume any who so dared to venture out.* Zvi dug his toes beneath the moist sand. He doubted with sincerity what the 'Over Lords' preached: that the ocean was endless. He knew that there was something laying beyond. Beyond anything that any of the inhabitants of this land knew or would recognize. There was something out there. How different, he could only begin to imagine. But there was something. For that he was sure.

This was one of the questions he dared not ask. Because it would identify him as a non-believer, a trouble maker. He would be exiled from the community and left to his own resources, far from any civilized area. Others had asked forbidden questions and were never seen again. His family would also be shunned and life made almost impossible for them.

There would come a time when he would know the answers. But not now. Even in the twilight the water glistened with millions and millions of tiny glittering specks. The ocean appeared to be on fire. This was a land of beauty and intrigue. No one went hungry or without, but all were governed closely with a tight rein.

He turned his attention to the mountain of lights and wondered why the lights issued forth from the peak, as they did. Was there something mystical and unknown inside of the mountain that no one could explain? And why were all forbidden to climb up the slopes?

He wandered along the sandy shore until he came to the other end of the village, then followed a well worn foot path into the hills behind the village. Here he stopped to look down on the streets and buildings and to dream again about the endless ocean.

Was he so much different that the others? Was he the only one to question and wonder about the unexplainable? Or were there others like him, only too conscious of the 'Over Lords' guards to make public their concerns. He had been warned once about his overt thinking and told if he disobeyed again he and his whole family would be punished severely.

AN ESOTERIC JOURNEY

BY

RANDALL PROBERT

An Esoteric Journey

by Randall Probert

Printed in the United States

www.randallprobertbooks.net

ISBN 978-0-9852872-2-1

The cover photo was purchased from iStockPhoto

Disclaimer: This book is a work of fiction and the dialogues of
Judaism and Islam and the suspicions surrounding the Gulf War
were created by me to create a modem for Brahm to test Zvi's
understanding and worthiness in his search for Truth.

Published by
Randall Enterprises
P.O. Box 862
Bethel, Maine 04217

He stood there in all the grandeur of Brahm's land, but was left with an emptiness within. Beauty surrounded him and the air was filled with a constant melodious humming. It was a sound that he was so used to hearing, that he hardly ever noticed it now. It emanated from every living thing. Even himself. No longer listening to the ever familiar melody, he sat down on a moss covered rock. In a short while he would have to go to the central meeting place to hear a repetitious sermon by one of Brahm's Over Lords or a priestly subordinate.

Deep within himself Zvi knew there was more to life and creation than was being told by the Over Lords. All of the Over Lords teachings and sermons did little to answer his questions. Therefore he knew there was more than what the masses were being told. People were being told only what Brahm wanted the masses to know and no more, to keep them dependent and obedient. But Zvi was different. He didn't like being led or told what he could or could not believe. He wasn't a cow being led to a pasture. But how could he resist and not endanger the welfare of his family. They were content to live as they were and believed what the Over Lords preached without ever thinking about doubting any of them.

Zvi needed more than the prosaic materialistic teachings. He needed adventure and more importantly, truth. "Some day I'll know the answers," he said as he stood up and stretched. The sun was already up. He wasn't aware that he had been there that long. He started back, not wanting to be late for the morning's services. He was a gardener and today all whose position was as a gardener had to attend this morning's service and listen to the Over Lord. Zvi would attend and only act as though he were interested.

*   *   *   *

Before Zvi was back from the hills, the big bell in the central meeting place began to ring. All gardeners in the village

5

left their homes and families and started towards the central meeting place to hear the days tirade on being obedient to Brahm. On the faces of all was an expression of complete joy and happiness. Even Zvi wore a mask expression of happiness.

The Over Lord waited patiently until everyone was seated in the outdoor arena before starting his deliberation. After everyone had taken a seat and all were quiet the Over Lord started a chant to dispel any negativity and create a purely positive aura around the congregation "Aaauumm, Auauuumm."

Zvi participated and he could feel a joyous vibration surge through him and engulf the entire group, forming a separate entity just above their heads. Each one was opened spiritually so that Brahm's message could flow through each more easily.

When the chant was over the Over Lord began his oration. "All is given to you my children from the Great Brahm. He has provided well for your happiness and well being. If you hunger, Brahm will feed you. If you are thirsty, Brahm will give you water. There is nothing that you can desire that Brahm can not provide for you. Does He not let you live in his world where all is happiness? Brahm is every thing and everything is Brahm. He is in all and all is in Him.

"There is no thought, deed or word spoken that Brahm is not aware of. He knows all. Worship Him and you shall rejoice in His kindness and His love for you.

"Though I warn you, speak derogative about Him or belittle Him in any way and His wrath will fall down around you. Worship Him and love Him and Brahm will be your protector."

The Over Lord kept the tirade going telling all the gardeners how loving and merciful Brahm was. Zvi gave his full attention to the Over Lord and what he was saying. He didn't dare do otherwise. He knew there were spies amongst the gardeners whose primary function was to pick up on unfavorable thought forms emanating from a discontent. If he let his mind wander and mistakenly start thinking about what was really troubling him, then these spies would pick up on these thought forms and he would have a severe penalty to pay. He had been warned earlier of an overt act and now he knew he would be watched more closely. The only time he had the privacy of his own thoughts were rare moments when he could be alone.

"In closing today's sermon, let me remind you of your loyalty and obedience to Brahm. Then and only then will he embellish you with His love.

"Go now and be cheerful in this land of plenty and of light spirit. May Brahm's blessings go with each of you."

Zvi left the meeting feeling as empty as ever. All it amounted to was an insidious manipulation of the masses. Control the desire of the individual, or masses, and Brahm controls the individual as well as the mind and one's own initiative to think. Well it was over at least until all the other groups had attended and then it would be the gardeners turn again. Tomorrow and for the next several days would be a relief. Tomorrow the tradesmen, then the builders and so on until each group had attended. The artists were the last to attend, being they were purposively at the highest level of citizenry. Then what—where did one go from there? Another question no one dared to ask the Over Lords. But some day Zvi would know. He'd have the answer. Of that he was sure.

Zvi walked with his friend to the central park where they were planting flowers and cleaning up the shrubbery. It was still too soon to think openly so Zvi asked his friend, "How did you like the Over Lord's talk this morning?"

"I thought it was marvelous. Didn't you? Everything we want is provided for us. And look what we do for work. We plant flowers and keep the shrubs and grass clean and everything looking so nice. And all that is asked of us is to appreciate Brahm and what He gives us." Varian replied

"Yeah, I guess you're right. Everything seems to be perfect. Anything we want is there for us. What could be better?"

Varian thought Zvi's tone had a bit of sarcasm in his reply. "You sound a little bitter. Are you doubting again the Blessings of Brahm?"

Before answering Zvi looked to see who might be near enough to focus on his thought form. Everyone had more or less gone their own way. He felt safe enough to add, "It's not that I'm doubting the love of Brahm or his power, but Varian, haven't you ever wondered about the endless ocean? Or what's inside the mountain of lights that issues forth such an array of colors? Or why no one is allowed to climb the slopes? Don't you ever have questions that no one can answer?"

The two walked on in silence. Zvi thought perhaps Varian had been offended and wasn't going to answer. But instead., Varian was drawing from deep within himself before answering. "I honestly don't think that there has ever been a time when I have thought that I needed to know any of the answers to your questions. I have always accepted what the Over Lords have said about the Brahm and I put my trust and faith in Him."

"But—isn't there a time when you want to know a little more than what we are told?" Zvi asked.

Again Varian thoughtfully took his time before answering. "If I did and let's say I did learn a bit more . . . would it do me any good? I believe Brahm has given each of us as much knowledge as we each can handle. With more knowledge, then wouldn't our desires become more, and more intricate? And I'm sure that kind of behavior would only offend the Great Brahm and bring His wrath down around me. To answer your question my friend, no I have no need for more knowledge or to know the answers to your questions. I am quite content as I am."

Zvi let it drop. It was obvious that his friend was satisfied with his plot in life. They walked the rest of the way to the central park in silence.

The park was situated on a side hill over looking the endless ocean and a far distant valley to the west of the village. Other workers were already busy with their daily chores when Zvi and Varian arrived. Masons were laying new walkways. Some were paved with small stones of red and green jade and white milky quartz. Others were paved in cement and lined with clear transparent quartz crystals and other precious gems. Other builders were building picnic tables and fireplaces, patios and terraces. A new amphitheater for the new string orchestra that was forming in the village. Other gardeners rolled out huge rolls of grass turf and fit the strips so close together that the lawns looked natural. Other gardeners planted shade trees that began growing as soon as the roots were embedded in the rich soil and watered. Zvi's and Varian's job was to follow behind the tree gardeners and builders and plant shrubs and flowers.

There was no bickering or grumbling among the workers. Each had a specific job to do and it was done. There were no supervisors or foremen standing watch. No safety inspectors. No health inspectors. Each task was completed with a conscience and was done right.

By the end of the day the park was finished and a two day holiday was declared to celebrate. The string orchestra had been practicing and were ready for a concert the next night in the huge new amphitheater. The crowds gathered early to stroll through the park and see its beauty.

Overtures of soft floating melodies were played and their vibrations blended with the ever present humming, that truly made the sounds of God. The group played their last piece as the sun was setting below the horizon of the endless ocean. Streamers of golden light reflected off the water's surface, sending them shimmering into the air, some streamers literally staying in mid-air and vibrating with the sounds of music. Some streamers shot up and blended with the pastel colored sky. Everything had a golden glow about it, even the people and walkways. Everything vibrated with the melodious music and life.

When the concert was over and everyone had left the amphitheater, Zvi walked alone along the walkways, smelling the flowers and listening to the humming that emanated from everything. He stopped to watch the ocean surf lap against the sandy shore, feeling a sense of awe. The music that night had set something stirring inside of his being, like an electric wave oscillating back and forth. It made him wonder about the constant humming. Where did it come from? Why did everything vibrate with the same all engulfing sound? All the Over Lords had ever said, "listen and you shall hear the voice of Brahm. For it is everywhere about you." But they had never explained it beyond that.

Zvi left the park and wandered towards the outer limits of the village. It wasn't long before he found himself crossing the long valley to the west. There was no concern about his family worrying about him. In this land of Brahm's, there was complete trust. No one ever violated another's privacy by asking about their personal lives.

During the night Zvi walked across the valley to the opposite side. There was no need for alarm from the animals that stalked the wilderness. They like himself were an extension of God's own being. Only an occasional night hawk or owl fluttered near. The pastel sky made it light enough to see without any trouble. He wasn't afraid of getting lost. Besides, he was being guided by the ever constant humming. The cadence had changed. Almost, it seemed for his benefit. The vibration pulled him along, destined to show him something. But what?

At the distant border of the valley, the rich green grass land was fringed by a lustrous green forest. He took a cool drink from a stream emerging from the forest and then sat down leaning his back against a silver birch tree. Instead of watching the valley, he looked intently through the trees, as if he might be expecting to meet with someone.

It was evening of the next day. Zvi had sat leaning against the silver birch tree the entire day; what had only seemed like minutes were actually hours. Strange though, how he wasn't tired or hungry. He took another drink from the cool stream and started back across the immense valley.

The next day while doing some gardening in the other end of the village Varian said, "I looked for you the other evening after the concert. Thought sure you'd be at the festival dinner."

"I didn't go to the dinner. I stayed out at the park and walked around for a while and listened to the surf. Then I walked across the valley to the other side."

Varian gasped with surprise. Shocked that anyone would be so bold to make the journey, to the other side of the valley— let alone by oneself. "What ever possessed you to do a thing like that?"

"Not sure actually. I started out for just a short walk. Wasn't long before I realized I had gone a far distance across the valley. Almost like I was being guided by something."

"By the devil more than likely," Varian said sourly.

"What do you mean by that?" Zvi asked.

"Haven't you ever heard the stories about that side of the valley?"

"No, apparently I haven't."

"Haven't you been listening to the Over Lords?"

"Not as well as you, I can see."

"The Over Lords tell of an ancient one that was banned from the village, almost at the beginning of time. He was accused of sorcery. Dabbling in the psychic phenomenon practices. He was sentenced by The Over Lords to live for eternity away from the village and to have no contact with anyone."

"You said he was accused; was it ever proven that he was a sorcerer?" Zvi asked.

"There you go again Zvi, doubting the teachings of the Over Lords. Haven't you learned your lesson yet?"

"I'm not doubting anyone Varian," he said in defiance, "you clearly said accused, not that he had ever been proven a sorcerer. There's a big difference."

"I'm not sure. I only know what the Over Lords have told me." Varian replied. "The forest he lives in is enchanted with his evil psychic undulations. It is said that one could disappear completely, if you were to enter that forest."

"How can that be?"

"I don't know for sure. But it has to do with the sorcerer's

11

negative powers, and something about a portal that opens to another time."

"Sounds too strange for me to believe," Zvi said. "Someday I might return to the other side of the valley and see for myself this ancient one you speak about."

The sorcerer subject was forgotten and they both went back to work harvesting vegetables from the community farm to be distributed later by the merchants. All day while picking corn and beans, Zvi kept thinking about what Varian had said about the one called the ancient one. Was he indeed a sorcerer? And had he devised a portal where one could step through to another time? It all seemed too fantastic to be true. But he had always been intrigued by the unusual and unexplainable.

After supper that evening Zvi went for a walk in the newly finished park. Others were there and no one seemed to pay any particular attention to him. He walked down to the shore and sat listening to the surf slap against the sand. It made a soothing sound. The pastel sky was particularly colorful. He tried to see the streamers of light issuing forth from the peak of the mountain of lights, but the top was lost in the clouds.

This land of Brahm's was so tranquil and serene. There was no ugliness. No quarreling or harsh words. And Brahm provided for every need.

Then why did he feel so much like a prisoner? Just then he noticed a lone person dressed in black watching him. He must be one of the Over Lords spies. Immediately Zvi began to think of Brahm and his world in more favorable thoughts and became gracious for all that Brahm had provided. He didn't want the spy to focus on his negative thought forms about Brahm. After a few minutes the stranger wandered off, satisfied that there was no discontent coming from Zvi.

Zvi watched as the stranger walked among the other people in the park, trying to find someone with a negative thought form. "There's one reason why I feel like a prisoner. I'm not free to think as I may without fear of being persecuted. This land of Brahm's is indeed almost perfect, but for myself, I must find my own answers. And I think they begin at the other end of the valley," he said to himself.

*   *   *   *

Two days later Zvi was ready to leave. He didn't discuss with anyone what he was doing. If his family knew, repercussions from his action could fall upon them. Once he left and entered the sorcerer's forest, he wasn't sure if he would ever be able to return. So he kept his plans to himself.

He waited until the sun had set and all was quiet. Before leaving the garden, he stopped to listen for any movement that might detect that he was being watched. When he was satisfied, he walked down the main street in full view to see if any one would follow him. Always he kept the gracious image of Brahm in the fore front of his thoughts, so if any spies were out and around they could not focus on his true intentions.

Once he was at the edge of the valley he stopped and waited. No one had followed. He continued on and forgot about Brahm and the spies. The air was still and the cadence of the steady humming had changed and the pastel skies were beginning to cloud over with dark menacing boulder like clouds. Not common in this tranquil land. A little further and the birds stopped their chirping. Lightening flashed ahead and thunder vibrated the ground under his feet. This had never happened before. Never had he witnessed lightening cutting through the air. Or the ground tremble from the deafening roar of the thunder that followed.

He knew he would be soaked from the rain so he sought shelter. He found an over-hanging cliff under a large boulder. But the rain never came. The lightening flashed continuously across the now darkened sky and the thunderous roar was making him nervous. Had he been wrong and made a mistake, trying to cross the valley again?

He waited until the lightening had stopped and he felt composed. It was almost dawn, yet the skies were still darkened. He thought about turning back, but knew he would be blamed for this strange unexplainable storm. No, he would venture on. He left the security of the boulder. The dark clouds were beginning to clear away and the first radiant golden rays of the sun brought forth a sense of strength and firmness of mind.

It wasn't long before the day was it usual self in all its splendor. But suddenly the ground he was walking on began to rumble and the surface moved like waves on the ocean. Suddenly the ground opened up behind him and the quaking ground rumbled louder as the open gap in the ground widened. The gap extended from side to either side as far as he could see. Return to his home now was out of the question.

Screams, shrieks and wailing issued out of the bowels of the ground. The hair on Zvi's neck stood up and he was convinced now that this valley was indeed the land of the sorcerer. But he couldn't turn back now. Mostly because of the gaping hole behind him and partly because he was still curious enough to find out for himself and see if his answer might lay hidden at the end of this journey.

He regained some composure and started out once again to cross the valley. The day was warmer than what he was accustomed to. Sweat beaded his forehead and he was needing a drink of cool water. Some hours later he came across a spring bubbling out of the ground. "Odd," he said, I don't remember this being here. He laid on his stomach and just started to touch his lips to the cool liquid when the smell of ammonia aroma burnt the membrane tissue in his nose.

In disgust he jumped to his feet and kicked sand into the ammonia spring until he had completely buried it. Aloud he said, "Oh what have I gotten myself into. I can't turn back and I'm not sure if I'll live to see the other end of this demented place!"

He started out again not knowing what he would find

next. The quake had loosened the soil and formed ridges and ravines. Making the journey rugged and more taxing. By the time the sun had set, he was only about half way across. He was so tired he wasn't hungry, but unless he found water soon, he wouldn't make it to the other side. The sorcerer's forest—what could he expect?

Discouraged he sat down on the ground with his back against a rock. The sky was clear, its usual pastel colors, and there were no strange storms raging about. "Perhaps I'll get some sleep tonight at least." As he said that he stretched his legs and kicked out a stone by his left foot. Water was oozing out of the sand where the stone had been. He dug out a hole and waited for the dirty water to clear. After drinking his fill he sat back against the rock and fell asleep.

It was a fitful night of sleep. All night he had dreams about the strange encounters during the previous day. The storms that were never seen in this land before, only heard stories told of them. Nor the ground opening up in gapping ravines. The only answer then, it had to be the work of the ancient one, the sorcerer. Did he know Zvi was crossing the valley and this was only his way of trying to stop him?

Morning came and with it a welcoming sigh of relief. Before leaving, Zvi went to get another drink of water but it was gone. Nothing but dry sand where the water had been.

He checked the sun's position before leaving to make sure he was still traveling in the right direction. As unbelieving as it might appear, the hills on the far side of the valley had disappeared from sight. By now he wasn't too concerned. He chalked it up with all the other strange encounters, as the work of the sorcerer.

The morning air was clear and cool, and the usual pastel colored sky helped to make his spirits a little better today. "But what will I find next? Is the sorcerer trying to scare me away, from ever reaching his enchanted forest? Or is this the work of the Over Lords trying to keep me from talking with the ancient one?" He didn't know who was responsible for trying to keep him from reaching the other side, but he was more determined than ever now, to find out why.

Zvi had been so deep in thought that he hadn't realized he was walking into a deep ravine. This too wasn't here before. Probably opened up by the quake he thought. He stopped to look around and for the first time he saw that the ravine was filled with snakes. Twisting around each other, squeezing and striking out at anything in its way. Some were huge beyond proportion. Some had two heads and tongues of fire. It was the ugliest, most grotesque sight he had ever seen. They were so busy fighting amongst themselves they had not seen him. He backed quietly out of the ravine and detoured along way around it. A sudden shiver went up his spine.

When he was finally beyond the snake filled ravine, he sat down and wiped the sweat from his forehead. The sight of that grotesque mass had unnerved him. He didn't want to think about what might have happened, if even one of those snakes had seen him. And what bothered him even more, "What's out there waiting for me now? What else will try to stop me?" He knew he had to keep going. If only to see what the next obstacle might be. The truth he was seeking he knew would be at the end of this journey.

He got up and started out again. Nothing unusual happened and he was nearing the foothills of the enchanted forest, the land of the sorcerer. The sun had set but he didn't want to spend another night alone in the valley. He found the same cool stream of water that he had drank from when he was there only days before. Everything seemed normal again. Everything looked as it had when he was there before. He took a drink from the stream and while his face was turned towards the water he noticed a dark shadow moving across the ground. He rolled over and started to stand up when he saw a winged bat of gigantic size gilding through the air toward him. As the bat gilded closer, he saw that the head of the creature was actually a human's head.

Mouth open and shrieking a high pitch scream. He ducked and the bat flew past him and disappeared into the forest.

But Zvi hadn't realized there was another larger bat behind the first. When the first bat disappeared into the forest, he stood up and turned around just in time to see the other larger creature coming at him. There was no time to duck or defend himself in any way. All he could do was to bring his arms up in front of his face. The bat came closer, screaming its hideous shriek and gilded through Zvi without ever touching him.

In amazement he dropped his hands and watched it, as it too disappeared into the forest. Where the first bat had gone. He couldn't believe what he had seen. He turned back around to see if there were any more. "It's only an illusion," he said. And then he added, "All of this strangeness, the lightening storm, the quaking ground and the ammonia spring, all nothing more than illusions. That's why the snakes didn't attack me. They couldn't, they weren't really there!"

He heard a branch break behind him and turned to see what was coming now. Much to his surprise, he saw standing where the bats had disappeared a man dressed in an off-white robe. His hair was cut short and he had no facial hair, his eyes were silvery blue and piercing. He smiled at Zvi and said, "No, I'm not an illusion. Welcome to my side of the valley."

Zvi stood there, by the cool stream; speechless. This was without a doubt the one called the ancient one or sorcerer. But he looked so friendly. "Are you responsible for all that has happened?" Zvi demanded to know.

"The illusions, yes my friend they were all of my doing."

"Then Varian was right. You are nothing more than a sorcerer!"

"Oh—I've heard that I'm some times called a sorcerer. But I suppose that that's only because the others don't understand. The illusions, as you have said, were my doing. They were all harmless, I assure you."

"Then it was for my benefit! A practical joke! Is that it?"

17

Zvi found himself getting angrier and angrier.

"They were not created to be a joke. But they were for your benefit, as well as my own."

"Then will you explain for what purpose you saw fit to scare me?" Zvi demanded.

"You were here before."

"Yes," Zvi replied.

"You were here before, I saw you."

"And?" Zvi interrupted.

"As I said I saw you and knew you would be back—"

"How could you know?" he interrupted again.

"I could read your thought forms. They were positive and of a good nature. You are an inquiring soul. A need to know, that others of your village do not have."

"Then why did you have to terrify me with all the illusions?"

"Because I needed to know how pure your search was and how strong of heart and spirit you were. The illusions as you finally understood them, were only created to test you. To see if you would turn back if the going got rough. When you didn't turn back, I made each illusion there after more malicious, stronger. To see if you would break from your original quest."

"Then are you a sorcerer?" Zvi asked.

"No, by no means. Although there are those who would address me as such. Only because they can't see the truth."

"Then what are you, if you can create all this magic with illusions?"

"First of all the illusions were not magic. The word magic is a very poor word to use indeed. It has no meaning, actually, when you try to apply it to any circumstance. What am I? That, you have come here to learn, and I can not tell you in one sentence alone."

"What do I call you then?"

"I am called by some as "The Ancient One." Although those who are close and know me well simply call me "The Old One.""

"May I then call you Old One?" Zvi asked.

"By all means. Yes."

"If then, those close to you call you The Old One, how old are you?"

The Old One laughed a hearty laugh and took Zvi by the shoulders and said, "Come, we will return to my hut and you can fill your stomach and rest."

Zvi felt reassured of his reason for coming to this side of the valley now. He felt very comfortable in the presence of the Old One.

"My friend, you asked how old I am. I am as old as time." The Old One's words resonated with a deep rolling effect down across the valley's floor and were lost before reaching the outer limits of Zvi's village.

CHAPTER TWO

As suggested Zvi ate a hearty meal of pinto beans, alfalfa roots and a herb tea made from a special plant that the Old One said grows only on this side of the valley. Afterwards he lay down to rest. The Old One went outside for a walk behind his hut.

The Old One's hut wasn't very elaborate. He had what he needed to exist, that was all. It was clean and tidy. The floor was planked over and rubbed with some kind of oil that glistened. The four walls were of stone and the inside was stucco. The roof was covered with thick layers of dry grass.

Before closing his eyes for sleep, Zvi thought about his trek across the valley and all the illusions the Old One had manifested for him . . . to test his desire for truth and his understanding.

He had gained just enough truth already, so he understood he could never return to the village and live only according to Brahm. To exist only.

Zvi fell asleep as he was looking at the inside of the hut. His eyelids became so heavy, he could no longer keep them open. He resigned to a deep peaceful sleep. Just before awakening he had a rather confusing dream. He was in some kind of a machine that flew through the air at incredible speeds. He was in control and flying over what appeared to be a battlefield. These were instruments of war and he wasn't familiar with them. He saw himself release a charge of explosives that exploded on contact below him on the battlefield and as he was pulling up to leave, the machine he was in caught on fire and he knew that it would explode.

Zvi opened his eyes and found himself in the Old One's hut and he soon forgot about the disturbing dream. The Old One wasn't there, so he went outside and walked around the little clearing that the hut had been built in.

"Aye, I see you are up and I hope are feeling refreshed," the Old One said.

"I'm feeling fine, thank you."

"Come let us walk beside the cool stream. There it is not so warm." They followed a well used path beside the stream that flowed away from the hut, higher into the hills. There was little conversation until they reached the height of land. It was actually only a low lying hill, but still the highest point of land around. The top was absent of trees, only low-growing underbrush on top of a ledge cap. There was a slight breeze that cooled them after their climb.

The Old One sat down on some cool moss and asked, "Tell me Zvi, what is it you're looking for? No one comes to this side of the valley unless they are looking for something. Some find it and some go away disappointed for not having found it."

Zvi started telling the Old One about how he felt. The time passed unnoticed and even after the sun had set, he was still telling the Old One about his doubts and how he felt about the Over Lords and about Brahm.

"It isn't as though I don't appreciate Brahm or how he provides for all my needs; but at the same time I feel imprisoned in a world that I have no control over.

"What we are told by the Over Lords only raises more questions, which we are not allowed to ask. We are told to worship Brahm faithfully but that faith is based only on what the Over Lords tell us. It's only theory which lacks participation and truth."

"But," interrupted the Old One, "aren't you given the necessities as long as you do your share of work and follow Brahm's wishes?"

"Exactly. As long as we do as we're told. The dialogues

of the Over Lords are more of a school of obedience than a school of knowledge. I'm forced to accept regimented ideas regardless whether I agree with them or not. The Over Lords have brainwashed the masses into submission, and through fear they keep everyone obedient."

The Old One stood up, stretched and said, "It's time to leave. The night is half over. Tomorrow we shall return here and continue our conversation."

The next day they both were up early and ate a hearty breakfast then packed a small lunch with some herb tea and went back to the hill top.

"Zvi, look over there," the Old One pointed. "There's another village not so different from your own. It lies way to the horizon. It would be several days traveling from here. There are other villages too. But they can't be seen from here."

"I never knew there were other people or villages, although I always believed there had to be others. The Over Lords made us believe we were Brahm's chosen few."

"There are many, many more villages. Some are quite like your own and some are very different. This land is but a single continent and there are literally thousands of continents in Brahm's world."

"Old One—who or what is Brahm?"

"I'll tell you, but not today." the Old One replied. "There are things that you must do for yourself, before I can tell you of many things. The mind, Zvi, is a very powerful instrument and unless you have the right knowledge of its use, then you could create a lot of unnecessary trouble for yourself.

"Once you have developed the use of your mind, then wherever your mind travels then your body will follow. And that will require your body as well as your mind to be alert and fine tuned—as sharp as a razor's edge—because there might be a time when you could find yourself on the proverbial knife's edge."

Zvi wasn't sure he understood what the Old One was

saying, but he would follow his instructions. "How do I fine tune my body, Old One, and how do you mean?"

"Tomorrow morning, you'll have to return to your village. The trip back will be easier than the trip out. There will be no illusions. I'll give you a set of instructions to follow daily. Once your body is in shape physically, then you can return here and we'll start your lessons.

"What do you mean, Old One, by fine tuning my body physically?"

"Living in this land of Brahm's, the inhabitants become complacent and lazy. Your muscles are weak and flabby. When the body is in good physical condition then the mind is more alert, more responsive and more readily accepts new ideas. I'll be teaching you things that'll be completely foreign to you, Zvi, and you must be prepared physically as well as mentally."

They talked endlessly, not even stopping to eat a lunch. Zvi was digesting all he could of the knowledge the Old One was imparting. They talked until the sun started to set. "Watch the sun set, Zvi. We have talked enough."

Indeed the setting sun was worth watching. He had never seen such a brilliant display of golden streamers of light shoot up into the pastel sky before. It was gorgeous beyond description.

The next morning Zvi was up early. He wanted to be on his way so he could start the lessons the Old One had given him. Their farewells were short. "Before I leave, Old One, there is one more question I'd like to ask."

"Yes what is that?"

"I've heard about a mysterious forest. That it's enchanted. Is this so?"

"Yes. But until you have prepared your mind and body, we will not speak of it again. When the time is right, a path will be revealed that'll take you there."

* * * *

The return journey was quick and easy. Zvi was feeling so jubilant that he began to run. This was part of the Old One's instructions, to prepare his body physically. While he ran he thought about all that had been said. In particular about Brahm's world and that there were thousands of continents and not merely villages. *Why had the Over Lords thought that it was so important to deceive the people?* He understood why the Old One's powers were mistaken for sorcery. The Old One, it seemed, used his abilities for good while sorcery deals with the negative. Perhaps the Over Lords were jealous of his abilities.

He hoped to return as soon as possible, but that would all depend how soon he could be ready physically. He was determined and he would work at it faithfully.

The sun had set by the time he reached the outer limits of the village. He remembered what the Old One had said, "When you enter the village and as long as you are there, do not think of me or the lessons I have given you. Think always of Brahm and how thankful you are for his charity. But do not over do it or the spies will pick up as fast on that as they would a negative thought form. At all times be careful and do not speak of me or your lessons."

As Zvi walked along the roadway he placed an image of Brahm in the foremost part of his thoughts and was serenely happy for His Charity. He walked through the park and said hello to some friends and eventually home.

No one asked where he had been or why he seemed so happy now. It was customary to give each their privacy and not interfere with another's personal business. Not even the Over Lords would question his whereabouts unless they found something in a negative thought form.

The next day Zvi went to work as usual. "My you look happy today," Varian commented.

"Yes, I feel happy."

"We have some new work today. The flowers and shrubs at the temple need to be trimmed and replanted. The Over Lord

24

wants the gardens and grounds to look extra special for the temple festival."

"Grand; I have some splendid ideas." Zvi replied.

Varian was surprised with his friend's enthusiasm. "What ideas do you have?"

"We could line the walkways with large white rocks, crystals if we have any, and plant flowers with varying colors between the rocks. Red and white roses around the pulpit and yellow roses around the temple itself. We could even plant a few cedar trees on the lawn. Space them far enough apart so the view of the temple won't be blocked."

"I like your ideas Zvi. Where will we find the crystal?"

"I think I know where there are a few along the shoreline. Why don't you start planting the flowers and I'll go see."

Zvi knew the crystals would be heavy and the effort of carrying them from the shore to the temple grounds would be affecting one of the Old One's instructions. He would be building body muscle. The first state of his lessons towards knowledge.

The crystal rocks were heavy and Zvi understood now what the Old One had said about his muscles being unused and flabby. One by one he carried the heavy rocks and set them in place at the temple gardens. Varian was busy with planting, but neither did he offer to help Zvi. That was alright too; he needed the work out.

By the end of the day Zvi's muscles hurt, but after he cleaned up and ate supper, he felt strong enough to go for a run. To run he had to go to the village outer limits, because no one ran here and if he was seen, it might raise some suspicion.

The temple festival came and went and everyone was pleased with the flower array in the gardens and the rock crystals that lined the walkways. The Over Lord came up to Zvi after the ceremonies were over and said, "You have done a splendid job, Zvi, with the gardens and the walkways."

"I didn't do it all myself, sir, Varian helped."

"Yes, but he tells me the idea was your own. He also told

me how vigorously you worked. I hope this sudden enthusiasm means your submission to Brahm's will."

"Thank you, sir, for the compliment and yes I'm finding it easier and more enjoyable now with complete surrender to Brahm." Zvi didn't dare think about how he really thought. To do so now would only betray himself.

After things had quieted down and the people had returned to their homes, Zvi went to the village limits for his nightly run. The cool night air felt refreshing as he ran. He was running faster and longer distances, but still his muscles would be tired the next day. He wondered if he would ever get the muscle tone the Old One said he would have to have. But he would prevail; he had to. That was his only solution to gaining the knowledge he so desperately needed.

*   *   *   *

Each day Zvi would do the heaviest of their work, leaving Varian to the easier task of planting. He was up early each morning before anyone else had awakened and he would do calisthenic exercises and then lift weights. But always in his own privacy. Everyone around him noticed a sudden change with this attitude and alertness, and little by little a leaner, healthier body.

Finally, one day after a long fast run, Zvi too saw the change and knew it was time to return to the other side of the valley. He waited for the twilight darkness and left quietly. As he walked up the road towards the village limits, he was happily thinking about the Old One and his return to the other side, to start his training and his quest for knowledge.

He had forgotten about Brahm, the Over Lords and their spies. He had let his guard down. Neither did he see the spy that was following him. As Zvi approached the edge of the vast valley, he paused to listen to the night sounds. The crickets chirping, the night birds flying in the cool night air after insects.

And the forever constant humming. There was another sound also. He turned to see what was making the noise and saw the spy running towards him. Immediately, without any hesitation, he began running across the valley. The Over Lord's spy ran harder trying to catch him, but he was no match for Zvi. Already his physical training had paid off.

The night air filled his lungs. He slowed and looked back and began to laugh at the spy. There was no danger. But also in that same moment Zvi realized he would never again be able to return to the village. He would forever be an outcast like the Old One.

*   *   *   *

Zvi reached the Old One's hut a short time after the sun had risen over the horizon. For some strange reason the pastel colored sky was a different shade of golden light. Brighter, it seemed, and the colors more distinct. Or was he simply seeing them through a more disciplined mind? There was a sharper definition between colors. Even the outline of the trees, hills and blades of grass seemed to be more defined.

"Good morning," the Old One said. He was sitting on the porch, as if in anticipation of Zvi's arrival.

"Good morning Old One. What's been happening? Everything has changed."

"How do you mean?" The Old One asked as he got up and walked down the steps to meet Zvi.

"Everything seems to be more defined. Each tree, shrub and even the different colors seem to be better illustrated."

"I assure you, my young friend, that nothing has changed here. It is rather, quite possible that it is you who have changed. It is quite obvious that you have taken my council seriously. You have a virile sinewy body instead of flabby, limp and unused muscles. You have disciplined your body and now your mind is more alert and you can see things differently.

"You have just begun to open the subjective awareness in

your mind. No, no, don't worry, more will come as we progress with your discipline and training."

"Old One, I must tell you of one serious problem before we go any further with my training."

"Oh, and what might that be?"

"As I was leaving the village I was careless. I was thinking too much about you and everything you have said and did not see the spy following me. He ran after me into the valley, but he tired soon and returned. The Over Lords now know of my disobedience and I will never be allowed to return."

"And does that disturb you?" The Old One asked.

"Only that my family might be ostracized from the rest of the community."

"Do not worry too much Zvi, that will be their problem to deal with the best they can. We all have choices to make. They all have had the same opportunity to explore deeper into the mind for more knowledge; but instead they have chosen to be complacent in their thirst for truth. They have chosen to submit to Brahm. They are satisfied with the little knowledge the Over Lords have given them. If they were not, they too would have crossed the valley looking for answers. You can not be responsible for the plight of some one else's existence. We each have to choose and decide what it is we desire."

"Now that I can never go back to the village, where will I go from here?" Zvi asked with real consternation in his voice.

"Well my friend, when one has taken a step ahead, it is usually senseless to watch where he has been. Perhaps in time you might even decide to leave this place in search for even more answers. Who knows? Only you. And then only when the time is right.

"But for now let us not trouble the mind with petty worries about yesterday or tomorrow; we are here today. Now. Let's live today for today.

"You must be hungry after your journey across the valley. Come I will fix you something to eat."

While Zvi ate his meal, the Old One arranged sleeping quarters for him. "When you have eaten, you can rest. You must be tired after your journey."

While Zvi rested the Old One went outside. He smiled to himself with satisfaction. He could see in Zvi's aura a virtuous young fellow whose quest for more knowledge was as clean and unblemished as the cool stream that ran by his hut. Zvi reminded him of all the other seekers of knowledge who had passed through here and he had helped along the way. But there was a difference with Zvi. He would need more than edification. Zvi would need experience. But not until he was prepared.

The Old One stepped off the porch and followed a well used path that led to a small pond. There were many varied species of flowers growing along the path, some popping up in rock crevices and spotted here and there in the velvety green moss. His hut had been built at the very edge of the forest and the landscape in front of the hut and towards the setting sun was more like tundra vegetation. The trees were sparse and scraggly.

The Old One stopped at the edge of the pond and sat down. The water's surface was calm. So calm in fact that it looked more like a mirror than water. The Old One gazed into the depths of the water as if he had been hypnotized. Then the humming that filled the air became more resonate, rolling from the hill tops to the valley and across to the horizon. Then a voice so powerful and sonorous that the ground vibrated with each syllable. "Old One!" The voice rolled, filling the air. "I understand there is another being dissatisfied with My World. That he wishes to know more about Me and My identity! That this one, deep within himself, believes there is more beyond My World and what I can give him. Is this true?"

"Yes my Lord, it is true. This one has a pure heart and wishes to learn more about Your world and what lies beyond."

"Teach him well, Old One!" The voice bellowed. "I will not make it easy for him." Brahm had spoken. All was quiet again.

The Old One remained sitting beside the pond long after Brahm had spoken. It was clear now that Brahm would make Zvi's progress very difficult. In the end though, this will only strengthen and finally cement together the knowledge that he searches for.

When Zvi awoke and not finding the Old One at the hut, he instinctively followed the same path to the pond.

"Hello Zvi," the Old One said without turning to see who was approaching, "come sit by the water."

"Do you know why you decided to follow this particular path?" The Old One asked.

"Not really," Zvi answered. "I was looking for you and took this one without giving it much thought."

"That is because I sent you a thought form, telling you I was at the pond and to follow this path." He just looked confused and the Old One continued. "You received my thoughts, the same as the Over Lords spies could receive yours. The only difference; you weren't aware of it. You interpreted the thought form as instinct."

"Do you mean you can make other people do what you tell them simply by sending them a thought?" Zvi asked.

"Yes, that too is possible. Only I was asking or rather instructing your mental faculty to follow a certain direction because you wished to find me.

"If I, you or anyone were to use the ability of controlling one's action through the use of thought forms then that would be wrong. Some might call it sorcery. Black magic perhaps. And certainly a negative aspect of what I'm trying to teach. I only mentioned it so you would become aware that you possess the ability, the same as the Over Lords and their spies, once you learn to discipline your mind and realize most of all that you do in fact have the ability."

"Where do we start with my lessons?" Zvi asked.

"My friend, we have already started. Look back and see for yourself how much you have learned." The Old One replied.

He sat silent, thinking about his first visit at the Old One's hut and the illusions he had over come. Yes perhaps the lessons had indeed already started.

"To answer your questions more seriously, I first will teach the finer art of self-preservation. It is indeed an art, because you'll learn to use your mind more than your body. As you progress with this you'll also be awakening your mind. At times we might regress for a short while, but other than those few times, every day will be filled with lessons and instructions of some nature.

"But now, for the rest of this day let us sit here by the pond and talk."

"Old One, once I have learned all, where will I go from here?"

The Old One laughed with a joyous rumble. "My friend when you have learned it all, then the only place suitable would be beside God Himself." He laughed some more. Not in derision, but rather at the simple meaning of an offhand remark. The Old One himself was limited in his knowledge, compared to knowing all.

"You said God Himself. Do you mean Brahm?"

"No. I mean God. The Supreme Deity that sits over all," the Old One replied.

"Where is this God? In the village we are taught that Brahm is God and He sits over all."

"My friend, God is within you and all creatures. The universal center is within each of us. All you have to do is look."

"How do I do that Old One?"

"You look deep within yourself. I'll explain more as we progress and I'll give you some exercises to practice.

"You asked earlier where you will go from here? When the time is right, you'll know what direction your destiny will take. I will tell you this though, your destiny has already been confirmed. I don't tell you this to confuse you but only to answer your questions. This too is another lesson.

"The sun is beginning to set. We have talked enough for now. I'll walk back to the hut and prepare us a meal. You, my friend, have some running to do. Tomorrow we start disciplining your mind by using your body," the Old One said and then stood up.

While Zvi ran, he began to think about everything the Old One had said, and wondering if he would ever fully grasp what the Old One was trying to teach him. Everything had come so fast that it all seemed a blur. Would he fail and disappoint the Old One?

When the meal was finished the Old One sat on the porch in contemplation and Zvi went for a walk back to the pond. He was still trying to absorb and understand what the Old One had said about Brahm and then about God being "within each of us." Were Brahm and God two separate entities? If so, then why hadn't he ever heard about the concept of God, the Supreme Deity. All his life the Over Lords had said Brahm was God, Brahm was All. There was no other God but Brahm. Now the Old One had made clear distinction between Brahm and God.

But where does one find this Supreme Deity, God? The Old One said God was within each of us, and all we had to do was look within. Then if God is within me, then am I God? But how can this be?

*   *   *   *

The next morning the Old One got Zvi out of bed early. "Come on my friend. We have a lot of work to do today. We'll have a nourishing meal first, then we'll walk to the hilltop for another lesson."

On the way to the hilltop Zvi thought again about what his friend Varian had said about the enchanted forest and a portal of some sort. The Old One had said there was such a portal, but wouldn't say much more about it. Was the forest Varian had told him about as strange as it had first seemed? But then at first, the Old One had been called a sorcerer until he had discovered the difference. Whatever the answer might be about the enchanted forest, it would have to wait until the Old One had decided to explain.

When they got to the top, the Old One sat down on his usual mossy carpet and Zvi sat on a rock. "Do you know the difference between the objective mind and the subjective?" The Old One asked.

"No, I have never heard of the terms."

"That is not surprising living under the tutelage of the Over Lords. The objective mind uses facts to discern an object; relativity. The use of scientific observations. It belongs to the sensible world and being observable. You can touch it, see it, smell it, measure it. It exists actually independent of the mind. It is the use of your common senses. Knowledge of a certain object derived by perception.

"Pick up that stone by your foot. Feel it. Does it have rough edges or smooth? Is it heavy or light? How large is it?

"All of your deductions about the stone came from what your senses perceived. You can see it and touch it."

"Okay I understand that. Now what is the subjective mind?" Zvi asked.

"This one is more difficult to understand. But you use your subjective mind as much as you do your objective mind. When you crossed the valley the second time, you were beset by my illusions. Your objective thinking told you there was something to fear and you were terrified until the bat appeared to fly through you. It was your subjective thinking that told you that the bat was not real. Because if it had been an actual bat, it could not have flown through you and if it had knocked into you, you would have felt it. Since you knew that the bat could not possibly fly through you and you did not feel it strike you, your subjective thinking deduced that the bats were in actuality only illusions. And since the bats were only illusions you also deduced that the rest that had beset your journey across the valley were also unreal.

"Your subjective mind allows you to make judgments and come to conclusions by your awareness of your own state of being. When you questioned Brahm's sincerity and the Allness of His World and Being, you were using your subjective mind.

"This is simplifying it, but that's what the subjective mind is. We will be using mostly the subjective thinking part of your mind and using the Shao-Lin arts to open its awareness and its acute perceptibility."

"What are the Shao-Lin arts, Old One?"

"Shao-Lin is a name of a famed temple in another world. Its actual meaning is young forest. But it more appropriately is referred to as a form of self-defense, used to protect oneself from attackers. But I will not be enlightening you or encouraging you to fight, but instead to exercise the mind and increase your awareness and your confidence of your own knowledge and abilities.

"Now go find a lotus flower. Pick it and come back," the Old One said.

While Zvi was gone the Old One closed his eyes and turned his attention inward and smiled; Zvi would be an appreciative student. One who had a vivacious desire for learning. He would prepare him well, as Brahm had counseled.

Zvi came back with a large white lotus. It also had a transparent golden tint around each petal. He was supporting the flower in both hands. It was that large. "Old One, isn't this a water lily?"

"Yes indeed," was his reply.

"Then why does it grow on this hilltop amongst the moss and rocks? I thought it would only grow in shallow water."

"Many things occur here by nature, that elsewhere might seem strange.

"Now sit in a comfortable position. Relax and look at the

34

blossom. See how each petal is bathed with a golden transparent aura. Smell its sweet nectar.

"Now close your eyes. Good, now tell me what you are holding in your hands."

"A lotus flower." Zvi replied puzzled.

"And how do you know this?"

"I can feel it in my hands. The soft texture of the petals. And I can smell the sweet nectar."

"Good. You can open your eyes now. You knew you were holding a lotus blossom in your hands because your objective mind knew what it was by your own senses.

"Now look at the blossom again. Look deeper into the blossom. See how each petal is arranged. Do you see the veins running out to the petal's edge from the center? From which flows the lotus's life sustaining nectar?" Zvi nodded his head. "Now look even deeper. Look at the center of the blossom. Smell the sweet perfume?" Again Zvi nodded his head. "Look deeper into the blossom. Concentrate all of your attention on the lotus flower."

The Old One was silent then. Letting him quietly contemplate the depth of the lotus blossom in his hands. Several minutes went by and then the Old One asked "Zvi what do you see?"

"I see a flower, Old One," he replied puzzled.

"Tomorrow we will start with some easy Shao-Lin exercises."

"What about this blossom, Old One. It is too beautiful to throw away."

"Embed the stem in the moss beside you. There is enough moisture in the moss to sustain the flower's life and it will soon sprout new roots."

"Come, the day has passed already and it is time that we return to the hut."

*   *   *   *

Again the next day, on top of the rocky pinnacle the Old One began the day's lessons by first saying, there are three important things you must remember in practicing the Shao-Lin arts. First and foremost you must learn to relax. Not just your arms or legs. But every muscle in your body. If you remain rigid, your reflexes are slower and you can be easily knocked off balance. And that brings us to the next fact. You must be as flexible as the branches on a willow tree. Not in just your body, but as importantly in your mind. You must be flexible and willing to listen to others if there is something of importance being said. Idle gossip, however, should not be given a passing thought.

"When doing a particular exercise you must do so with complete and full effort. Let the force of life spring from the soles of your feet and issue forth from the crown chakra at the top of your head. Every move must be given your all. And in order to do this your body as well as the mind must be relaxed.

"Later you will be applying these techniques to your thinking. And then you'll surprise yourself with the sudden understanding and clarity."

For the rest of the morning the Old One demonstrated the different kicks, turns and punches he would be teaching Zvi. Time after time the Old One would land a full impact of a thrust on Zvi's chest, arm or leg. And each time he would fall. But he wasn't discouraged. He trusted the Old One. If only he could remember to move fast enough.

"You're as stiff as a piece of stone Zvi. Remember to relax and move with the thrust and not against it. Learn to watch with your mind as well as with your eyes. Try to anticipate my moves and counter move."

It was difficult to do anything the Old One was saying. His moves were lightening fast. And with each thrust there was a renewed sensation of pain. But he kept trying. Not that he wanted to be a precision fighting tool, but rather he wanted the expanded awareness that the Old One had said would come with the physical training.

"Interpret my thought forms, Zvi. Use your instinctive reasoning."

All he could do was try. By mid-day he was sore, tired and hungry. "That's enough for now, Zvi. Let's rest and eat our meal. I too am feeling the effort."

They ate their meal in silence, and when Zvi had finished he lay back on the moist moss, watching the pastel colored sky. "Zvi, do you know what is most pernicious about the social structure you left behind on the other side of the valley?

"The lack of imagination. The Over Lords have kept the people there in a superficial atmosphere. Each are convinced that Brahm and Brahm alone will take care of their every need. Therefore there is no need of ever imagining that there could ever possibly be anything beyond Brahm. Each is kept in compliance by a very clever form of brain-washing.

"To illustrate how important being able to imagine is, I'll tell you a story about a leaf that could imagine."

Zvi sat quietly listening to the Old One. "There was a leaf, strong and healthy, perched on the very top of a large maple tree. This leaf was different from the others because it could feel the vibrations of life emanating from all the other leaves. And it knew it wasn't alone. But this leaf was alone because it could think and it tried to imagine how it would look and how all the other leaves would look. You see, Zvi, although this leaf didn't have the senses that we do, it could, however, perceive the presence of all the other leaves. This is what I've been saying about subjective thinking.

"Now back to my story. Since this particular leaf was so different from all the others, it became lonely. It began to wilt and die because of its loneliness. It wanted so much to be able to see the other leaves and to know for sure that it wasn't alone. Then one day as a final request, it wished it could see the other leaves before it died. The request was granted and the leaf could see."

"What happened to the leaf after it could see?"

"It died. So much strength had wilted from the leaf that it didn't have enough left to survive. But it died happy, knowing that it had been right all the time when it imagined there were others like itself.

"The point I'm trying to make Zvi, you can aspire to great heights of understanding if only first you imagine that you can. If you, lets say tomorrow morning, start with these Shao-Lin lessons we have studied today and imagine that you have already mastered them—well you would be surprised with the effects.

"The other people in your village, Zvi, couldn't possibly imagine that there could ever be anything beyond Brahm or His World. That's why they are content to stay under the tutelage of the Over Lords. But you, Zvi, are more like the leaf. You have already imagined beyond Brahm's existence and you are on your way to discovering it.

"Now if you only could imagine that you are already a Shao-Lin master maybe you wouldn't be so bruised." The Old One laughed.

"But Old One how do I imagine that I can already master the Shao-Lin arts?"

"Create in your mind, an image of yourself performing the techniques we have worked on today. See yourself going through the movements until each exercise is completed. This won't make you a Shao-Lin master instantly, but it will help you to become one." Zvi nodded his head that he understood.

"Now before we continue with your lessons there is a demonstration that I think you might gain some benefit from." They left the hilltop and walked down to the cool stream by the hut.

The Old One stopped next to a large maple tree. Zvi sat on a rock next to the stream in the shade. The Old One stood in front of the tree in quiet contemplation, studying the tree, every feature and the grooves in the bark. Then he raised his right arm level with his shoulder and pressed his finger tips against the tree. Zvi watched in fascination as the Old One's fingers began to disappear into the heart of the tree. First his hand disappeared then his wrist and forearm to the elbow. He turned and smiled at Zvi and withdrew his arm from within the tree.

Zvi began to laugh. "You had me believing for awhile that your arm was inside the tree. Then I remembered the illusions you created and beset on me," and he laughed some more.

"My friend," said the Old One with all seriousness, "believe me when I tell you, this is no illusion."

Zvi stopped laughing and stood up to examine the Old One's hand. "It is all there and is fine. You still do not believe what you saw do you?" The Old One laughed.

"I find it difficult to understand. How could your hand pass through that tree? It is solid!"

"As I tried to explain before, you must first know that you can do it and then you must see yourself doing it. Then it becomes a simple matter of doing it. It all begins with imagination."

"Will I ever learn enough to be able to do that?" Zvi asked.

"Is it the unusual that impresses you to want to do it? Or are you asking, will you develop to the level of using your hidden abilities effectively?"

"Will I develop to that level?"

"That will depend entirely on you. I will tell you this, there is another world outside of Brahm's domain that exists with a lower vibratory frequency that you could walk through what would appear in that world as solid objects, without any difficulty."

"How can that be Old One?"

"In that lower world, matter is very coarse compared to this world. Here everything vibrates at a higher frequency and objects are not as coarse. And at the same time there are worlds that exist at a higher frequency than this world. And everything there is also not as coarse as here and the colors there are also more vibrant and colorful."

Zvi sat silent for awhile, digesting the Old One's explanation. He was beginning to understand that the Old One was very subtle about how he imparted knowledge. It was a little at a time and given in such away that he had to stay alert and think about what was being said.

"Now my friend if you are rested we must return to teaching you to be a Shao-Lin master. Come, we have regressed long enough." They walked back to the hilltop and on the way Zvi thought about the Old Ones' stamina. He never tired. Never showed any signs of weakness. And for whatever reason Brahm and the Over Lords did not interfere here with his enlightenment. He was a separate entity, it appears, in Brahm's World of which He nor the Over Lords had any control over.

For the rest of that day they worked on the same techniques as in the morning. Only this time before they began, "Before we start, Zvi, sit in quiet contemplation for a few minutes. Go inside yourself like I taught you and see yourself already mastering the techniques that we worked with earlier."

Zvi sat on the hilltop with his face into the cool breeze and all else was an empty void, except for the images he created on his inner screen. There he watched himself working through the techniques with fluent agility.

"Now if you are ready, we will begin," the Old One said. "Keep the image you saw only a few moments ago, at the forefront of your mind. Relax and don't step into my thrust— much better. See how easy it can be, once you have prepared yourself."

Zvi was no Shao-Lin master, but he had improved considerably since morning. He was using his mind now as well as his body and he surprised himself with the improvement.

Each day was a repetition of the day before. Early morning was set aside for new techniques and exercises, the mid-day meal and a rest period for conversations of enlightenment. Then a repeat of the morning's activities. Usually with greater success. And as each day passed, Zvi noticed a subtle change in his thinking and how he viewed things. No longer when he looked at a rock, did he see just a cold stone. He saw every crack, crevice and its composition. He perceived what the interior of the stone was like and could judge accurately the weight and size. When he looked at a tree; he saw the inside and counted the growth rings; heard the water passing through its veins to the branches and leaves. A flower was no longer a simple pretty blossom. He visualized himself standing at the center of the blossom looking out at the petals. He smelled their sweet nectar and he tried to imagine what each flower was feeling. Did it know it was surrounded with beauty or did it just exist, unknowing and subdued. The colors of his new world were profoundly more vibrant with each passing day. There were new colors everywhere about him that he never before had seen, let alone even contemplated there were such brilliant arrays.

Yes this world for Zvi was unfolding into a greater awareness with each day. "Or am I the one that is changing?" He spoke out loud.

"Did you say something Zvi?" The Old One asked.

"I was actually talking out loud to myself. I am suddenly surprised how different everything is now. I am aware of an abundant amount of life around me that I never noticed before. Each day the colors everywhere become more vibrant. Like turning on a light switch."

"I like most your statement about you recognizing how much life is around you. Perhaps you can see for yourself now how fast you are progressing with your training and how you, yourself, are disciplining your own mind."

"I have already achieved more than I could have imagined only a short while ago. But the more I learn, Old One, the more I realize just how much I don't know. And how much more I want to know."

The Old One laughed and stated, "That is a statement from a true scholar. Not only are you realizing how far you have progressed, but you also realize how far you still have to travel. It will all come in time. One day you'll awaken and it will suddenly be right there in front of you and you'll wonder why you couldn't see or grasp the reality of it before."

*   *   *   *

The Old One was pleased with Zvi's progress. He was learning at a fast pace. Not only the Shao-Lin techniques, but once he started using his mind along with this body, his mind became very open and acute. His perception was extraordinarily keen. He had mastered all the techniques the Old One thought were beneficial. There were more, but they would direct Zvi's attention towards too much of an aggressive fighter. And that was not his purpose of becoming a Shao-Lin master. Rather to awaken his thinking and his cognizance of his own abilities. Now that that was almost completed, it was now time to instruct him in more recondite wisdom.

After their evening meal the Old One said, "Zvi, let us walk to the hilltop and settle our meal."

"What is there, Old One, another technique you want to show me?" Zvi laughed.

"It is a splendid evening to sit in contemplation and watch the sun set. Come."

At the hilltop the Old One took his usual place and this time Zvi sat beside him. "Before we sit in contemplation over the wonders of the magnificent array of colors the setting sun will provide for us, Zvi, see that lotus flower that you set in the moist moss some time ago?"

"Yes, Old One. It has blossomed beyond its' own solstice. It has become more and more sculptured with each passing day."

The Old One laughed, "And I see along with the acuteness of your thinking, your vocabulary has increased also. To answer your statement, Zvi, yes the lotus blossom has changed with each day. The same as you have also changed my friend. When you first came to this hilltop with me, you were only a budding flower. This lotus blossom demonstrates your progression. It has actually grown along with you, Zvi.

"Pick the blossom again Zvi. And again focus your attention on the blossom. Contemplating its beingness. Go deep within the flower, Zvi."

He sat silently gazing into the depths of the lotus blossom that he held cupped in both hands. Time passed unnoticed and so too did everything else, except the flower he held in his hands. While Zvi sat contemplating the lotus blossom, the Old One sat quietly watching the sun set and the array of kaleidoscopic color patterns in the pastel sky.

It was a long time before Zvi stirred. It was good, the Old One thought. It means he is deep within himself. Besides, the Old One was enjoying the changing sky.

"Tell me my young friend, what did you experience on this trip to the center of the blossom?"

"It was breath-taking Old One. I saw the flower as I never have before. It was so beautiful. And the music from the humming vibrated from all the petals so sonorously. The fluids of life sounded like rivers in the blossom's veins. I have never before experienced anything so wonderful."

"Good my friend. You have seen more on this trip to the blossom's center than before. This means you are progressing well. But you still have more to learn.

"It is late. Come we must return to the hut for rest. Tomorrow we will talk more," the Old One said.

When the evening meal was eaten, the Old One walked outside to be alone with his contemplation on the inner worlds. Zvi remained behind to clean up after the meal.

The Old One stepped off the porch and found a comfortable moss covered rock not far away. He sat silently watching the sky. But his only view was of an inner world. "Old One!" a voice rumbled through the mountains and valleys. Vibrating through every living thing. "I have watched the progress of the curious one. He learns fast. But still he only sees

43

the lotus blossom. He must be better prepared if he is to travel throughout my Kingdom in search of knowledge. He is still like a young bird that has his full plumage, but cannot fly. His journey, Old One, will not be easy. He has already chosen that for himself." Brahm had spoken.

"My friend," said the Old One, "do not worry so. Zvi has a strong character and an unquenchable thirst for knowledge. He is progressing faster than some who have passed through here. This one will not cede so easily. He is just beginning to understand that most of the answers to his questions can be found within his own being. He only has to learn to recognize them."

*   *   *   *

The next morning the Old One and Zvi were again seated on the pinnacle. "Old One," Zvi asked, "The endless ocean—is it really endless, as the Over-Lords say?"

"What do you think Zvi?"

"No I don't believe it is endless. I believe there is something more at the other end. Like there is on this side of the valley."

"For many, Zvi, the ocean is endless. If some were to try and cross to the other shore, they would be consumed by their own fears. For although the ocean is not endless, the journey to the other shore would be of great magnitude. For those that could not make the journey, then indeed the ocean would be endless."

"But why do the Over Lords keep it mysteriously secret?"

"To control the imaginations of the masses. If the mass of inhabitants honestly believe the ocean is endless, they will not venture to cross it or imagine what else is out there. It's called a form of mind control, Zvi. The same as believing that obedience to Brahm will earn you nirvana."

"What is across on the other shore, Old One?"

"Another continent in Brahm's world," the Old One answered.

"Then why do the Over Lords keep it in secrecy?"

"Because the inhabitants there are of a different culture and a higher level of consciousness. If the people of your village or of any of the villages on this side of the endless ocean knew of the inhabitants on the other shore and the high aesthetics there, then the masses would know that the Over Lords had been lying to them. The Over Lords would lose there control over the people and chaos would erupt. People would want to leave their homes for what they might imagine to be a better place to live."

"Would it? Would the other side be a better place to live?" Zvi asked.

"For some. Some one like you. But many would be disillusioned and find nothing but confusion."

"Why would some be disillusioned and not others?"

"The aesthetics there vibrate at a higher frequency and most would not understand what they saw. They have not, let us say, earned the right to passage to the other shore. Until each can unburden themselves with the disillusions of this side of the ocean, they can not travel to the other. And for them the ocean is indeed endless."

"How could the aesthetics be so different that people from this side of the ocean would be disillusioned?" Zvi asked.

"Look at yourself Zvi. Have you not noticed a very prominent difference in the way you see things? Are not the colors more splendid than when you first arrived? And hasn't your awareness, more of late, been more attuned. Look how you viewed the lotus blossom yesterday. Do you think that any of the other people of your village could have gone to the depths of the flower that you have traveled?"

"Then it is more to their level of understanding that prevents them from crossing the ocean." Zvi replied

"Exactly."

"Will I travel to the other shore Old One?"

"Perhaps. But possibly you might find the aesthetics dull and might choose to travel beyond to yet another continent with even higher vibrations."

"Earlier when you were talking about another world that is coarser than this one: where is this other world, Old One?"

"It is right here, Zvi."

He looked confused. *How could that possibly be?* The Old One, sensing his confusion added, "The reason you can not see it is because, as I said before, the vibrations of that world are much lower than they are here so things in the other world are invisible to you, as you sit here. The only way to see into that other world is to be there in a body compatible to that world."

"You mean, Old One, that that other world occupies the same space, only we can not see it because we are in this world?"

"Good my friend! You are catching on."

"But how can two objects occupy the same space at the same time?"

"Because of the difference in vibrations. The lower world vibrates so much slower than the frequency of this world. Everything is here, as we speak. Only you can't see it because of its low vibrations."

"Why does everything have to be so difficult to understand, Old One? Why is there so much mystery about Brahm's World, and as I am now learning, about the other continents in this land of Brahm's? Why is truth kept from everybody?" Zvi asked.

"First, truth isn't kept from everyone. Only from the masses. For the strong at heart and the curious, the answers are always there. There in front of you. All you have to do is know how to look for them. Once you have enlightened your awareness, then the search becomes easier.

"Truth is kept from the masses because if all answers were given freely, then knowledge would be meaningless. Before you can have any desire, you must first earn the right to have it. This law is even taught by the Over Lords, except in a different context.

"Understanding is purposely made difficult so the aspirant will learn to use his own faculties to see and hear, so he can interpret the truth for himself. To do this, one must learn to use the subjective mind. We talked about that already. See how everything comes together. Good."

"Old One—before when you started my training with the Shao-Lin techniques, you said the physical training was to awaken my awareness and not for fighting. That puzzles me."

"How?" asked the Old One.

"There is no fighting or quarreling in this land. Then why would anyone wish to become a Shao-Lin Master? Other than to discipline the mind. I mean where would anyone ever use the techniques to defend one's self?"

"My young friend, there are worlds with much coarser vibration that exist below this world where fighting seems to be a prerequisite to survival."

Zvi sat in silence thinking about that. Never in his life had he ever been accosted, or anyone else. Fighting and bickering was not rational behavior. There were no rules or laws against it, it just never happens. There never was any need to fight. "These coarser worlds you speak of,Old One, must be barbaric in nature. Why is there such a need to fight in order to survive? Are those worlds that crude and uncivilized?"

"Yes, in a way my young friend, they are. And the people of those worlds will remain there until they learn different. They are so low on the consciousness scale, that most can not even imagine a world like this. Or for that matter the higher worlds beyond this one."

"At night when I dream, Old One, I see strange images of flying machines. Sometimes I am inside one of them looking out a window at people fighting below on the ground. These dreams bother me because I am so unused to fighting. If fighting only occurs in the coarser worlds, then why am I dreaming of fighting and of a world that I never knew existed until I met you?"

The Old One thought carefully before answering. If he said too much Zvi might be warned about his journey that he would soon embark upon. If he knew of the dangers

47

and turbulence that lay in-wait of his arrival—then he might not choose to go. "This, Zvi, might only be your subtle body traveling to other worlds while you are asleep. Showing you how life could be in one of the coarser vibrant worlds."

*   *   *   *

Each morning brought a new day of discovery. The Old One seldom reiterated a previous lesson. If he did, it was only to stress a point. Some days were spent on the hilltop and others were spent walking along trails and paths through this strange land that at one time Zvi only knew as the residence of the sorcerer. Now he seldom thought of his life in the village or his family and friends. He had detached himself. They were as free as he was to pursue their curiosity and imaginations.

Each day the Old One stressed the importance of knowing and understanding that the center of the universe and creation was actually within each living being. He instructed Zvi how to go within and see this center. Much the same as he had done with the lotus blossom.

When Zvi had finally mastered the technique of going or looking within his own being, the Old One asked, "Zvi, how would you like to take an incredible journey?"

"Where will we go?"

"I will stay here while you take the journey."

"Where to, Old One?"

"From the center of creation out through one of your own arteries to the very end of a capillary. Once you reach the end of the capillary you can return as I have previously taught you.

"Use the same technique as we have been using to go within and center your attention on the heart center chakra. When you have reached this center, then take as much time as necessary and feel comfortable with your surroundings. Then locate the main artery and start your journey."

"What will I be looking for, Old One?"

"Nothing in particular. Only take notice of what you do see so you can tell me."

Zvi nodded his head indicating that he understood. He relaxed, placed his attention at the heart center and within moments he found himself within his own body. Inside the heart. He was first cognizant of the sound of his heartbeat. The same sound he had heard within the lotus blossom. And much to his surprise everything was very luminous. He found himself suspended in a medium that resembled, almost exactly, galactic space.

He couldn't see the main artery. Everything was in a macroscopic concept now. He focused his attention on the artery he wanted, and instantly he began to move forward through the galactic-space like medium. He began to follow his imagination to the location of the main artery. The walls of the heart could not be seen. Everything was so immense.

As he moved along to the entrance of the main artery he began to notice objects in the main stream that represented very closely to stars in the skies. They were actually blood molecules, cells and oxygen molecules. All flowing along the fluid blood stream from the heart. But from his position there was no current flow and he or his awareness was also a small molecule, traveling through that seemingly galactic space. And all the time ever aware of the rhythmic heartbeat that pulsated from all around him.

He traveled on and on and the blood and oxygen molecules looked like comets with a fiery tail as he passed them. How strange, he though, the inside of his own body looked so much like the starry universe.

Finally he came to the end of his journey. He focused his attention back on the outside world and he returned. The Old One was still sitting beside him looking out across the landscape.

"And how was your journey my young friend?" The Old One asked.

"Beautiful. But that does little to actually describe it fully. I would not have believed it, if I had not seen it for myself. Inside of my body is no different than looking up at the star filled heavens above."

The Old One smiled to acknowledge Zvi's new discovery. "Does that journey substantiate (that the) center of the universe being within us all?"

"Yes it does. I can now appreciate better all that you have been teaching."

"Good. Now would you like another journey?"

"Yes. Where to this time?"

The Old One looked up and said, "Out there. A trip through the macro-universe."

Instantly the Old One was in his subtle body and waiting for Zvi. "Follow me." They were off on a sublime journey through the universe.

Once they were beyond the limits of Brahm's world the colors became more luminous. The darker galactic space was not black, instead it was more transparent. The fiery stars were golden and not yellow. Solar flares erupted and shot out into space like a giant roman candle. There were many, many more celestial bodies that could be seen now, than were ever possible from Brahm's world. Towards the center of the galaxy there were so many stars and worlds that the center looked like a solid mass of iridescent colors. The spiraled arms reached out from the center like giant octopus legs.

They traveled on beyond the Milky Way Galaxy and the colors became even more luminous and the ever present humming had changed. It was becoming softer and the music was coming from all. Even Zvi could feel the new vibrations emitting from himself as he sped quietly from galaxy to galaxy. They traveled beyond Omega Centauri, Alpha Centauri, Orion Globual, Ursa Major, Hercules, Virgo Corona Boreclis, Bootes, Hydra, Ceigus Zolm and many more. Each growing in brilliance and magnitude.

Zvi looked back; all the galaxies combined looked as if

they were composing the contour of some figure. But they had not reached, in their journey, the limits necessary to view the panorama of all the galaxies, to witness the grandest embodiment of all. He could only but guess what the embodiment might be. Behind the galaxies they had already passed, a crystal blue aura illuminated from their outer limits. The very extreme edge of the aura was tipped with a radiant crystal white shimmer.

"Old One," Zvi asked, "can we travel to the outer limits and beyond?" I would like to see what embodiment all these galaxies combined synthesize."

"We could travel to that point, but you are not ready for what you would see. There are other and more important lessons for you to learn before you can behold the grandest sight of all.

"Now it is time for us to return. Take us home Zvi," the Old One commanded.

*   *   *   *

Zvi's enlightenment continued and with each day the lessons became more difficult. The Old One was being sure he would be prepared; as Brahm had spoken, discipline and nurture his mind. He was pleased with Zvi's zest of the unknown and his eagerness to learn and his ability to retain what he had learned. Not only that, but he understood, and could use the knowledge and demonstrate its effectiveness.

The final test was coming. There wasn't much more that he could teach Zvi now. Not until he had a chance to use and see the effect of his knowledge thus far. Others had taken the test before him. Some had failed and had then fallen by the way side and others had passed and had moved on to other worlds, some more vibrant and some much coarser.

The day finally came when the Old One knew Zvi was ready. "Zvi, today we go back to the hilltop." He didn't say anything about a test, because if Zvi knew he was being tested then his response would be artificial.

51

"Find a comfortable position, Zvi, and pick the lotus blossom again."

He did as he was instructed and waited as he carefully watched the Old One.

"Zvi, I want you to again focus your attention at the center of the blossom. Only this time I want you to go much deeper into the flower. No, you won't have to do anything different. Cup the blossom in both hands and go as far as you can possibly go." The Old One was quiet then. He sat back and relaxed. He watched Zvi with intense interest.

He knew when Zvi was within the flower. There was a noticeable subtle calmness that prevailed around him. All tension had disappeared from his muscles and from his face. He could almost see him descending into the blossom. And feel the rhythmic heartbeat vibrating through his being. Smell the sweet aroma of the blossom's nectar. And see the unparalleled beauty.

Zvi was smiling. Apparently he had found happiness within the blossom. A luminous golden light began to illuminate from him and encompass his entire body. The Old One knew, by the presence of the illumination, that Zvi had reached his final destination. That he had traveled within the blossom as far as it was possible to go.

The Old One waited patiently. Zvi was in the middle of the greatest ecstasy imaginable. He remembered the same test given him almost an eternity ago. He remembered the joy he had experienced, while he traveled deep within the blossom. Song birds went about there daily rituals as if neither being were there. Some birds perched at their feet and filled the cool air with their songs. They perched on Zvi's head and shoulders as if he was nothing more than a limb on a tree. Perhaps they could smell the sweet nectar of the lotus blossom that Zvi was enjoying.

Morning had passed and mid-afternoon was coming to an end. The sun was setting its golden brilliance against the pastel sky. The Old One noticed a change. Zvi was returning. He had been within the blossom for a remarkably long time.

Much longer, in fact, than he had when he had traveled within the blossom.

Zvi slowly opened his eyes. There were tears blurring his vision. The Old One asked, "Why do you weep, my young friend? Did you find sadness?"

Zvi remained silent until his eyes had dried and he had regained his composure. "No Old One. I do not weep because of any sadness. But instead of the complete rapture and the wonderment of the entire experience. It was so astounding that words alone will not do it credit. But yet at the same time it was such a subtle discovery."

"The day has passed; as you were within the blossom. There is much to tell. For you were gone so long. Do not rush because the day is almost over. What you have seen and discovered can not be told quickly. Even though the evening air is cool, God's Breath will keep us warm.

"When you feel relaxed, and if you can, tell me about the adventure of your esoteric journey within the lotus blossom."

Zvi didn't feel relaxed. He was excited and wanted to tell of his journey. "It was different this time, Old One. As soon as I was inside the petals, I noticed the change. The sound of the blossom's heart beat was there but this time it was more profound and there was a different tone and this kept changing the further I traveled. The petals structure was more—well more stately, for a lack of words to properly describe it. The colors of the entire blossom were vivid and more lustrous than before. There was depth to the colors. And the colors seemed to be made of several layers laminated together. Each were transparent allowing the color from one lamination to tint the next.

"The sound of the blossom's life fluids rushing in the veins out to each petal was deafening. The deeper I went the more it seemed like rivers of water rushing through my own veins.

"Then I began to experience a feeling of complete serenity. An ecstasy of joy that I have never known before.

And this too grew as I traveled further. It became so great that I thought I might explode from the sheer joy of the experience. I didn't know how much of this I could endure.

"I decided to continue with my journey. I lost all cognizance of everything except the blossom. There was no more exterior world. Nothing existed now beyond the lotus blossom. I continued on but there was no longer any movement, but things still continued to change.

"My attention was still placed at the very heart of the blossom and towards this point I journeyed forward. At last I found myself standing at the center where the life fluids of the flower are dispersed. At first I thought I had reached the end of my journey, but you said to go as far as possible.

"I had traveled to this point before and then returned. I decided or perceived, as you have taught me, that there was more to this journey than where I was postured. So I decided to wait and see.

"While I waited I suddenly realized that I wasn't there at the blossom's center, in body. There was no part of me physically there. But I was very much aware of everything around me. If you understand what I'm trying to say." The Old One nodded his head that he did. "I waited and enjoyed the serene beauty all about me. I don't know how long I waited, but after some time I began to experience a knowingness that was seeping into my awareness. I was becoming even more aware of everything. The beautiful sounds, the sweet fragrance of the nectar and the sheer elegance of the blossom. The rhythmic heartbeat was now my own. Coming from within me! As well as the rushing river in the petal's veins. I had traveled beyond any description of emotion or happiness. I had become that in itself.

"I waited with this perfect serenity all about me. Then I realized that I had actually become one with the lotus blossom. That the blossom's heartbeat was mine, the sounds of the rushing water in the petal's veins was also now my own. The sheer beauty of the blossom was also now myself.

"But even with this knowledge, I knew the journey had not yet come to its final destination. I waited, bathing in this new concept of myself. Then I felt myself going deeper within the blossom, but I was already at its life center. But still I seemed to journey beyond the limits of the blossom's life center. Then it happened, Old One! I saw the purpose of the journey and the purpose of all the discipline and the training. I then knew. I knew that I had not become one with the lotus blossom! I now understood that I was the blossom. The heartbeat was my own and the sounds of rushing water in the petal's veins was my own. I sustain life in the blossom. I am the lotus blossom—therefore I sustain my own self!

"The journey was over and I started to return. I wept when I opened my eyes because of the emotional impact of my discovery."

The Old One smiled and said, "You have come a long way since you first came to this side of the valley. You have progressed well, my young friend."

The Old One had taught Zvi all he could for the present. There was more, much more to learn, but for now he had enough and was prepared well enough for his endeavor into the less vibrant worlds. There was no need of telling Zvi that this journey in the lotus blossom was only to test his awareness and discipline, his progression thus far. Nor would he tell him of his next endeavor into the less vibrant world. There would be no need.

"Come, Zvi, see how late it is, we must return to my hut for nourishment," and the Old One started down the trail to his hut.

"This experience took all day, Old One?"

"You have been on a long journey, Zvi. Into the depths of the blossom and beyond its narrowness into the greater expanse where you learned that you were indeed the lotus blossom. A journey of such magnitude takes time."

Zvi didn't say anything more. He followed the Old One quietly back to the hut. But he contemplated on the way of the day's experience and its ultimate meaning

*   *   *   *

Zvi was up before the sun. He didn't sleep much during the night. His mind was so wide awake and thinking of many things. When he first laid down he dropped off into a deep relaxing sleep. But he awoke soon after and then sleep was impossible. He had an unexplainable urge to do something. There was something that he was sure that he had left undone. There was something he was supposed to do. Try as hard as he could, he just could not think of it.

Not wanting to disturb the Old One, he decided to get up and go for a walk along the stream. The sun was still below the horizon, but Zvi didn't need the sunlight to find his way. In his new state of awareness, which he was now for the first time realizing, his perception had also changed. Everything was illuminated with a golden glow that encompassed all. The trees, rocks, each blade of grass, the flowers, everything was illuminated with this golden glow.

He walked to the streams edge and knelt to take a drink of the cool clear water. Even the water sparkled like thousands of diamonds clustered together. After his drink he started to follow the stream upstream. He hadn't gone very far when he noticed a well worn trail on the other side that came down the embankment. He waded across and up the embankment on the other side. *How strange* he thought, *I have never noticed this trail before.*

The birds were out early that morning in search of food, and filling the air with their songs. Zvi stopped to listen and realized that no longer were the sounds of their chirping the same. The sounds now came in soft rolling waves of enlightened music.

The trail left the stream and veered off into a steeply rising forest. The trees were large here. Much larger than he had seen on this side of the valley. Their tops made a canopy over head, filtering out most of the sunlight. The ground was covered in most places with a thick carpet of moss. Smaller trees; seedlings, punctuated the moss like a pin cushion.

On top of the steep ridge, the trees were not as large and they grew closer together, like a solid wall, and the trail continued on through this wall of trees. There weren't as many birds on top of the ridge and their chirping no longer came in soft rolling waves. Instead, it was coarser and often with broken intervals. The golden illumination that had earlier encompassed everything was now gone. And the air was thick and moist. The ever constant humming that filled Brahm's world was still there, but that too had changed. It was barely audible now.

He walked on looking cautiously ahead and to either side. How could an area in Brahm's world have such a sudden change. There was no evidence that anyone ever used this trail. There were no footprints in the soil, no over turned leaves or broken branches. Only the trail, and it continued on through the thickening trees.

The evergreen trees had closed in on the trail and Zvi had to part the branches. The trail continued on. The sun had come up by now and the day was exceedingly warm he thought. He came to more branches and when he parted those and walked through, he noticed a rock laying by the side of the trail and decided to sit and rest. He sat down and when he looked down at his feet, panic shot though him like a bolt of lightening. With a horrifying consternation, he looked at his hands. They were calloused. His attire—instead of a loose fitting robe, he wore an Air Force uniform with captain bar insignias. He could only explain knowing that the uniform was Air Force by instinct. He wore heavy black boots instead of sandals. Nervously he looked around him. There was nothing familiar about anything that he saw. He looked behind him and the trail was no longer there.

Zvi panicked and raced back in the direction he thought he had come. The trail was nowhere to be found. He stood still, listening. The constant humming had completely faded. The beautiful music of the birds was gone. He looked up at the sky.

The pastel colors too, were gone. Everything he had ever known of Brahm's world was gone.

Suddenly it occurred to him he must have by accident stumbled through the portal of time that his friend—had told him about. "That's odd" he thought out loud, "I can't even remember my friend's name." Right then he wished he had listened to his friend and stayed away. But then he would never have met the Old One and would never have learned so much wisdom. Would he ever see the Old One again? Tears started to well-up in his eyes and his throat tightened, as he thought of the unlikelihood.

After some time he finally managed to compose himself. He straightened his uniform and walked in the direction the trail had originally been going. He found the rock where he had sat and walked on.

The ridge was now going down into a forested valley. He turned to look at something behind him. But when he turned to look, he forgot what it was he had turned to look at. He walked on and off the ridge.

The Old One, Varian, Brahm's world, and even Zvi was now left behind and forgotten

CHAPTER THREE

It was a hot day in August. August third. The day after Saddam Hussein had invaded Kuwait. People world wide were on edge. Wondering what the United States would do. The servicemen and their families were particularly concerned. All those who had been on leave were ordered back to their bases and any future leave cancelled.

Anywhere you traveled, the only conversation was about Iraq and Kuwait. Would the United States support Kuwait and declare war against Iraq? If the U.S. did, what about the other Arab Nations? Could Hussein ally the Arab world and turn Kuwait's invasion into a (jihad) holy war?

If Hussein declares it a holy-war, then what about Israel? Would Hussein be another Hitler and exterminate the Jews? What if someone became a prisoner of war who had a Hebrew name? Would he be executed for being a Jew, simply for having a Hebrew name? These and many more thoughts were on the minds of men and women everywhere. Zachary Breinstein was one of those who was worried. He had only been home for a week on his thirty-day furlough, when his commanding officer had telephoned and ordered him back to Plattsburg Air Force Base in upstate New York. He flew an F-15 fighter bomber and he knew his squadron would be sent over in case of further fighting.

*   *   *   *

Zachary opened the kitchen door and before he could close it Rachel exploded, "Well where have you been? You said this morning that you were going for a short walk up back! Do you know what time it is? It's four in the afternoon! It doesn't take six hours to walk out back and come home. What have you been doing all this time. If you didn't want to spend what very well could be your last few hours with your wife and daughter, then just say so and we'll leave!"

How could he possibly explain to his wife where he had been, or why he was gone for most of the day. He didn't know himself. He could remember leaving the house about mid-morning and then sitting on a rock on the ridge, where he could look out across his valley in the Green Mountains. The next thing he could remember was wandering around aimlessly looking for something that he could identify with. All that took six hours? He didn't know what had happened, so how was he to explain it to Rachel. "I laid down and fell asleep. I must have slept longer than I thought," he told her.

"Sometimes I think you come home just so you can roam around the forest out back. You spend more time in those damned woods than you do with your family. Supper is about ready. Go wash up."

Two hours later Zack was saying good-bye to his daughter and wife. He didn't have any idea how long he'd be away. "It'll depend, I guess, on what Hussein does. If we're coerced into a war with Iraq we could be over there for a long time."

"Have you ever stopped to think what would happen to you Zack if you're shot down and captured?" Rachel asked.

"I know, with a name like Breinstein I wouldn't be treated as a prisoner of war. I'd only be a Jew to them. A threat and the enemy of their damned Jihad," he replied.

"Will you be able to let me know where you are, once you get stationed?"

"I don't know for sure. I will if I can."

Their good-byes were short and Zack drove down the

driveway and on to Plattsburg. He would miss his daughter most of all. Little three year old Becky. All she knew was that her Daddy was going back to his job in New York. She didn't yet have any concept of war. He would miss Rachel, but lately their marriage had hit a hard spot and kept getting progressively worse. He didn't know for sure if she would be there when he returned.

He made one stop in Burlington to pick up his friend Vern. He, too, was a captain and fighter pilot and squadron leader.

The ferry to Plattsburg had already left, so they had to drive to Rousse's Point at the Northern tip of Lake Champlain.

"What do you think of all this, Vern?"

"Looks to me as Hussein's bitten off more than he can chew." Vern replied.

"Think he'll try to unite the other Arab Nations to support him?"

"If he thinks he is going to hang onto Kuwait, he'll need help from somewhere. I don't think he'll get any from Russia right now. Their whole economy is too shaky. And besides, I don't think Gorbachev wants to take up sides against the U.S. right now."

"This would be a prime time for Syria and Jordan to throw in with Hussein, if only to wage a holy war against Israel," Zachary said. "I can't imagine someone in Hussein's position threatening to take on a nation like the U.S. with all of our superior technology. The man's insane."

"What do you think would happen if you should be shot down, Zack?"

"What do you mean?"

"The Muslims don't like the Jews—and Breinstein isn't exactly an Irish name."

"Just because one has a Hebrew name doesn't necessarily make him a Jew," Zack said flatly.

All the way to Plattsburgh, the war in the Middle East dominated their conversation. Nothing positive had been said yet about the twenty-third fighter squadron going to Kuwait. But why else would the entire squadron be called back. Not only the pilots, but also the maintenance crews and support personnel. The only question left unanswered really, was how soon. Zack knew that most of the pilots in the Twenty-Third would be excited about going over. They would welcome the challenge of combat flying, instead of the dull routine low-level practice runs. In a way Zack too liked the idea of the challenge of flying in combat. The thought stimulated his blood.

At the base entrance the security guard directed them to a briefing room in the main administration building, "Yes Sir. Col. Lowell Davis's directive. You're to go there immediately. The meeting is suppose to start at 2100 hours."

"Thank you Sergeant." Zack replied.

"Must be important, Zack."

"Yeah, looks that way doesn't it. Sounds as if it now has become more of a question of when do we leave."

Zachary and Vern were the last to arrive. The briefing room was filled with the other squadron pilots. All talking nervously with one another. All conversations were the same. "We'll give Ole Hussein a licking and show him some American guts."

When Col. Davis entered the room, everybody stood at attention and all talking stopped.

"Be seated gentlemen. This won't take long. It's probably obvious why some of you were called back. Iraq under Saddam Hussein's direction invaded Kuwait on August second and now he has annexed the country. Some of the Kuwait leaders managed to escape and are now asking for our help.

"At the present all that we have been told is that President Bush has delivered a message to Hussein to get out of Kuwait. For now he isn't saying that he'll use military force to put him out, but this squadron and others have been ordered to 'red alert' and to fly our fighters and maintenance crews to Saudi Arabia— Riyadh's air field.

"Arabia's people are afraid Hussein will attack their oil fields next and they have agreed to let us temporarily use Riyadh as a reconnaissance base to fly surveillance over Iraq and Kuwait. We aren't the only fighters ordered over, and I'm not at liberty to say how many. Reconnaissance aircraft are ordered over as well as B-52 SAC command and KC-135 tanker crews. This probably is just the start of a massive build up and our job is to get there immediately and fly surveillance around the clock.

"Tomorrow you take off at 0500 hours. Then and only then will you be given orders to your destination. There'll be an envelope in each cockpit. After take off you will set course for 70 degrees East and then open your envelopes and follow your directives."

"Gentlemen this is not a practice, believe me. It's real and has all the elements of getting bigger. Now get some rest and report to your hangars promptly at 0500 hours. We'll then leave immediately. Good night men." The colonel finished and left the briefing room. The pilots left also and there was little talk among them as they left. As the colonel said, this would be the real thing.

*   *   *   *

Not much was said for the rest of that night. It's one thing to talk jubilantly and joke about flying combat, but now they knew for sure. It was real and no longer a game. They would be away from their families and loved ones for—for how long? Col. Davis didn't say. Each pilot returned to his quarters feeling somewhat mellow.

The next morning at 0500 hours sharp the pilots were all at the side of their fighters waiting for the signal to board and start their engines. Col. Davis was the flight commander and would take-off first. The signal was given and the pilots boarded. Their support crews helped to fasten their safety harness and equipment and then removed the ladder and gave the signal to start their engines.

"Thanks, Mac," Zack said as he gave him the thumbs up sign, "see you in Saudi Arabia."

"I checked out your engines early this morning, Captain. The port engine seems to be okay now, but watch her fuel pressure and the aft temperature."

"Okay, Mac, thanks."

The ground crew connected the APU unit and Zack threw the switch for his port engine and then the starboard engine. The high pitch whine of the engines was deafening and hurt his eardrums. He put his helmet on to soften the noise. After the engines were running, the APU unit was disconnected and moved away from the plane. Zack methodically went through the pre-flight check-off and checked each instrument reading. The fuel pressures, the first stage compressor pressures and then the aft compressor pressures. Oil pressures and temperatures. Fuel capacity, the hydraulics. He tested the aileron, flap, rudder and stabilizer movements. All were functioning properly.

He was cleared for take-off. He closed the canopy hatch and tightened his helmet and oxygen mask. He slid the throttle control forward and the engines came to life. He taxied onto the runway and as he was turning on to the main runway he slid the throttles full forward and as the engines roared he was thrust back into his seat and the pressures against him kept increasing as he taxied faster and faster down the runway. When he attained lift off speed Zack eased the yoke back and the fighter's nose came up and he shot up into the air. He set course at 70 degrees East and then opened his orders.

They were simple. Fly to Keflavik, Iceland and refuel at the airbase and then proceed onto Sussex England. From there he would leave England at 0500 hours and proceed directly to Riyadh, Saudi Arabia. The orders also said that KC-135 tankers would be standing by out of Israel if he needed refueling. The quadrants were given; all he had to do was follow orders. That's how everything seemed to be in the Air Force; follow orders and everything is supplied for you. Somewhere in the deep recess of his mind he had heard a familiar echo of a similar adage.

His new course took him over Maine, New Brunswick and Labrador and then the Southern end of Greenland. Greenland was already blanketed with a skiff of snow, and small icebergs could be seen floating in the waters just off the coast.

As he left Greenland behind, Zack noticed his port engine was operating hotter than normal. He checked the air pressure and it was normal, but the fuel pressure had dropped slightly. It wasn't long before he noticed the affects in the controls. The port engine was fluttering, causing the plane to yaw from side to side.

"Breinstein to squadron leader," Zack called on the radio.

"Go ahead Breinstein, what is it?" The Colonel asked.

"I'm experiencing problems with my port engine. The temperature is hot, and the fuel pressure has dropped slightly. The engine is fluttering and the plane is difficult to handle. It's yawing from side to side."

"How much fuel have you left, Captain?"

"About three hundred pounds, Colonel."

"That should be plenty. Shut down your port engine and peel off to starboard. Capt. Warren will escort you to Keflavik."

"Zack," Vern called, "you going to make it?"

"Yeah, it handles sluggish with only one engine though. Have to keep steady pressure on the yoke to starboard."

"I'll stay with you off your port wing. If you have to bail out, I'll get an exact reading for the rescue crew—water's cold, old buddy," Vern added.

"Thanks, that helps."

His landing at Keflavik was rough. When the base commander heard of Zachary's problem he ordered the air traffic control to assign Capt. Breinstein the number five runway, just in case of a mishap.

*   *   *   *

Once on the ground Zack breathed a sigh of relief. That's the first time he had had to secure an engine. The fighter was hauled to the maintenance hangar and Keflavik's top crew went right to work on it.

"How long do you think it'll take Sergeant?" Zack asked.

"If it's what I think it is, Captain, it won't be long at all. Maybe an hour or two."

"What do you think it is, Sergeant?"

"I think the fuel nozzle has been wire-drawn."

"What's that, Sergeant? I'm not familiar with the term."

"The nozzles are designed concave to allow the fuel to atomize in a finer spray. Sometimes the nozzle metal has a defect in it, or a spot of weak material. Or maybe the burner is misaligned. The nozzle has a scratch in the hole, like you had drawn a thin wire through it repeatedly, pulling to one side. This drops the fuel pressure and the combustion can temperature rises because there is turbulence in the can now, instead of a smooth gas flow.

"If the problem continues with a replacement nozzle, then the burner alignment will have to be checked. Maybe even another engine bolted in place, while this is inspected."

"If it's a defect in material, Sergeant how soon will it show again?"

"Oh, probably within a couple hundred hours. But the nozzle should be inspected after each flight until your own mechanic is satisfied. I'll make a note in your maintenance log so he'll know."

The repairs were made and the remaining flight to England was uneventful. There at the Sussex airbase the fighters were refueled and Zack's port engine inspected. The next morning at 0500 they began their systematic take-off. The roaring jets thundered across the English Channel to France, Italy and across the Mediterranean.

During the flight over the Mediterranean Zack began to imagine what it would be like to point his F-15 straight up and break through the Earth's gravitational limit into intergalactic space and travel through the universe, instead of flying recon-missions over Iraq. Or at least he tried to imagine himself flying off into outer space. He could almost see the Milky Way Galaxy with its spiral arms streaming out into darkened, airless, cold space. He began to wonder what lay beyond the Milky-Way Galaxy and the other galaxies known to man. How many more were out there that man couldn't see, even with the most powerful telescopes? What kind of configuration did all the galaxies combined form? How he envied the civilizations that could travel from one end of space to the other. To do so would mean traveling faster than the speed of light, and at the present, his civilization didn't have any means of travel that came anywhere near close to that speed. For now at least he would have to be satisfied to imagine he was traveling in space.

His thoughts were interrupted then by the command leader's voice on the radio. "We are approaching the coast of Israel. The KC-135s have been notified. Any pilot needing to refuel, drop down to 6500 feet. Those who have enough fuel will maintain their present position and speed and proceed to Riyadh."

Zack checked his fuel indicator and he had about two hours of fuel left. Enough to reach Riyadh.

At Riyadh, Zack secured his fighter and left it in the hands of a skeleton maintenance crew to check the burner nozzle. In the last two days he had flown through several time changes and almost half way around the world. He, like the other pilots needed sleep.

A meeting was scheduled the next morning; an orientation of local customs and the purpose of the routine surveillance missions over Iraq. The pilots all gathered in the briefing room. "Men," Col. Alfred Freedmont addressed the group, "I don't have to dwell on the seriousness of the plight of Kuwait or the direction that Iraq has chosen. Before we discuss military business there is another matter that should be addressed first.

"At the present we are only guests, invited to Saudi Arabia to monitor Saddam Hussein's movements. If Hussein continues to declare this insurrection as a holy war, and our intelligence believes he will, he will also try to unite support from all the other Islamic nations. He desperately needs the support of Saudi Arabia. And so far, King Fahd hasn't completely denied Hussein of his support. But at the same time he is also worried about an invasion across the border from Hussein's elite guard. Our only objective right now is to monitor Saddam's movements.

"During our stay here in Saudi Arabia we will be constantly surrounded with Muslims. They have the same belief as do the Muslims in Iraq. Their customs are different from our own and we can not, at the present, afford to accidentally offend any of their customs.

"Their women are to be treated courteously and with royalty. I do not want any snide or rude comments or jokes to leave this base. You are not to engage them in idle conversation or solicit sexual overtures.

"An incident will be dealt with severely. Keep your minds on your primary goals here.

"You will be kept informed of any changes with Hussein's actions and any change in his military movements will have a direct bearing on your routine recon-missions. Things could escalate without any advance warning.

"As far as your flight missions, I'll turn the meeting over to Col. Davis. He will be in charge of the flight schedules and the command. Good day, gentlemen and welcome to the Middle East."

"Each morning I'll have posted on the bulletin board the day's schedules. The schedules will rotate every two days. You'll be assigned into teams. No one is to fly alone. And you will not engage the Iraqi air force unless they come after you. You will not pursue them into a dogfight. But be absolutely positive that they are aggressive and not just trying to scare you off. If your indicators warn that they have locked their radars on to you, then take the necessary procedures to defend yourself.

"We are basically flying recon missions to monitor Hussein's movements and the build up of supplies and men. At this time we do not know what the President's intentions are, although word is coming down to expect a massive military build up of Allied Troops and supplies.

"Your regular maintenance crews have been delayed, but are expected to arrive in a couple of days.

"Capt. Breinstein, how is your fighter handling now?"

"Okay, sir."

"Good. Have it inspected after each flight."

"I want to caution you all that this is not an exercise. It is very possible that some time in the near future we'll be at war with Iraq and whomever Hussein can find for support. The Soviet M-29s are the best Russia can produce, but I don't think they'll stand up to our advance electronics, radars, and our fighters. Don't become careless and over confident. If you are shot down, chances are that you'll be put on public display and become hostages like those still being held in Iran.

"Capt. Breinstein I'd like to talk with you privately. The rest are dismissed. The schedules are posted. Pick up your orders and proceed."

Everyone else left the briefing room and Zack walked down to Col. Davis's desk. "Yes sir, you want to see me."

"Yes, Captain, sit down. I don't mean to be offensive, but have you considered the possibilities if you were shot down and captured?"

"I don't understand sir. I have, but then who hasn't. And why single me out?"

"Captain, your name Breinstein is Jewish. In case you haven't heard, the Islamic nations have declared a holy war against all Jews. You would not be treated in the same capacity, if captured, as another pilot, let's say whose last name might be Smith!"

"Colonel, Breinstein may very well be a Hebrew name, but that doesn't make me Jewish."

"Maybe not, but you'd never be able to convince the Iraqis of that. They'd take it at face value. To them being Hebrew would be the same as being Jewish.

"My point being, you would not be treated the same as other prisoners of war, under the Geneva Convention. You would be held under their terms of their damned jihad, or possibly executed. I'm only telling you this, Captain, in the event that you're shot down, so that you'll take precautions."

"I appreciate your concern, Colonel, but if I am shot down, I don't see anything that'll change who I am. I'm a good pilot, Colonel, and I do not intend to become a statistic or an M.I.A."

Zack left the briefing room and walked back to the barracks. He was confused why so many people were so worried about him having a Hebrew name. He wasn't Jewish! Do all Muslims hate the Jews so much? Why?

These thoughts were interrupted by Vern's excitement. "Hey! Hey Zack!" Vern bellowed over the nose of incoming transport jets.

"What is it, Vern?"

"I checked the schedules and you and I are a team. We take off at 1400 hours."

"What's our destination? Did it say?"

"Only that our flight plans would be sealed in an envelope and to open them just before takeoff. No one else is to know our flight course. Not even the other pilots. Only Col. Davis. A lot of secrecy involved. I feel more like a piece of machinery than I do a human being sometimes Zack."

"Well I suppose it's safer if no one knows ahead of schedule where we're going." And what Vern said about being only a piece of machinery, triggered a response that hit him square in the gut and was turning his stomach upside down. There was an echo from somewhere reminding him, perhaps of another life, he wasn't sure, where he had been victim of persuasion and had rebelled against the grasp of some entity, that he now couldn't remember.

Vern saw the consternation on his friend's face and asked, "Zack are you feeling okay? You look troubled."

"No I'm fine. I was just thinking of something, that's all."

"Care to talk about it. Wouldn't want anything eating away at your insides this afternoon while we're over Iraq."

"I'll be fine really. Something you said awakened an old echo that's all."

Vern forgot about it and Zack tried. But he wished he knew why it had troubled him so. And where or when had it all started. The feeling was real and he was sure he had experienced a similar circumstance before. Maybe someday he would remember. For the present he had a recon-flight over Iraq and he needed an alert mind and body.

Transport planes were landing about every forty five minutes. Some were filled with troops and others with high sophisticated technical radar and radar laser equipment. The President wasn't wasting any time. By all appearances the United States was going to invade Iraq. The only remaining question was when. With the U.S. air superiority the battles would be fought and won in the air. The ground troops obviously would have to hold and secure those advancements. The greatest fears circulating throughout the airbase was Saddam's unpredictable use of gas warheads, and the Soviet made Scud missiles.

"Do you think Saddam will attack before we finish our build up?" Vern asked.

"If he doesn't want the living hell kicked out of his country, he'll attack as soon as possible. The longer he delays the better our chances are, and the sooner it'll be over." Zack replied.

"I don't know how you feel about all this Zack, but it excites the living hell out of me. For four years we have flown only practice runs, preparing for the day. The day is here now, and now we find out for ourselves if we're as good as we think. Also, we'll be putting up our best against the Soviet's best. It's the excitement of the chase and the hunt that I find stimulating."

"Yeah me too Vern, but in a different way I think."

"How do you mean?"

"It's hard to explain. Almost like I have been sent over here for a far greater reason than flying against the Iraqis in Soviet migs."

"What do you mean Zack?" Vern asked quizzically.

"As I said, it's hard to explain, but I think there's more to this, for me that is, than freeing Kuwait. Maybe I have to find something or discover for myself, who I really am."

"You're Zachary Breinstein, of the United States Air Forces." Vern laughed.

It was close to 1400 hours and it was time for Vern and Zack to get into their flight suits and open their orders.

Zack climbed into his cockpit and gave the ground crew the thumbs up sign and the A.P.U. unit was connected. The whine of the turbines was deafening. A sound he could never get used to. The sound was so alien. The engines ignited, he closed his hatch cover and opened his orders. He and Capt. Warren were to fly north along the Persian Gulf and continue along Kuwait's coast to Iraq's border. Then follow Iraq's border north and climb to 20,000 feet elevation over Baghdad to Jordan's eastern border and then drop back to 6,000 feet elevation. If any of Iraq's fighters were intercepted outside of Iraq's airspace they were to pursue and push the Migs back into Iraq. If they were fired on, then they were to use any means necessary to take out the Iraqi fighters. Over the Jordan border they were to see if any of Jordan's forces were moving towards the border. Then return to Riyadh, along Iraq's southern border.

*   *   *   *

Capt. Warren and Breinstein left Riyadh's airbase and proceeded to the Persian coast and then north to Kuwait. Even from the air and at 600 knots the damage done by the invading Iraqis was evident. At 600 knots though it was difficult to focus on anything in particular. But the damage and the number of

Iraqi troops in the city itself and apparently stationed at its strong holds was prodigious to the ordinary mind.

Along Iran's border the activity didn't seem to be as hurried. There was no troop movement from either country. Apparently Iran's Ayatollah wasn't worried about Hussein. But would he support Hussein if the U.S. declares war against Iraq? "Probably," Zack thought out loud.

From 20,000 feet over Baghdad, there wasn't much that could be seen. Later when the flight recorders were examined and the images enlarged, then a closer perspective would prove beneficial. Enlarged enough so a dime could be seen lying in the streets. But what Col. Freedmont was more interested in, was possible munitions factories and storage depots and communication headquarters. They would be primary targets if the U.S. decided to invade Iraq.

Over Jordan's border Vern and Zack dropped down to 9,000 feet and there they saw long convoys of trucks traveling towards Iraq. Zack banked his fighter to starboard and Vern banked to port to circle and make another fly over. There was no military equipment that they could see, but anything could have been concealed within the truck trailers. Probably they were munitions and food supplies.

On the ground back at Riyadh, Zack and Vern removed their flight recorders and left them with intelligence security for developing. "It'll be interesting to see what will be on the film. Especially over Baghdad," Vern commented.

"Yeah, but we won't know. Not until we fly over with the intention of taking out the installations. Security. Remember Vern. We're only told as much as intelligence wants us to know."

"One hell of a concept isn't it Zack. We're only puppets ,damn it! We're responsible enough to fly a $20 million dollar plane and "Intelligence" says we're too irresponsible to know what we are flying over and taking pictures of. Like they're programming some stupid pinhead! Intelligence throws a stick; we fetch and get a pat on the head," Vern scowled.

Zack didn't reply. He was too immersed listening to yet another echo that he couldn't understand. For whatever reason Vern's vociferation about being only a puppet for Intelligence, had stirred something in him and had aroused that familiar echo again. It was like he was only acting out a part in a play that had already been rehearsed.

There was never any silence at Riyadh. Fighters and huge transport planes were constantly landing and taking off and troops were coming in daily. Some were carrying supplies and others were carrying troops. Young kids mostly. Too young to be faced with the ravages of war. The base was crowded, but confusion wasn't a problem. That alone impressed Zack. Probably because everyone did only what he was trained to do; therefore staying out of the way of someone else. Was that the product of a suppressed imagination and obedience or a byproduct? Which ever; Zack still preferred to be a free thinking being. But was he really? Didn't he conform exactly to the military's way of thinking. He did exactly as he was told and nothing more.

The next day was an exact routing of the day before. The third day was rest. Zack slept late and then went for a walk outside the base confines. He had just taken a shower after getting up and already he was covered with a thin film of dust. Even when there wasn't a breeze, sand and dust filtered through the air. His boots filled with sand and it worked through his clothing. The dry heat was suffocating. He didn't know how these people withstood so much dryness and extreme heat. But then probably they would think the same about the cold snowy winters in the Green Mountains of Vermont.

He found a supply truck that was headed for Riyadh and asked the driver, "Corporal, how long will you be in Riyadh?"

"Two hours, Captain."

"Do you have any extra room?"

"You looking for a ride to town sir?" The driver asked.

"Yes if there's room."

"In the back if you don't mind. The front is full."

"That'll be fine Corporal."

Riyadh was not what Zack had imagined. For the most part the city was very modern. The streets were clean and sparsely lined with palm trees. Probably the modern lifestyle and cleanliness was due largely to the rich petroleum fields. There were two major differences between Riyadh and the western world communities: here the buildings, streets and parks were spacious, not crowded together like most of the western world. There were also fewer vehicles.

"Captain, we'll be leaving the depot at exactly 1500 hours. If you're not here sir, –well we can't wait," the driver said.

"I understand Corporal. If I'm not here when you leave, I'll find another way back."

He left the depot and found a clean restaurant with air conditioning. When he walked inside silence blanketed, like a plague had swept over. Everyone stared at the American in uniform. Some pointed and others talked, whispering in Arabic. Zack imagined what some of the comments might be. He glanced at an attractive woman with a younger woman, maybe a daughter, and instantly the two pulled their veils over their faces. He turned away, remembering what Col. Freedmont had said.

As he ate his meal he noticed that people were curious about him. Some would stare openly while a few stopped at his table and offered a phrase of good-will and encouragement. Little of which he could understand. But their amiable grace was clear.

When he had finished eating, Zack went back out into the scorching heat. There was still an hour before the supply truck would leave. He decided to walk about the city. He turned off the main street into a busy avenue of shops and traders. There didn't seem to be the menace of Hussein's wrath in the atmosphere, as the traders and shopkeepers went about their daily routine of trying to better their rivals. At one shop a loud argument was drawing spectators. Zack stood in the background listening. The argument was in Arabic and Zack didn't understand any of it, although their anger was obvious. Apparently one had cheated the other.

As Zack was about to move on he felt a tug on his pant leg. In perfect English, a blind beggar sitting on a doorstep said, "Alms! Alms for the destitute," and he extended a leathery hand towards Zack. "Alms—my young friend. You see I have no eyes, with which, would allow me to work and support myself. I do not ask for much. Only enough to buy a loaf of bread perhaps."

Zack turned to look at the beggar tugging on his pant leg. He was appalled with the appearance of the beggar's face. Two empty eye sockets were set in a rather clean shaven, wholesome face. Void of any visible stress or sagging, rippling skin. It puzzled him; the beggar's use of clear English. Apparently he was well educated and probably had held a substantial job. After the shock had subsided Zack reached into his pocket and gave the old beggar all his change. "Here, Old One, take this," Zack put the coins in the beggar's hands.

"Blessings my friend and may the Great Deity that watches over us all, sit with you, as you fly your fighter over Iraq."

"How did you know that I am a fighter pilot? You cannot see."

"One does not always need eyes to see my friend. I perceived your presence was near. You had your hands in your pockets, which is common in western culture. Your speech is English and the material of your pant leg is made with machine and pressed with a permanent crease."

"That only indicates that I might be an American serviceman." Zack replied.

"That is true, Captain," a pause and then, "your insignia over your pocket identifies you as a fighter pilot."

Zack stood silent, gazing at the old beggar. The old beggar chuckled to himself and then Zack asked, "How do you know this? You can not see either my captain bars or my fighter insignia."

"When one becomes blind, it then becomes necessary to use other faculties that lay hidden and dormant in the far reaches of the mind. As you can very well see that I am old. I am older than time itself it seems. And I have made good use of that time and I am now able to reach out beyond this physical shell and perceive where I have focused my attention."

Zack was speechless. For some unknown reason, what the old beggar said made some sense to him. But he couldn't figure out why. He didn't know how the old man reached out beyond his physical shell, but Zack understood that he had indeed done just that.

The old beggar said, "I can perceive from your silence that you are troubled."

"No, not really. Something you said started to almost sound familiar. It went away."

On the way back to the base Zack kept thinking about the old beggar and what he had said. It troubled him. More so because he knew that somewhere, he had been told a similar recounting and he couldn't recall when or where he had been at the time.

The next day Zack spent most of the morning on his back on his bed, with his fingers intertwined behind his head. He was trying to understand why the old beggar had had such a profound effect on him. Then his thoughts would shift to the present; his being in the Arabian desert. A place so alien to him. He missed the sound of the wind blowing through the trees. The rain splattering on the rooftop and the sounds of the water gushing in a river. Here there was only the constant roar of jet engines.

His thoughts wandered back to the old beggar. He remembered he was going to give him enough money to buy himself a nourishing meal and he had been so transfixed with the beggar's prattling he couldn't remember for sure now whether he had given him the money. He decided to return to the city someday soon and look for the old beggar and buy him a decent meal.

For now he dragged himself out of bed, showered and put on a clean uniform and went outside. The day was hotter than the day before. He found most of the other pilots that weren't flying recon, gathered in the officer's mess drinking coffee and telling stories about their flights over Kuwait and Iraq. Zack got a cup of coffee and sat alone at a table, listening to the others.

"Hey, Zack, thought you were going to sleep all day. What did the noise bother you?" Vern said jokingly. "Come on over and join us."

"No, that's okay. I'm going to finish my coffee and then go for a walk."

After Zack left the mess hall one of the other pilots asked Vern, "What's gotten into him, Vern? Ever since we arrived here, he's been awful quiet. Is there something wrong back home?"

"I don't know for sure. He doesn't say much. I think everything is okay at home. He's just more reserved than the rest of us. Zack needs a lot of time for himself."

Zack found some old rags in the maintenance hangar to wipe his fighter down with. He was meticulous about he care of his jet. He kept it clean of grease and oil spots and polished the outside lovingly. He removed the dustcovers from the turbine intakes and inspected the compressor blades. Then wiped the inside of the turbine cowling.

When he had finished he sat on the leading edge of the wing and watched the arrivals of B-52s, KC-130s, KC-135s and the huge C-154s. There was no end to the constant supply line of troops and supplies. He knew in his own mind that President Bush had all the intentions of invading Iraq. If all he had wanted was to liberate Kuwait, the Air Force could have accomplished the job with one SAC command and two fighter squadrons. There was more to this battle than simply freeing Kuwait. Intelligence knew the answers, but Zack doubted if the pawns on the desert playing board would ever be told the real reasons.

A smaller jet than the huge transports just landed, and from the insignias on the fuselage Zack figured it would probably be high ranking officials—the ones who would be safe in their bombproof shelters, directing the movements of various troop units and flight wing commands. They and they alone would get all the glory if Iraq was defeated. None of the young fighter pilots or the pilots of the huge bombers. Nor probably would the Intelligence personnel that were on the ground in Iraq and Kuwait receive any recognition, only the high and mighty generals that would be far from any danger.

Generals, Colonels, Majors, and Admirals were useless, until time of war or the threat of War. "Perhaps wars are fought only to amuse the idle curiosity of our military giants," Zack said aloud.

The more he saw of the Mid-East the less he wanted any part of it. The people, no matter what sect, were always fighting. It seemed, if there wasn't a good enough cause, then some holy-war enthusiast would invent a reason. This is certainly a land of unrest. It always had been and probably always will be.

Now that he had himself distraught about he military and the Mid-East, Zack climbed down off his F-15 and returned to his quarters.

The next day, Capt. Breinstein and Warren had orders for night patrol over Jordan to the Turkish border, and intercepted four Turkish sukhoi SU-7s and escorted them back to Riyadh. Turkey's Prime Minister had offered his support to the Alliance with his expressed understanding that his support was only to stop Hussein from further atrocities and not to invade Iraq.

For the next two nights their orders took them deep into the interior of Iraq, a low level flight at near supersonic speeds. They were to record several communication installations that Intelligence had located, and needed more information whether or not the facilities could house Mig fighters or scud rocket launches.

Word began circulating around the base at Riyadh that

additional troops and supplies were being stockpiled in Dhahran as well. Carriers, battleships and destroyers were either already in the Persian Gulf and the Mediterranean or were on there way. Great Britain was sending troops and supplies as well as France, Egypt and even Syria. Enough war materials were delivered daily to completely wipe out the entire Mid-East. "Perhaps that's what the President has in mind," Vern said.

"I don't know," Zack replied, "but there sure is one hell of a lot of equipment over here already and more arriving everyday. I only hope this doesn't escalate into a bigger conflict than just helping Kuwait."

"I think it's too late for that already Zack. Hussein can't back down now. He's got to keep up the charade, if he wants to save face. He's boasted too much to his own people and to Muslims all over the world, to haul in his guns now. He's committed to playing the cards he has already dealt."

"I wonder how long Gorbachev will support the Alliance. Hussein has already pleaded for help from the Soviet Union," Zack said.

"I doubt if Gorbachev wants to be drawn into a war right now. The Soviet's economy is too unstable and I doubt if the other Soviet political leaders would support Gorbachev even if he decided to send aid to Iraq."

"Let's hope so, Vern."

The next day Zack went back to the city, hoping to find the old beggar. He wanted to talk with him as well as buy him a decent meal. He went back to the street with all the shops, where he had met him before. He walked the length of the street on both sides. The old beggar wasn't there. But nothing said he had to work the same street everyday. So Zack methodically checked all the mercantile streets in that area of the city. The old beggar was not there. He went back to the first street and went into the shop that the beggar had been sitting in front of on that day. Zack approached the owner and asked, "Do you speak English?"

The owner replied, "Yes, a little."

"Two weeks ago I was in front of your shop and there was an old beggar sitting on the sidewalk. I would like to find him. Do you know who I am talking about and where I can find him?"

Suspiciously the owner asked, "Are you the police?"

"No. I would only wish to talk with this beggar."

"Why would you want to talk with a beggar?"

"He is a wise old man; I would like to see him again and talk."

The shop owner found this to be strange. "No one here ever wants to talk with old beggars. You say he is an old wise man. Then why does he have to beg?"

"Look! Can you help me?" Zack was exasperated.

"There has been no beggar here. They're not allowed on this street."

"Perhaps you might have seen him on some other street. He is blind. His eye sockets are empty and he was wearing a white robe. It was torn and dirty and he was barefoot."

The shop owner thought about it and then replied, "No, I have never seen him."

Zack thanked him and went back out in the street. He went from shop to shop inquiring about the identity of the old beggar. In all cases it was the same. No one had ever seen a blind beggar in the area. There wasn't much more he could do, except to return to the base.

The old man's words of wisdom, and his peculiar abilities intrigued Zack. For the present at least he would have to forget about him and concentrate on the Mid-East conflict and his flying. It was growing in magnitude everyday.

CHAPTER FOUR

The Old One left his hut and followed the path to the hilltop. The day was inexorably beautiful. There was a translucent golden aura that bridged the pastel sky's horizons. The music emitting from the land of Brahm was eminently beautiful on this particular day. And as the Old One stood atop the hill a light breeze blew into his face and he smiled with satisfaction.

The hilltop began to stir. The Old One knew what to expect. Soon the land was quaking and the air began to tremble. Brahm's voice rolled across the valley floor to the hilltop where stood the Old One. "Old One!" Laughter filled the sky and its deep thundering roar deafened the Old One's ears. "I hope you have indeed prepared the curious one well. I have sent him to the very ashcan of all the universes! There he wanders in complete dismay. He has already forgotten all you have taught him!" More thundering laughter filled the air. The Old One showed no consternation. He gazed steadfastly out across the valley below and smiled. "Do you hear me Old One? You have lost this one. He can never return. Because he has no memory of My Land! He walks the land below searching for all eternity, but he'll never find the hidden wisdom now!" More thunderous laughter.

The Old One spoke with an even, fluid reciprocation. "You speak in haste, my old friend. Has not the Great Brahm perhaps forgotten that Zvi has just entered the world below and during the process, one looses all memory of your world. You have given him an incredible obstacle to deal with. He will have to first find his way clear of the obstacle, and then I am sure the knowledge he has received here will seep into his conscious mind. And once it does, he will once again recognize who he is and he will return.

"It could be said, My Lord, that the test and circumstances you chose for my young friend might not have been a little harsh? You have set him into the middle of a dispute that has carried on since the beginning of that world. He will be persecuted purposely for his namesake alone."

Brahm laughed his thunderous roar. "Old One, do not get sentimental! I purposely made his venture harsh because of his nature and fortitude. A lesser test would not have served any purpose."

"I was not complaining, My Lord. I simply pointed out a fact. The venture is indeed harsh, but once Zvi begins to look within himself for the answers to his present circumstances, then he'll rise above the obstacles. And once he has done this, then he will remember his lessons here and once again he'll discipline his mind. Even if he is in the ashcan of all the universes."

"You are sure of this one, are you not, Old One?"

The Old One looked up at the pastel sky, with a broad smile he said, "Yes. Yes I am, My Lord."

"What makes you so sure?"

"Because of the depth he traveled when he discovered he was the lotus flower and his recognition of the difference of being one with it. That understanding alone will carry him beyond your obstacles, My Lord, and beyond the Ashcan and beyond, even of your limitations. He can perceive that there is more than the limits of the understanding of your world. He does not put limits on himself nor of his understanding."

Brahm had been rebuffed.

CHAPTER FIVE

The days kept getting increasingly hotter. Water became more precious than gold. No one went far from their tent or barracks without carrying plenty of water. Work was slowed to a moderate pace. Outside activity, unless performing some vital act, was discouraged altogether. For the most part the troops were bivouacked in tents. Only the officers and special trained personnel maintained some semblance of civilized living in four walled structures with a roof. Water was a precious commodity for all, and showers were limited. Clothes had to be worn for several days at a time. Body odor was so poignant, especially in an enclosed room, that the smell caused Zack's eyes to sting and water.

Air recon-flights were increased. "Gentlemen, if ever it would be advantageous for Hussein to attack, it would have to be now. His army is well accustomed to fighting in this heat and we're not. On the ground we would lose as many men from heat exhaustion as from enemy bullets. Our flights have got to be increased to ward off any surprise air attacks.

"The AWAC aircraft and our satellites surely can spot a sudden movement, and if that does occur we must have our fighters already in the air to intercept Iraq's before they reach Saudi's airspace.

"There are two aircraft carriers in the Gulf now, and the F-111s will be flying routine patrol flights also. As well as a third carrier in the Mediterranean and another recon-squad from Dhahran. If you spot an Iraqi fighter outside its airspace, bring it down. If it is within Iraq's airspace, intercept it and order it down. If it refuses to comply, take it out. Is that clear?

"It can be well assumed that Hussein has his own intelligence people here, and is well informed about our military strength as well as the effects of this damned heat. If he is any kind of a strategist, he'll take advantage of the heat and use it to his advantage.

"If you encounter anything at all that even remotely looks suspicious, fly over it if it's on the ground and the flight recorder will have it on film, or if any, and I mean any aircraft are seen in the air, investigate it. There's information that Hussein has ordered some of his best fighters to Iran. At the present we are not sure what this means. If you encounter one in route to Iran, follow it until it lands. Under no circumstances initiate an air battle over Iran. If you are fired upon then take the appropriate measures. Take it out. So far, Iran hasn't committed any support to Hussein. That's how we want to keep it." Col. Davis nervously wiped the perspiration from his forehead and left the conference room.

On the way back to their barracks Zack asked, "Vern, have you stopped to think why we're here in Saudi Arabia?"

"Yeah, to push Hussein out of Kuwait and bomb the hell out of Iraq if we have to. He illegally annexed a country and stole the richest oil producing fields in the world."

"Haven't you ever stopped to think that there probably is a lot more behind Desert Storm besides freeing a tiny country like Kuwait, that should probably be part of Iraq anyhow? It's a dispute between two Arab nations, not ours."

"What's eating at you Zack? You've been edgy ever since we arrived in Riyadh. Intelligence knows what it's doing. That's their business. And ours is flying these fighters where and when we're told. Sure there's more to this than we're told, but again that's Intelligence's business. Anyhow, I can't wait to intercept one of those Russian Migs. We'll show Hussein who has air superiority. Each time we go up I hope we intercept one of their Migs and he wants a fight. Stop worrying Zack."

"It just all seems a little too circumstantial to me."

"You mean you think that this sudden interest to help out an Arab nation, and a Muslim one at that, is only a cover up for something else?"

"Wouldn't surprise me in the least Vern. If we knew just a fraction of what goes on behind the Intelligence's closed doors it would be appalling."

"Lets just suppose you're right Zack. Then what's the real reason we're over here?"

"I don't know—a cover up or something else maybe. Maybe by defeating Hussein, it would give our people an added incentive to overthrow Iran while we are here."

"You're making too much of this Zack. Let it alone. If you don't, you could be called in for subversion."

"Vern, we have flown thousands of hours over Iraq, Kuwait, Iran, and Jordan. Not one encounter has been reported. We've photographed every square mile of Iraq. There's something in particular that Intelligence is looking for."

"What's that?" Vern asked.

"Don't know. But I do know their looking for something in particular."

"How do you know that?"

"I'm not sure—call it a hunch, a gut feeling. It's real, Vern. There's something there that Intelligence feels is worth sacrificing millions of dollars for, not to mention human lives."

*   *   *   *

When Zack wasn't flying recon-missions over Iraq, he flew low level practice runs in the Saudi Desert. Preparing for the day when Iraq would be attacked. Still, Intelligence was looking for something in particular. Whatever it was, wasn't showing up on satellite photos, the AWACS radar screens or on the fighter's flight recorders. There was something there. Zack was sure of it. Because that could only explain the number of repeated flights over the same installations.

One afternoon Vern and Zack were ordered to fly recon into Iran. Information was coming back to Desert Storm headquarters from ground intelligence that Hussein had sent more of his prized Mig fighters into Iran. Vern and Zack were ordered to intercept the Migs and if they couldn't turn them back to Iraq, they were to take them out.

Between Dezful and Iraq, Vern spotted two Soviet Migs flying at ground level. "Zack, 4 o'clock below us. Do you see them?"

One of the Migs turned back for Iraq and Zack followed it until it was in Iraq's airspace. Vern pursued the other Mig. It was obvious from the beginning that these two intended to see whose flying skills were better and who had the best fighter. Vern banked to port and descended to come up on the tail of the Mig. As soon as the Iraqi pilot saw what Vern was doing, he put his fighter into a steep climb for about 10,000 feet and then banked hard to port and did a 180 degree roll back and came up behind Vern.

Vern was nervous. It was evident he was up against an experienced pilot. He did a 360 degree roll to starboard and then a 180 degree back roll. He couldn't shake the Mig. The Iraqi pilot anticipated each movement and then countered to keep Vern in his radar.

Vern's radar alarm went off, signaling that the Iraqi pilot had locked his radar onto the F-15. Vern released his dummy rocket for the Iraqi's missiles to follow. Then he banked hard to starboard, then a 360 degree roll to port and came up behind the Mig. The Iraqi's missile had followed the dummy rocket and exploded on contact. Now Vern locked his radar onto the Mig and fired one starburst missile. The Iraqi Mig exploded. Almost instantaneously.

"Damn! Did you see that Zack!"

"Yeah. That's some pretty flying buddy."

"Guess we know now which side has the better pilots and fighters," Vern said feeling smug. "We'd better return to base; my fuel is low."

On the way back Zack was oblivious to his present situation. He was listening to a strange, yet somehow familiar voice that came at him from somewhere afar. The voice was telling him of another place, another world, where the people were strictly obedient to an unknowing deity. That as long as they were obedient, they would be provided for.

The voice went on to say that the inhabitants of this world were not free to believe as they wished. Their obedience was only coerced persuasion. An artificial contrivance. A cold piece of unfeeling, unthinking mechanics, that could only function if told what to do.

The voice stopped and Zack could hear himself inside his own mind saying almost the exact same thing. "I'm only a piece of machinery in this modern day military and I do only as I am told. Nothing more. I'm not a free independent individual that can react to a situation as I see best. There's rules and regulations that must be followed. Follow the established procedures, no matter what the consequences. It's a suffocating atmosphere.

Then he saw the old beggar sitting on the sidewalk in Riyadh and listened to him explain about using perception to see, and not the physical eyes. Zack laughed out loud and wondered how Col. Davis would react to that. If he told the colonel that he was bringing his F-15 in for a landing with his eyes closed. "Don't worry, Colonel, I'll perceive the runway." He laughed some more.

Back at the airbase in Riyadh, Vern was ecstatic about his first ever air battle. And against the Soviets best fighter, the Mig 29. No denying the Iraqi was certainly experienced, but his Mig couldn't maneuver as well as the F-15. It was faster but its response was slower.

"How did it feel, Vern, to kill one of those air-camel jockeys?" another pilot asked.

"It was exciting! Almost pissed my pants when he'd locked on. Thought I'd had it for sure."

Zack stood in the background listening. He couldn't find

anything exciting about killing another human being. Whether he's an enemy or not. He was a highly skilled and trained fighter pilot and he would do his job when it came to it. But that didn't mean he had to glorify in it.

Zack lay in bed that night with his hands folded under his head. Eyes wide open and staring at the ceiling. Too many thoughts were running rampage through his mind. He found question after question without answers. No one was telling the truth. Especially the Intelligence Agency. Hussein was lying as well to his people and his military leaders. Both sides were lying to the world. This war wouldn't be fought over oil wells or the liberation of Kuwait. Although that would be the excuse used to invade Iraq. And that probably would start as soon as Intelligence found the installation they were so concerned about.

Zack was just another pawn on the chess board. He was expendable, manipulated into strategic positions and sacrificed, if needed to protect something of more grandeur. He wasn't free to think for himself or believe as he wished. He was told every move he made. When to go to bed, when to get up, when to eat, when, where, and how fast to fly his F-15. Every detail of his existence was being programmed daily for him. The only thing he did for himself was eat and maintain a healthy body. And then that too was a prerequisite. He was a slave. A slave to what? Who was the master? As he was a slave, then so too was all the entire military. Even Intelligence.

Was he alone in this concept; or were there others like himself that could see the fallacy. Logic predicated that he couldn't be alone. But he and those like him would certainly be a small minority. Why were so many willing to follow so blindly into battle an idealistic establishment? Had everyone been programmed to respond in the manner in which the leaders wanted? Had he been programmed? Yes. But there was a flaw in his programming. Zack believed he had a right to think for himself and to doubt anything that didn't look or sound right.

He listened to Vern's snoring in the bed beside him. He

was a machine also. The same as he, too, was most certainly only a small piece of the military machinery. A start button that set him in motion in the morning, another that turned on his already programmed mind and another button that stopped all action and laid him down each night to sleep. "Robots, that's all any of us are!"

This ballyhoo of stockpiling men and munitions was increasing faster than anyone could possibly have ever imagined. Already there were enough supplies and munitions to take out Hussein. Battleships, cruisers, destroyers and carriers in the Mediterranean and the Gulf; B-52s, fighter jets, sea to land missiles, ground to air rockets, a new defensive missile called the patriot, laser guided missiles, a bomb called the smart bomb, the new M1A1 tanks with their incredible speed advantage and the night attack capability. Enough weapons to launch a major invasion into Russia. Was this what Intelligence was trying to do? Show the Soviet army the military strength the Allies had so the Bear wouldn't interfere?

Rumors were beginning to circulate that Hussein had nuclear capability. And that was Intelligence's prime prerogative; to find the installations that housed the components and the planning. Other rumors had Hussein saying that if he was attacked he would deliver his first nuclear warheads on Israel and smash the Jews once and for all, gaining support from the other Arab nations to launch his holy-war against the Allies.

It was becoming more evident each week, as more supplies arrived that this was not going to be an attack to just liberate Kuwait. Hussein's troops had dug in around Kuwait's frontal border with Saudi Arabia and the coastal areas. But Saddam failed to realize, that all of his defenses would be useless against a huge, highly technical superior army.

It was becoming more and more evident that a war with Iraq was not only a possibility, but a certainty. Everyone at Riyadh was ready with anticipation for the President's signal to move on Hussein's army.

The only man who could stop this foolishness was Saddam himself. If he complied with the U.N.'s terms to leave Kuwait and leave his machines of war abandoned in the field. Intelligence knew he couldn't stop now. Saddam had been pushed too far and Intelligence wanted his nuclear capabilities destroyed. And the only way that was going to be accomplished was to invade Iraq.

It was also evidently clear that Hussein and his elite guards would be facing the Alliance alone. A pitiful prospect, in light of the Alliance's superior weaponry.

*   *   *   *

Christmas was over. A solemn holiday, in the dry sandy desert of Saudi Arabia. Zack had received a care package from home. A brief letter from Rachel and a longer one from his daughter Becky. Becky was too young to understand the importance of war or why her daddy was gone. As Zack read her letter, he could almost hear her chipper little voice. He missed her more than he did his wife. Becky was so much more alive. Inquisitive, where Rachel was complacent.

Christmas didn't mean much in a Muslim state. There was no seasonal music on the radio, no brilliant displays in shop windows. But what Zack missed most about the holiday was the snow covered land. The snow always seemed so peaceful and serene. A blanket and underneath was the mother earth. Gone to sleep for a brief period. In Riyadh there was only brown sand. The heat was gone but it too would return in March.

It was New Year's Eve. A somber place to be indeed, to see the old year out and greet the new. Zack's squadron got together for a little celebration, socializing and drinking. The conversations all centered around how soon would President Bush give the order to take out Iraq.

Col. Davis was overheard talking with the Base Commander that all preparations had been finalized except some new information from ground Intelligence in Baghdad concerning new communication installations set up in public school buildings and hospitals. "I would expect Commander that as soon as these are officially located we'll start our air attacks. It could be within the next few days."

"Let's hope so Lowell. Our ground troops won't be able to swelter the summer heat. If we're going to invade Iraq, it'll have to be soon," the Commander said.

The next day while the rest of the squadron laid in their beds with a hang-over, Zack took a shuttle bus into Riyadh. He wanted to make another attempt at finding the old beggar and spend a few minutes talking with him. When the invasion starts, there won't be any free time and he'd be confined to the base.

He checked first the street where he had previously talked with him. He wasn't there. He methodically checked each street in that area of the city. The old Beggar was not there. He asked several people if they knew of a blind beggar. Those who could speak a little English said no.

Finally he bought a bag lunch and went to the park to sit. The park benches were full so he looked for a shady spot beneath a palm tree. There was only one tree that afforded any shade and there was an old man dressed in an off-white robe, sitting with his back to the trunk and chanting to himself.

The old beggar's chanting produced a humming sound that seemed vaguely familiar. As Zack came closer, the humming was more pronounced. The man too seemed somewhat familiar. The chanting stopped. The old man lifted his head, as though he knew someone was approaching. Zack saw the empty eye sockets and recognized his friend.

"Hello, Captain", the old beggar said.

"How did you know it was me? I did not say anything, nor have you touched the fabric of my uniform?"

The old beggar smiled and said, "There are rumors in the city of an American Officer who searches for an old blind beggar. Since I am both blind and old, I assume that I am the one in search of. Few if any will walk across the park to find a beggar. We have so few friends you see. So when I heard your footsteps in the grass, I assumed you were looking for me. And I see you have brought lunch with you. That I can smell, Captain," and the old beggar chuckled.

Zack gave the old man his lunch. "Thank you, Captain. Sit down. There's enough shade for us both."

The old beggar finished eating and then asked, "Captain, why have you been searching for me?'

"I wanted to talk with you and buy you a nourishing meal."

"Well the lunch was nourishing and I did enjoy it. Thank you. Now what did you want to talk about?"

"First, I would rather you called me Zack, instead of Captain. And what may I call you?"

"You would have difficulty with the pronunciation. You westerners have a difficult time rolling your A's and R's. So call me an old friend or old man. I don't mind. For surely you can see that I am old."

"I like old friend better." The old beggar nodded his head to acknowledge Zack's reference.

"When we talked before, you were explaining about perception sight. You hit a familiar chord. I was sure I had talked with someone else before about the same topic, but I couldn't remember where or when. But the familiarity brought a harmonious feeling of tranquility. A peaceful aura stayed with me after talking with you. That's until I went back to being a fighter pilot."

"You do not like being a pilot then?" the old beggar asked.

"I like flying yes. But it doesn't have the same effect on me like talking with you. I mean the feeling I had last time."

The old beggar chuckled, "Yes I know what you mean."

"Not long ago my friend and I encountered two Iraqi planes. One returned to Iraq and the other was shot down by my friend. He was so happy about taking out the Mig and killing the pilot. And back at the airbase everyone wanted to hear his story. Like he was a hero for killing someone. I realize we have a job to do, but I didn't find any excitement in a man losing his life."

"Would you have felt better if the tables had turned and the Iraqi had taken out your friend?" The old beggar asked.

"No, of course not," Zack replied.

"Sometimes my young friend, in this earthly life, one may find oneself in a situation where you must kill another human being in order to survive. I'm not saying that you should enjoy it by any means. But until man raises his level of consciousness, then man must survive by the law of the land. If he doesn't then he will be killed."

"I know you're right, but until the other day I never stopped to realize that when we take out another fighter, we're taking a life also. It has always been just a target. Another plane or a spot on the ground. I never considered before that a human life would be lost."

"Maybe this will help you to be a better pilot," the old beggar added. "There is more troubling your mind, is there not my friend? I listen to your words, but I also hear an emptiness in your voice."

Zack didn't respond immediately. He looked away from the old beggar and watched as children played gleefully across the park. He was debating whether to say anything about his feelings of not being free to be who he really was. But what was that? And he wondered why he felt so comfortable talking to this man that he hardly knew. Would he or could he understand? A beggar only had to answer to himself. There was no timetable, no programming. He wasn't just another piece of machinery; essential at that.

Zack turned back to look at the old man sitting beside him. He was smiling Maybe he does understand, Zack thought. "In my country we live in a democracy. Probably the most democratic society in the world, where we are free to choose whatever we wish. But I'm not free and neither is anyone else!" Zack stood up and hit the palm tree with his fist and walked away and then returned. The old beggar sat with his back against the tree patiently waiting for Zack to continue.

After Zack sat down again the old beggar asked, "Why don't you feel free my young friend?"

"Because every facet of my life is programmed for me. What I do, I only react to what I have already been programmed to do. I'm told where and how to fly my plane. What objectives, installations, targets and even how to respond to an encounter with an enemy aircraft."

"Yes, but is not this only discipline of being a good fighter pilot? It's a derivative of your training. Without the training and discipline would you be an effective tool. Excuse me, let me phrase that differently. An effective pilot."

"You're right, but my whole life is like that. Even my personal life. I'm told when to go to bed, when to get up, when to eat and what I'll eat. I'm told how to dress and where I can or cannot go. What my demeanor should be and I am never free to believe as I may. I am constantly being told what's best for me to believe. Our Intelligence Command sometimes appears to be a lesser God. They think all should bow to them, that they are the only ones with a logical brain who might be able to perceive an answer!" The old beggar smiled and Zack asked, "Why do you smile? Do you think I'm crazy?"

"On the contrary my friend. It is they who are insane. But I smile because I see you remembered something from our last discussion. One's ability to perceive."

"Sometimes I feel like I'm suffocating. I haven't any space I can call my own. And I am more disturbed now than ever about this war with Iraq that we are about to start. If I believe only what we are told by Intelligence, then we are in the right. But if we're being told nothing more than lies than this is wrong."

"What do you think Zack?" The old beggar asked.

"I don't know what to think. I want to believe the Intelligence's reports and know that I am doing the right thing and support my country."

"But," the old beggar interrupted, "your gut reaction tells you different."

"Yes. Exactly. I feel I'm being manipulated into this and into believing the reports are all true. There seems to be little truth and honesty now, among men and nations."

"You should not upset yourself so much my friend. You are not here because you choose to be, are you? No, I didn't think so. You, your friends and your country have been pulled into the middle of a war that has been waging since the beginning of time. The Muslims against the Jews and vice-versa. That's what this war really boils down to. Not the invasion of Kuwait or the blatant theft of the oil fields."

"I understand that. I guess what really agitates me most is the fact that we are not being told the truth. That instead of being a free thinking individual, I've become nothing more than a dispensable pawn. As long as I do what I am told and believe what I am told to believe, the military establishment will take care of me and provide whatever I need. I can't live like that old friend. Maybe it's okay for some but not for me."

Inwardly the old beggar was laughing. He tried hard not to let it surface and maybe embarrass his young friend. Then in a serious tone, "Where do you think you could go in this earthly world where you could escape those restraints?"

"I don't know. But there must be a place," Zack replied.

"As you have said, your country is the freest democratic state in the world; can you escape from restrained thinking there?"

Zack thought before answering. Even in his home of Vermont he was not free to be his true self and to know truth. "No I guess not. Even there I would always be subjected to someone else's ideas and beliefs. What do I do?"

"That will have to be up to you. Maybe someday, in your heart, you'll find an answer."

Zack sat under the palm tree for most of the afternoon talking with the old beggar. He felt good in his presence. He could feel the positive vibrations emit from this shabby old man. It wasn't long before he was feeling better about himself. Although no questions had really been answered. Still he sensed a difference.

"I have to return to base shortly. There's an early curfew now that war with Iraq seems so eminent. Come, let me buy you a decent meal in a fine restaurant."

"Oh that won't be necessary. You have already provided for a fine lunch. Besides, it doesn't take much anymore to sustain this old body. No, you go along. I have enjoyed this discussion as much as you. Maybe someday I can return your hospitality and provide you with lunch."

The old beggar stood. Zack looked into his empty eye sockets. Even without eyes he knew the old beggar was also watching him. "Thank you for listening to me ramble on. Goodbye."

"I wish you well Zack. For now, keep your attention focused on the present. There'll be time later on, to worry about truth. Learn to perceive the movement of an enemy. It'll help you with your flying."

CHAPTER SIX

Zack returned to the airbase and all was forgotten about he old beggar and his important words of wisdom. President Bush had given Saddam Hussein just twenty-four hours to get out of Kuwait or the Alliance would put him out.

Everyone cheered when they heard the news. If a war was going to be fought, the troops wanted to get it over with as soon as possible. They had been dug-in the sands of Saudi's desert long enough. They had trained day and night and were now ready. They needed to be engaged in battle before the eagerness wore off, and their spirits dampened. This was not going to be another Vietnam. A war of politicians and greedy cooperations.

The reports from Intelligence were clear now. Iraq had been developing nuclear capabilities and it was believed that Saddam would use his nuclear war heads if his scientist had gone that far in development. He threatened openly to destroy Israel if the United States invaded Iraq.

It was obvious now why Hussein had waited so long, instead of taking advantage of his tactical position during the early stages of the U.S. build-up of troops and supplies. He needed the extra time to complete his nuclear weapons. But as midnight January 17th approached, Intelligence still could not confirm whether or not his scud missiles were armed with nuclear warheads. Rumors were circulating that the scuds would be armed with nuclear warheads as well as with chemical gases.

No one on base talked anymore about their families or back home. All conversations were centered around Bush's ultimatum and how Hussein would react. What would he do first? Blow up Israel as he had threatened? Send his elite guard into Saudi Arabia? Or would he withdraw his troops?

The recon-flights had been stepped up. Movement of Iraqi troops had been reported. Convoy lines of supplies and men on its way to Kuwait's coast. Shipments coming across from Jordan. And reports that Iraqi troops were well dug in along Iraq's borders.

At 1800 hours on January 16th, six hours before the official start of the Iraqi invasion, Col. Lowell Davis summoned all of the squadron pilots for a briefing.

"Gentlemen," he paused and cleared his throat and wiped the sweat from his forehead.

"Gentlemen at midnight we invade Iraq's borders and push forward into Kuwait. This is no longer just a possibility. Even if Saddam Hussein agreed now to move his troops out of Kuwait, there isn't enough time left before the deadline for the communications to reach all of his units. And as long as there is still a single Iraqi troop within the borders of Kuwait the President said to move forward and liberate Kuwait and push the Iraqis back to Baghdad or until Hussein surrenders.

"This invasion will be grander than the invasion of Normandy in WWII. Air strikes will begin from Riyadh and Dhahran simultaneously at 2400 hours. Our naval carriers in the Gulf and the Mediterranean both will be deploying their fighters. The French, British and our armored divisions will start advancing towards Kuwait and the Iraqi border. The naval battleships will deploy cruise and sea to land missiles.

"The carriers in the Gulf will deploy their fighters to Kuwait city. Our first assignment is to take out Hussein's communications installations along Iraq's border and then proceed to Kuwait's border and take out the communication installations there.

"Some of the installations are well dug in underground and some have been installed in public buildings. Our intelligence people have pinpointed the exact locations and buildings. Some buildings are set adjacent to others, but with your laser guided missiles you should be able to take out your target without destroying the adjacent buildings.

"Once we have taken out the assigned communications installations, then we'll concentrate on bridges, supply lines and scud launchers. These launchers are portable and maybe difficult to target. SAC wing command will fly B-52 sorties over Iraq's airbases and the dug in troops along the border and carpet bomb them.

"Your orders are on the table in front of you. They'll pinpoint the installations to take out. If you can't fire your missiles with the first fly-by, then make another fly over. It is imperative that these installations be destroyed. If you have any missiles left, then on your return flight take out bridges and supply lines. KC-130s will be standing by just off Iraq's border if any of you need refueling. When you return to Riyadh your crew chiefs have been instructed to refuel and rearm your fighters as fast as possible. In the mean time, you'll be given a new set of orders and new objectives. You'll be flying as many sorties each day as you can. If you feel that you're to exhausted to stay alert then notify ground command. You must be alert up there men. You can expect a heavy concentration of anti-aircraft firepower. It'll be like flying through a July fourth fireworks.

"If you're shot down we'll send out a rescue helicopter immediately. I have no other advice to give you other than how you have been trained. I don't think I have to stress the importance of this matter. Your sorties will be anything but routine. Those of you who flew in Vietnam, you'll be facing new weapons; anti-aircraft guns that fire more rapidly, surface to air rockets that'll seek out its target and mostly, the advancement of the Soviet made Migs. We are still not sure of the Mig's total maneuverability, its speed or firepower. We are sure that they don't compare to our advanced F-17s or F-18s and probably they lag behind the F-15s. But the Iraqi pilots have flown combat more recently than any of you. He'll be experienced.

"Let me reiterate, you'll be flying combat, not recon or practice runs. The Iraqi's will throw everything they have at you. Stay alert and watch out for your buddy. Good luck men." Col. Davis put his hat on and walked back to his quarters to study his own orders, and familiarize himself with his objectives.

Zack and Vern walked across the compounds to their quarters. Neither one offering a conversation. Inside they each sat at their desk studying their orders to destroy communication installations along Kuwait's border. "This is going to be different, Zack."

"How do you mean, Vern?"

"Flying combat. Now we know there will be enemy fighters on our tail and we'll have to fly through enemy anti-aircraft fire. On recon it was only a slim probability that we would face an enemy fighter, and we joked openly about it. Now it's right there in front of us. We already know what we'll be flying into in a few hours." There was no levity in his remarks. Vern was deadly serious. But then so were all the soldiers who landed on Normandy's beaches.

Zack had forgotten about his recent conversation with the old beggar. He was once again a cog in the mighty military machinery. Once again he was being programmed. Told where to fly and how to fly. What his objectives were and even how many rockets to fire at each installation.

"Think I'll lay down for awhile and get some sleep before we take off. I'd advise you to do the same Vern."

Zack laid back and closed his eyes. Instantly he found himself awakening in another world. One without wars or fighter aircraft or anti-aircraft guns or bombs. There was only peace and serenity. There was a golden aura surrounding everything. The colors were so vibrant and clear. There were birds singing and way off in the distance was the sound like a gigantic multitude of bees swarming. There were no people or animals. Only himself and the sound of millions and millions of swarming bees. For some unknown reason he sensed a familiarity with this place. He couldn't remember of ever being here before, but it did somehow seem familiar.

He stood in the middle of what appeared to be a beautiful garden of many varied flowers and shrubs. The fragrance of the sweet nectar was so aromatic that the membrane in his nose began to burn. Beauty encompassed him. He started to walk along a garden path and noticed he was wearing a white robe instead of his air force uniform. For some unexplainable reason it didn't seem strange. He was drinking in the joy and tranquility of this place and really didn't care much about anything else.

*　　*　　*　　*

"Zack. Hey Zack wake up. It's 2330 hours. Time to get into our flight suits and warm up the engines. You fell asleep fast."

Zack didn't answer. He was back in a world that was anything but serene. But the dream of that tranquility soon faded and his thoughts once again riveted on being a fighter pilot.

Zack climbed into his cockpit. A cold piece of metallic machinery. Unthinking and uncaring. He was programmed to fly an F-15 and now he was being told what his targets would be and how to execute the operation.

The crew chief climbed up to the cockpit and helped to strap Zack into his safety harness. "Thanks Mac. Anything I should know first?"

"She's running smooth kid. Give Saddam a piece of hell for me." Mac climbed back down to the ground and watched as the crew connected the A.P.U. unit to the F-15. He ran his hand through his graying hair and hoped for a speedy end to the war. He was up for retirement.

Zack gave the thumbs up sign and the crew stood back

away from the engine exhaust. The turbines began to whine and sing. The air pressure reached ignition pressure and Zack flipped the fuel switch to the starboard engine and to the port engine. The roar was deafening. Zack put on his specially equipped night combat helmet and closed the hatch cover.

Mac gave the signal that all was clear and Zack inched the throttles forward. Even with the heavy payload of bombs, rockets and fuel, the F-15 rolled out to the runway effortlessly. Vern was beside him. The signal came from the air traffic control tower and Zack and Vern simultaneously moved the throttles full forward and their F-15s sped down the runway. They used extra distance because of the added weight.

"How's she handling Vern?" Zack asked over his radio.

"Sluggish, like an over filled bathtub. You nervous, Zack?"

"Strange, but I'm not."

Night flights were always eerie. You traveled at tremendous speeds without any visibility. You read the instruments and hoped they were functioning properly. You didn't have the luxury of spotting a familiar landmark below or visual contact with other aircraft. You flew according to instrument readings.

Tonight held that same eerie suspense. And added to the suspense was the threat of enemy aircraft. It was difficult to out maneuver an enemy fighter because you were never sure of his location except what showed on the radar screen. You never knew for sure where he was.

Would this attack surprise Saddam or would his own intelligence be forewarned of the invasion? If he knew the attack was coming, that President Bush wasn't just bluffing, then he will have his fighters on the ready to intercept the attack. Zack rolled this idea around in his mind until it was beginning to affect his flying. "Hey Zack you got problems. You're yawing back and forth on my radar screen."

"No, everything is okay." He put Hussein's fighters out of his mind and concentrated on his flying.

Five minutes away from there objective. Still no alarm. Hussein was caught unaware. This first attack then would be a cinch. The next would undoubtedly be more difficult.

"You ready, Vern?"

"As ready as I'll ever be."

"I'll make the first strike; you cover me."

"Make it good."

A minute away from there target Zack saw the first signs of anti-aircraft fire. It was sporadic and ineffective. Most of the shells were exploding before they reached the fighters altitude. Still it was significant to visually see the fire power coming at you.

Zack turned on his night radar screen and energized his laser system. He locked onto the coordinates in his orders and scanned his radar screen for the communication installation. He missed seeing the installation on his first pass. It was camouflaged that well. "What happened Zack?" Vern shouted into his radio.

"Missed the installation. Didn't see it until I had flown by. The installation's a dug in substructure. The front is covered with sand bags. I'll fly around and come in at 90 degrees to it. I'll try to drop one in the front door, you take the roof."

"Any Migs yet?"

"Nothing. Only the anti-aircraft guns."

Zack swung around and guided his laser rocket to the front door. It blew up on contact and Vern's rocket leveled what was left of the substructure.There was four heavy armored vehicles near the installation and these were destroyed as well. Zack located a power transformer installation and guided a laser rocket into the center of the transformers. Vern located an ammunition depot and when it exploded the whole sky line was afire.

They both still had their full compliment of stinger missiles. Those would not be used unless they encounter enemy fighters. On their way back to Riyadh they didn't encounter any of Hussein's Migs or had any indication on the radar that any had gotten off the ground. The only aircraft spotted were other units of their own squad also returning to Riyadh.

At Riyadh while their fighters were being rearmed and refueled the pilots took the flight recorders over to Intelligence and then met in the conference room with Gen. John Henry McWilliams, Col. Alfred Freedmont and Col. Alex Hamilton.

There had been no casualties at all. No anti-aircraft hits, no mishaps of any kind. Each unit was successfully able to locate their objective and fire the laser guided rockets.

"Men your next sortie will be more difficult. Hussein's air force has without any doubt been alerted and will already be in the air before you reach your next objective. The only thing I can say is stay alert.

"Col. Freedmont has your new orders. That's all." Gen. McWilliams and his aide, Col. Hamilton, left the conference room and went over to Intelligence to observe the flight recorders and ascertain the amount of damage inflicted on the first invasion wave.

This time Vern, Zack and three other units were assigned to take out the landing strip northwest of Kuwait city. "I want each runway destroyed first, then target as many aircraft on the ground as you can."

"Col. Freedmont?"

"Yes, Captain."

"Has there been any scud missiles sent up yet?" Zack asked.

"No, not yet. But we can expect them anytime now. So far none of Hussein's air force has gotten off the ground. This may be because we have taken out some of his communication capability. But as Gen. McWilliams said, you will probably find some of them already in the air on your next sortie. Gentlemen you have your new orders. Good Luck and God speed."

Col. Freedmont left the conference room and Zack opened his orders. They were to fly low level supersonic flight until ten minutes away from the landing strip. Then they were to climb to 3,000 feet and slow their speed to 400 knots. The laser guided rockets would be fired from that altitude. After the runways were destroyed they were to come in at low level and destroy what aircraft they could.

Zack climbed back into his cockpit and started fastening his safety harness. Mac climbed up to the cockpit.

"How's she handling, Captain?"

"Like a dream once I'm off the ground."

"That's usual; you're carrying the F-15 maximum payload. Anymore and you wouldn't get off at all."

"How's the engines?"

"Okay."

"Notice any temperature change yet in the port engine?"

"I didn't have the time to look. I'll check on it this flight. Okay, Mac, I'm set."

Mac climbed down. The A.P.U. unit was already connected and he gave the all clear signal. The turbines whined and then exploded into a deafening roar as both engines ignited simultaneously. The runway was clear and Vern and Zack were back in the air at 615 knots at 400 feet altitude heading for the air strip outside of Kuwait city.

After his first sortie Zack never interpreted his targets as killing anything more than perfunctory objects. He couldn't see the faces of the men inside a bomb shelter or a communication installation. When one of his rockets exploded inside, he couldn't smell searing skin and blood or hear the screams of the dying and wounded. He dropped his load, flew out of the target area back to safety and left the ground war in Iraq. From the air, he was oblivious to the destruction. If he had been more aware of the destruction he might have started questioning again the Intelligence reports and the actual reasons for invading Iraq. And perhaps he would have listened more attentively to that familiar echo that was trying to guide him in his quest for truth. But he had been programmed and disciplined to the military's way of thinking and for now at least, his probing for truth would have to wait.

Upon the approach to the landing strip the Iraqi troops let loose everything they had for anti-aircraft fire power. The night sky was alight, like a roman candle. Some of the anti-aircraft shells exploded so close Zack could hear the explosions over the noise of the turbines. Zack released his first laser guided rocket and because of the air disturbance, he couldn't keep his laser guiding track on target and the rocket missed and exploded harmlessly. On his next pass he released two rockets and they hit one of the runways and destroyed it.

Two of the Mig fighters had gotten off the ground before the landing strip was destroyed. They had their radar guided missiles locked onto two of the F-15s, but missed their target. Before they had a chance to fire again, both Migs were taken out.

Zack concentrated the rest of his fire power on Iraqi aircraft on the ground and the maintenance buildings. He kept two stinger rockets for the return flight to Riyadh.

While the fighters were being refueled and rearmed the pilots met with Col. Freedmont in the conference room. The invasion was going better than anticipated. Apparently some of Hussein's communication lines had been destroyed in the first wave. That probably would account for the absence of Mig fighters in the air. The squad's next objective would be to take out the known stationary scud launchers between Kuwait's border and Saudi Arabia and Kuwait city and a scud launch installation at As Samawah. There was a concrete bunker at each launch sight. The laser rockets would have to be guided at the weakest appendages. Like a door or ventilation duct.

Vern was assigned to take out the bunker in Kuwait and Zack the bunker in As Samawah. They each would be accompanied with two other F-15s. The rest of the squad was assigned to the dug in Iraqi troops on the front line at Saudi Arabia's border. They were to destroy the anti-tank barricades, opening a hole for the armored division at dawn. They were also to take out the heavy artillery guns and the anti-tank guns. No Iraqi tanks had been reported in this area yet, which convinced Intelligence that they were well dug in, in a defensive line behind the artillery guns.

The fighters would reach their targets about dawn. The heavy U.S. 12th armored division was prepared to roll through on the heels of the F-15s, and destroy the tanks in the defensive line. Then move forward towards Kuwait city.

Zack flew over the concrete bunker and in his radar screen he thought he had seen where electrical conduit had been installed in the back portion of the bunker. These lines would probably be the main electrical entrances. Even if his rockets failed to penetrate the concrete, the electrical service would be interrupted and may possibly even explode the transformers inside.

On his turn around pass he spotted a truck convoy approaching As Samawah, probably from Baghdad. He would take that out after he had destroyed the bunker. The anti-aircraft fire was heavy. Zack learned from his last sortie to stay at a high altitude, even if he had to slow his speed. There he would be out of the reach of the guns. He held his fighter as steady as he could as he guided his rocket to the conduit service. When the rockets hit the bunker, there was a delayed explosion, and then the whole bunker just collapsed in its own hole.

Zack flew back and located the convoy. He came in low and fast at the head of the column. His stinger rockets hit the first two vehicles and those exploded setting off a domino effect along the convoy. In the rear was a larger fuel tank, too distant from the rest of the convoy to explode. Zack fired two more stinger rockets and the tanker went up in flames.

He still had three laser guided rockets left. He circled the bunker installation and decided to destroy the road and bridge to As Samawah.

Zack would fly two more sorties before he would be

relieved. At the end of his last sortie he was told to get some sleep. His fighter would be inspected, refueled and rearmed.

*   *   *   *

It wasn't a peaceful sleep. The constant noise of fighters and B-52s taking off and landing was unbelievable. He rolled over and covered his head with a pillow. Vern slept soundly however. The noise wasn't a nuisance.

Zack couldn't sleep so he rolled over on his back and tried to empty his mind of all thoughts. At least a peaceful rest would be better than no rest at all. But he couldn't stop thinking about the last twelve hours. He was a piece of the machinery. Finely trained and disciplined. He would do his job the best he knew how.

He couldn't let himself think of the targets as anything else other than solid material objects with no life. He knew if he started thinking about the people caught inside of the targeted installations and how many were dying from his bombs, he would start asking himself again about the purpose of the invasion; the real reason for the invasion, and he would not be able to fly his F-15 into combat effectively.

So as he laid in bed, his thoughts centered around how he could do his part, (flying), even more effective.

At 1800 hours Vern and Zack were called back to the flight line. "Sorry to disturb you, Captains, but there's been some scud attacks and we need you two to fly into Iraq and destroy the launchers. We have the coordinates from the last attack. Follow these and take out those launchers. They may be movable. If they are, they won't be in open view. You'll have to hunt for'em.

"Your planes have been refueled and rearmed and you're cleared to leave." Col. Freedmont handed them their orders and the coordinates of the last scud missile launched.

The coordinates took them to Ash-Shabakah. Not too far across the border. They flew above the reach of the anti-aircraft guns, and watched the ground below on the radar screens. There was no scud launch visible. "Vern let's split up. You take the east and I'll look to the west. Watch the anti-aircraft guns and Migs. If you find it let me know."

"Okay."

There were four main highway systems that came together at Ash Shabakah, making it an ideal location for a launch sight and a point of invasion into Saudi Arabia. Zack followed the highway towards Kuwait until he was too far beyond the coordinates Col. Freedmont had given them. He turned around and searched the area to the southern highway. Still nothing. He radioed Vern and told him he was turning back. "—haven't much fuel left. We might as well take out these bridges and highways."

Zack flew back over the southern route and guided a laser rocket to a bridge. The bridge exploded with so much magnitude that Zack circled back. From the destruction he surmised that the Iraqis had hidden a scud launcher under the bridge. He radioed Vern and then they routinely took out all the bridges in the area. They found scud launchers under two other bridges.

When they returned to Riyadh to refuel and rearm, they told Col. Freedmont about the launchers being hidden under the bridges. From that discovery any bridge found intact was to be destroyed. Later another pilot discovered a launcher hidden in a barn.

Col. Freedmont gave an explicit order that any building large enough to house a scud rocket launcher found in the vicinity of the coordinates from a launched scud rocket was to be destroyed.

Dhahran, Riyadh and Israel were routinely being barraged with the Soviet made scud rockets. Dhahran and Riyadh had not received a hit yet. The patriot missiles were intercepting the scuds before they reached the city limits. Israel however had sustained some minor damage.

Israel was threatening to retaliate with nuclear warheads and declared the state of Iraq would be totally destroyed.

However perverse, this seemed to be what Saddam Hussein wanted. For Israel, a Jewish state, to attack Iraq, a Muslim state. Perhaps Hussein was thinking he'd gain the support of the other Arab nations that way and drive the infidels from his Iraqi soil.

"Do you think Israel will restrain from attacking Iraq?" Vern asked.

"I don't know. The hatred between the Jews and Muslims has been going on almost forever. They attack each other out of pure spite and hatred. A tooth for a tooth and an eye for an eye. An animalistic way of thinking. If Iraq should score a direct hit, then no amount of persuasion from the United States will stop Israel from carrying out its threat to destroy Iraq with a nuclear warhead."

"Let's hope our patriot missiles arrive there in time." Vern replied.

The attacks on Israel, as well as Dhahran and Riyadh continued. The patriots were able to intercept most of the scuds, but a few did explode in relatively harmless areas.

The Soviet made scud missiles were probably Saddam's most technically advanced weaponry he had, except for the Mig -29's, which had yet not even gotten off the ground. The scud, unlike the U.S. made smart bombs and cruise missiles, did not have the capability to recognize a definite target and destroy it explicitly without destroying everything else around it. The scud was an instrument of mass killing that often didn't hit its programmed target.

The B-52's carpet bombing technique opened the heavily mined front lines and permanently destroyed Hussein's airbases. The new MIA/tanks were an artilleryman's nightmare. It had the capability of night maneuvers and could fire repeated salvos while moving. Hussein's tanks and heavy artillery was World War Two vintage compared to the U.S.'s high technology.

Intelligence had reports that several of Hussein's best fighters, the Mig-27 and -29 had flown into Iran and landed at Dezful and Bakhtaran.

"Gentlemen," Col. Davis cleared his throat and stood up and walked over to a wall chart of Iraq and Iran. "Intelligence has reports that in the last two days several of Hussein's best fighters have landed in Dezful and Bakhtaran. Iran has assured the Alliance that once the Migs enter Iran's airspace they will not be allowed to return and that the Migs will be kept under close security and will not be allowed to take off. Iran cannot be trusted to honor its word.

"We are sending specific sorties into Iraq and Iran with orders to take out any Iraqi Migs. Maj. Daniels will command one wing and will patrol the Iranian border and I will command another wing that'll fly to Baghdad and Al Amarah. We'll intercept and destroy any Mig found on the ground or in the air. The airbases at Baghdad and Al Amarah have not been totally wiped out. So if Hussein has anymore Migs at these two locations, he'll want to fly them to safety while he still can.

"They'll probably try low level flights. But watch upstairs also. If telecommunications spot anything that looks like a Mig, Intelligence will give us the coordinates. I can't stress enough how important it is to prevent Hussein from sending his best to Iran."

Vern, Zack and three other pilots were ordered to Baghdad. Col. Davis and three other pilots would go to Al Amarah. If there were no Migs located they were ordered to destroy the rest of what they could of the remaining airbases.

"We're going right into the ring of fire this time, Buddy," Vern said over his radio.

"Yeah, right down the camel's throat," Zack replied.

At Baghdad the five fighters dropped down to 3,000 feet altitude and first made a fly by, past the airbase. There were three Migs on the ground and several older fighters. Zack took the lead and came in at 400 feet. His first rocket hit one of the Migs in the midsection and it went up in flames. Vern hit another and one of the other pilots took out the third Mig. They made another pass and took out four more aircraft. Zack's rocket misfired and exploded in air.

The anti-aircraft fire was heavy but poorly targeted. They had apparently caught the Iraqi's by surprise. There was no attempt to try to get any of the fighters into the air. With the remaining rockets, they destroyed the landing strips and fuel storage tanks.

After the last pass they pulled into formation and headed back for Riyadh. As they started to climb Vern radioed Zack, "Zack! You have a fire in your port engine."

Zack had already felt the sluggishness in the controls. The combustion temperature was too high. "Try your fire retardant."

"I have already. The fail switch must have burned off."

Vern radioed the other three fighters and told them to return to Riyadh. He would stay with Capt. Breinstein.

Zack shut the port engine down but the excess jet fuel in the combustion can was still burning and the temperature gauge kept climbing. The hydraulic alarm went off. The fire had spread forward now, burning the hoses and auxiliary equipment on the engine casing. "The only chance I have now Vern is to get as much altitude as I can and dive. Maybe the air will blow the fire out."

Zack ignited the port engine. Pushed forward on the throttles and pulled the yoke back. He was climbing fast, but he knew he had only seconds left. At 15,000 feet he leveled off and cut both engines. "Of all times to have that damn burner tip screw up again," he said over the radio.

"Ride it down to the ground Zack. Hit your ejection if it doesn't look like it'll come out of it."

The nose of Zack's F-15 tipped forward and he was diving at about 70 degrees to the ground. The G-force wasn't that great but he started to spin. With both engines down he had no hydraulics to work his control surfaces. The fighter was spinning faster and faster.

If a plane's control surfaces are rigged properly, then in a hands-off position the plane is supposed to return to level flight.

When you're spinning out of control spiraling towards enemy soil, it's a difficult decision to let go of the controls. But Zack had no other alternative. He let go of the yoke and rudder paddles and the spin started to stop and he leveled out at 1,000 feet. There wasn't any waiting. He had to ignite both engines now or crash. He couldn't know for sure if the fire was out or not. Even if it was and provided he could make it back to Riyadh without encountering an Iraqi Mig, he would have to bring his F-15 in on its belly. He had lost too much hydraulic oil to extend and lock the landing gear into position. But he would worry about landing when he got to Riyadh. Right now he had to worry what would happen when he ignited the engines.

Vern was flying above Zack watching for enemy fighters. As Zack was leveling off, Vern noticed on his radar screen an Iraqi fighter approaching from the rear. He rolled hard to starboard and pulled his yoke back and climbed above the Iraqi Mig.

While Vern was flying attack with the Mig fighter, Zack flipped the ignition switches. In Vern's radar screen he saw the explosion. When Zack's engines ignited there was excess unburned fuel still in the port combustion can and when it ignited, the whole plane exploded. Tears filled Vern's eyes. He knew what must have happened. His best friend was dead. Torn apart by the explosion like some slab of meat in a grinder. He pushed his throttles forward and came up behind the roar of the Mig. So close he could see the flames inside the engine. He said, "This one is for Zack," as he fired two stinger rockets up the tailpipe of the Mig.

CHAPTER SEVEN

After returning to Riyadh, Vern went directly to Command headquarters to report Capt. Breinstein officially missing in action, presumed dead. Vern knocked on the CO's door and entered without waiting for a reply. "Yes, what is it, Captain?" Col. Freedmont asked.

"Sir, it's Capt. Breinstein. His fighter blew up."

"Did he get out, Captain?"

"I don't think so sir. I didn't see him."

"What happened? Was he shot down?"

"We were returning from Baghdad, the mission was a success, when Capt. Breinstein's port engine caught fire. The fire retardant system failed to function. He climbed to 15,000 feet and shut down both engines, and then dove, hoping to blow the fire out. At 1,000 feet he leveled off. At that time I'd spotted an Iraqi Mig and was engaging combat maneuvers. Breinstein's fighter must have exploded on ignition. I was first aware of it on my radar screen. I didn't see the actual explosion. After I had taken out the Mig I circled back to look for Capt. Breinstein. All I could see was burning remnants scattered on the ground. There was no sign of Capt. Breinstein, sir."

"Damn it!" the colonel said after Vern had finished. "He was an excellent pilot. Did he have any family, Captain?"

"Yes sir, a wife and daughter."

"They'll have to be notified. That's all, Captain, thank you."

*   *   *   *

Before Zack switched the ignition to both engines, he took a cursory glance at the temperature gauge. It was hotter than before when he made his dive. This could only mean that the port engine was still on fire. If he tried to ignite the port engine now, it would certainly explode. But his thinking wasn't synchronized with the movements of his hand. He had already flipped the ignition switch. Then automatically he hit the ejection switch and was ejected from the cockpit just as the plane exploded. The explosion was so close that Zack was dazed by the concussion.

He was thrown clear of the wreckage. The forward movement of the plane carried the debris away from him. His parachute opened and he clung to it helplessly. It seemed like an eternity as he was suspended in a weightless void. Complete emptiness. His eyes could not focus and his ears were filled with an enormous sonorous roaring.

When he hit the desert floor, his camouflage colored parachute drooped down around him. He lay there motionless. Waiting for some degree of consciousness to return. He knew that training had dictated that the parachute and any unnecessary gear should be promptly buried and he should leave the area as soon as possible.

Part of him wanted to leave and the other part wanted only to lay there undisturbed. He wasn't sure just how much time had passed before he could finally crawl out from under his parachute. He took the chute harness off and using his helmet, began to dig in the sand.

When Zack had finished, all that remained of his gear was a small survival kit which consisted of a gallon of water and some saltine crackers. He started walking southwesterly away from Baghdad. He had to put as much distance between him and his wrecked fighter as possible. The weather was warm, but not as hot as it had been on his arrival to this devil's land. But still,

116

he was concerned about his water loss. He only had a gallon and didn't know where or when he'd find any more.

There was a constant stream of aircraft overhead. B-52s and fighters, heading towards Baghdad and other targeted areas. They were all too high to notice him on the ground. He used their flight path for his compass. In time, that is if there is enough time, he should make it back to the Saudi border. There he hoped to contact an Allied troop.

For six hours Zack traveled, following the flight path, without stopping to rest. But now he had to. If not, he would die from exhaustion. He would never have believed how difficult it was to walk in the sand. The footing was soft and it slowed his progress. There was no shade anywhere. He had to stop though. That was certain. He'd rest until dark and continue during the cooler hours of night.

He kept this up for two days. Traveling by night and resting during the warmer daylight hours. The only shade or protection he had from the blazing sun was to gather all the bushes he could find and lay those on top of himself, while he rested.

By daylight of the third day he came to the Euphrates River near Ash Shinafiyah. His water was gone. As thirsty as he was he decided to wait for the cover of darkness before venturing to the river's edge. He could hear excited voices on the other shore as a squadron of B-52s passed overhead. The crowd was mostly women, with baskets full of laundry to wash. Some started to run for cover while others stood their ground shaking angry fists at the huge planes.

He made a blind from bushes that grew along the fertile river bank to conceal himself from those across the river. For the first time he was relatively comfortable. It was cool along the river. He slept soundly for several hours. By midday he started watching the women on the other shore with curiosity. Their behavior wasn't what he had expected. They wore for the most part brightly colored clothes and did not have the black veils covering their faces. They were slender, dark hair and quite pretty.

Iraqi power stations had been targeted earlier. That would explain why so many women had gathered at the river to wash clothes. It was as much a social gathering as it was to wash clothes. They chatted merrily with each other; that is until another wing of B-52s flew overhead. Then some would raise their fists and shout angry words or spit on the ground.

When the Iraqi women had finished washing their clothes in the river, some disrobed and bathed in the warm water, while others returned to their homes. Zack watched with only mild interest. His attention was riveted on his own unpredictable survival. If he had been caught watching the women bathe by their men folk, he would have been killed immediately. After the women left the river bank and all was once again quiet, Zack laid back and closed his eyes.

It was long after dark before Zack left the security of his blind to get some water. He drank as much as he could and then filled his gallon water bottle. This wouldn't be a safe place to cross, so he followed the river downstream away from the village. He walked all night before stopping at what seemed to be a deserted stretch of the river. There was still a little time before daylight, but Zack decided to wait until the next night before crossing. He wanted to know what was on the other side first.

The moon was still out and he was hungry. He would try catching a fish in a shallow pool. It wasn't easy using only your hands and guided only by the light of the moon. But after several vain attempts, he succeeded in trapping a small silvery fish. He had no choice but to eat it raw. It was food and it was nourishing. He caught another and another, until he had had enough.

Nothing stirred all day across the river. The only sound was the almost constant drone of the planes overhead. As he lay concealed behind his blind he wondered how the Iraqis would combat the constant bombing. The power and communications installations were destroyed. Their food supply line had been cut off. There was no running water. How could Hussein expect to fight against so overwhelming odds? But then Hussein was a crazy man, absent of logic or caring.

He waited until midnight before crossing the river. Still the only sound was from his own air force flying over head. Once on the other side, he crawled to the top of the bank and laid there, intently scanning the grounds around him. He lay there several minutes watching for any movement. Finally when he was satisfied that it was safe to move, he went back to the water's edge and walked downstream along the shore. He wanted to put some distance behind him from Ash Shinafiyah, before striking off across the desert again towards the Saudi border.

By daylight he had put ten miles behind him. He felt relatively safe and stopped for the day. He built another blind from bushes and lay down. He was tired and soon fell asleep.

At twilight the next evening Zack crawled out from under his blind and foraged for fish in the shallows. He found a variety of small fish and ate two raw. That's all he could stomach. He found no delicacy in eating raw fish, and he wondered why the Japanese found it to be so appealing.

It was dark by the time he finished eating and he began his trek again. The only guidance he had was the flight path of the planes overhead. The river was soon left behind and Zack found himself in a mysteriously quiet setting. All was silent. There was no wind, not even the slightest breeze. But there was movement all about. Dry tumble weed and sagebrush glided smoothly along the sand packed floor of the desert. If he looked closely the sand was stirring over the desert surface like blowing snow, drifting over a road surface. The desert was a mysterious place indeed.

The desert night air was cool. He could see his breath. The stars overhead formed a brightly lit, speckled canopy. Although he felt like running to get safely out of this God forbidden land, he cautioned himself against being too careless.

He proceeded with foresight, listening for the rumbling of trucks or tank engines, or the chatter of lonely soldiers. There was nothing. He was alone.

Before daylight Zack stopped and dug out a hole in the sand and then collected enough brush to cover the top. It provided a cool enclosure, hidden beneath the desert surface. He wasn't long going to sleep. All his thoughts were centered around the last few days. Would he get back to Riyadh? Or would he eventually become just another unfortunate statistic of war?

Zack hadn't been asleep for long, when he was awakened by the sounds of trucks and excited soldiers talking. He turned over in his brush covered hole and slowly lifted his head above the sand to see what the disturbance was. It looked like an entire company of Iraqi troops on the move north. Since they were crossing in the open desert Zack assumed that traveling was probably too risky for a column of this size to be on the highway back towards Baghdad. There were no tanks or armored vehicles. Only trucks carrying troops and more Iraqi troops walking. This could only mean a retreat.

Zack watched with particular interest. They were close enough so he could see by the insignias on their uniforms that these were Saddam's best—the often talked about and feared Elite Republican Guard. The Elite Guard was reported to be entrenched between Kuwait's border and Albasrah. What were they doing in the desert and retreating towards Baghdad? They were supposed to have been Hussein's main strength—dug in, in reserve to ward off a ground attack by the Allied forces. Their presence here could only mean that a strong hold in Hussein's defenses had been broken.

He guessed about a hundred men. Only a small portion of the Elite Guard though. But it signified that Hussein's best, instead of fighting was now retreating in the face of the Allied troops. Zack chuckled and said to himself, "Another bluff called on Saddam."

Zack was getting cramped. He turned his head slowly to

stretch sore neck muscles and move his legs. The truck nearest to Zack stopped. The door opened and a soldier stepped out. He barked an order and the soldiers in the body of the truck jumped out and circled Zack. Someone in the truck had seen him move. Now what would happen? Would he be shot on sight? His worst fears were coming true.

One soldier flung the brush back with the rifle barrel and then stood back pointing his Russian made AK-47 at Zack. Zack put his hands on his head and waited. A cheer went through the column as soon as it was discovered that they had captured an American airman. An officer stepped forward and was talking with another officer, probably a captain. The ranking officer was probably a colonel, although he wore no insignias except a patch on his hat.

After what seemed an eternity the ranking officer walked over to Zack and stood there with his hands planted firmly on his hips and said in perfect English, "Captain, you are now a prisoner of war, captured by Saddam Hussein's Elite Republican Guard. I am Col. Abdel."

Col. Abdel then ordered two soldiers to remove the captain from his hole and bind his hands behind him. Their treatment of an American prisoner was no more congenial than Zack had guessed it would be. After his hands were tied behind him one of the soldiers punched Zack in his stomach, using the butt of his rifle. Zack doubled over from the blow and groaned through clenched teeth. Then he was hit from behind with another rifle butt between his shoulders. This sent him sprawling to the ground, to the delight of the entire column, as some cheered. The pain in his shoulders was searing hot. Like a hot iron had been driven into his back. He didn't know if he could remain conscious or not.

"Captain, that is only but a little of the pain you have brought to the Iraqi people with your bombs and missiles. You will walk with those of us who are forced to walk. I will not remove a man from one of the trucks so a filthy dog can ride."

Zack heard the colonel. Only barely, between the pain in his back and stomach, and his anger. These people were no better than barbarians. He was dragged to his feet and accompanied by four Iraqi soldiers to the rear of one of the trucks. There he would have to walk in the dust of the column to Baghdad. Would the column be spotted by a fighter squadron, possibly his own, and attacked? It was very possible.

*   *   *   *

The Iraqi column had not gone very far before it stopped for the day. Like Zack had been doing, they too were traveling mostly during the cover of darkness. He was given a sparing amount of water and his ankles were shackled and then he was pushed down on the ground beside the truck. At least he was out of the direct sunlight. He watched as the soldiers ate meager meals of bread and cheese. Even that was appealing to Zack.

Some of the soldiers crawled in under the vehicles, to get out of the sun, and stretched out to rest. Others gathered in small groups and talked. The atmosphere around the troops was anything but cheerful. So Zack assumed that the war was not going so well for the Iraqi soldiers. How could they defend themselves against the awesome affects of the B-52s carpet bombing. Or the destruction of their heaviest artillery pieces; the Soviet made tank. They were being destroyed systematically by the Allied fighter jets and their pinpoint accuracy. Most never even firing a slavo against the invading enemy.

The soldier's morale was low. And their future was uncertain. For the first time Zack began to worry about his own life. Would the soldiers take out their revenge against him, because of the overwhelming Allied forces? Would he be killed before they reached Baghdad? If he survived the trip, what was the best he could expect then? A prisoner of war? Would he be kept a prisoner for the rest of his life, because his name was Hebrew?

Col. Abdel seemed to be particularly troubled by something. The anxiety showed in his nervous behavior and his quick remarks to the others. Zack watched him with curious interest. Had he deserted his position cowardly and left before the combined Allied ground force had made contact? Hussein's Elite Guard, his reputed best. The grim reapers of the desert. It was almost laughable.

This little pathetic column sure lacked the military discipline of the American soldier. The war and his present uncertain situation were suddenly of little importance. He pushed those thoughts aside and tried to visualize the images that were trying to seep into his conscious mind. The word discipline had a familiar vibration. A vibration that set into motion a series of disturbing images that Zack was only able to catch pieces and fragments of. There was something there of the utmost importance, if only he could grasp the meaning. It had nothing to do with his military training. It was a discipline training of a different nature. One that brought truth and answers.

Slowly the vibrations subsided and the fragmented images disappeared. But this bizarre sensation left him feeling inspired and more acutely aware of smaller details. He looked more intently at each soldier and noticed for the first time how poorly equipped they were. Their uniforms were poorly tailored from heavy coarse fabric and many wore low cut shoes instead of boots. Even the vehicles were old and poorly maintained. All the appearance of a rag-tag army that had not had much forethought before the invasion of Kuwait had begun.

At dusk the column moved out. The shackles were removed from Zack's ankles and he was dragged to his feet. "I hope you rested well, Captain," the Iraqi colonel said. "If you can not keep up, you'll be tied to the back of the truck and dragged to Baghdad." Zack didn't doubt for one minute that Col. Abdel meant what he said.

They moved away from the river and away from all highways—and out from under the flight path of the B-52s and fighter jets. Zack trudged along, an escort on either side. Escape was out of the question.

As the column moved slowly across the desert, Zack began to notice a subtle change happening among the Iraqi soldiers. The closer they were getting to Baghdad, the more sullen and surly they were becoming. The atmosphere seemed to be filled with a dark heavy cloud that hung over the troops. Quarrels started over nothing at all. Even Col. Abdel was edgy.

Col. Abdel had ordered the company to retreat to Baghdad and abandon their heavy artillery pieces and tanks. Without firing a shot! Retreat to Baghdad where the great Iraqi hero Hussein would take care of them. That was again laughable.

The column stopped at midnight. The soldiers rested and ate a meager meal of cold hard bread patties. Zack was given a cup of water and scraps. "How is the American doing?" Abdel asked and then spat on the ground in front of him.

Zack looked at the colonel and replied, "Better than some of your own men it seems." All along the long line, quarrels and arguments could be heard. Abdel didn't comment further on Zack's welfare. He ordered the column to start up.

By daylight Zack was exhausted. He was dirty, hungry and thirsty. He knew it wouldn't do any good to ask the colonel for water, so he slumped to the ground and leaned against the truck. The whole column was tired. No one wanted to argue or fight. The soldiers found what shade they could and laid down to rest.

Zack tried to sleep also, but his future was too uncertain for sleep now. He closed his eyes and tried to think of more pleasant things. Images of a picturesque valley filled his mind. The scene was quiet, the air clean and cool. Music floated across from the horizon in endless waves. The images were so real, so life-like. But he knew it was only a dream. Reality was in the desert of Iraq, shackled and his hands tied behind him. He opened his eyes hoping to find himself in the valley he had just seen in his inner thoughts, that he would awaken from the nightmare of the Middle East.

As the sun was beginning to set that night Col. Abdel removed the shackles and untied Zack's hands. "Come with me. I want to ask you some questions." Zack followed the colonel to the lead truck. Abdel brought out some aerial maps of Baghdad and the surrounding areas. He unfolded them and laid the maps on the ground.

"Show me, Captain, where you went down."

Zack studied the maps briefly and pointed to an area south of Baghdad. "Here, I'm not sure of the exact location."

"What was the purpose of your mission, Captain?"

"To destroy the airfield at Baghdad and take out as many aircraft as possible.

"Only the military installations have been targeted. The electrical power plant and bridges. The civilian areas have not been bombed."

"Have you seen any other columns from the air on the move to Baghdad?"

"No." Zack replied. The colonel was obviously concerned about his retreat from his post and returning to Baghdad and having to face Hussein. Regardless of the overwhelming odds of the Allied troops, he would be looked upon as a coward. A deserter. How many more of Hussein's troops would desert their position and retreat? Retreat to what, Hussein's wrath? That was pathetic.

Abdel scratched his head and rubbed his eyes. Zack almost felt sorry for him. He had only been following orders, the same as he had been. A machine, that had been programmed to think, act and respond in a predetermined way. It didn't make any difference whether you were an American fighter pilot or an Iraqi colonel. It was the same. Someone else held the purse string. And now the Colonel's future probably didn't seem anymore favorable or congenial than Zack's.

"This war was not supposed to happen," Abdel said in a flat toneless voice. "You Americans have so much supplies and weaponry. We can not fight, if we can't reach our enemy."

The colonel escorted Zack back to the rear of the truck and tied his hands. The signal was given to move the column. Tonight there was no talking at all. No one paid much attention to their prisoner either. Their retreat was in everyone's thoughts and what would happen when they reached Baghdad.

One of the trucks broke down during the night and another had a flat tire. By morning only twenty miles of desert had been crossed. The food supplies were almost gone and only enough water for two more days.

As the column rested that day, B-52s and fighters could be heard in the distance, to the east. Exploding bombs reawakened earlier fears in the Iraqi soldiers and they nervously talked in small groups. No one got any sleep that day.

Other Iraqi deserters started drifting in. Some were alone and barefoot. Some straggled in small groups of three and five together. All with the same horrifying tales of the thunderous bombings of the B-52s. And only small arms with which to defend their positions.

Even though these soldiers had deserted their positions and commanders, they were not treated with indifference or apathy. Instead they were regarded with understanding. *Would Hussein be so understanding when they reached Baghdad and he learned about their desertions?* Zack wondered. Col. Abdel was also wondering.

Dusk came and Abdel ordered the column to move out. No one was in any particular hurry. Out here in the desert at least, they were free from Hussein's wrath and temporarily indisposed of his war. Camouflaged in the desert, away from military targets or highways the soldiers had a spurious hope of security.

The sky towards Baghdad was alight with exploding bombs. To the east and south also. Zack wondered what his future would be under the concentration of Allied bombing. Everyone was watching the array of lights over Baghdad. The column slowed. Col. Abdel tried to encourage the men to move along faster. He told them if they didn't, their water would be gone and they'd die in the desert without any. One soldier cried hysterically and tried to run away from the column advocating others to join him, that Abdel was only leading them to a certain grave in Baghdad.

Abdel picked up a rifle and without forewarning shot and killed the man. A quiet whisper went through the line and no one else wanted to tempt the same fate. For whatever reason, Col. Abdel after shooting one of his own, looked intently at Zack. Almost as if he was seeking for his approval for his action. The column of bewildered soldiers moved out without further incident.

All that night Zack worried about his fate, once they reached Baghdad. No one had asked for his name or looked at his dog tags, but when it was discovered that he had a Hebrew name, his interrogator would make the assumption that he was a Jew. Could he convince the Iraqi's otherwise? If not, would he be killed for being a Jewish infiltrator? Subject to the wrath of destruction of the Islamic jihad? Could he expect any better fate as an American POW? He had helped to bring such devastation to the Iraqi people. Probably not.

At midnight Abdel stopped the column for a brief rest. The food was gone and the water had to be rationed. He brought a cup to Zack. Zack drank it and said thank you and then sat down in the sand to rest his weary legs. No one else was near and Col. Abdel sat down next to him. "If you were a Jew, Captain, you would probably be shot along with me."

Zack's fears were beginning to surface. He knew now what to expect as soon as he was discovered.

"Why will you be shot, Colonel? You didn't have much of an alternative."

"Yes I did. Saddam Hussein expected that I and my men to defend our position at all costs."

"Could you have defended it, Colonel?"

"No, impossible against such overwhelming fighting

power of you Americans. We would have been butchered before firing a shot."

Well, that was Colonel Abdel's problem. Zack had his own.

By daylight the column was not yet at Baghdad. They were close and Col. Abdel decided to continue in the morning light, as soon as they had rested.

In Baghdad, Col. Abdel stayed his troops at the railway station, while he went to Hussein's supreme command headquarters. The headquarters building had been specially built while the U.S. troops were transporting troops and arms to Saudi Arabia. Hussein was stalling and took advantage of the interlude to build himself a concrete bunker below ground. Col. Abdel spat on the ground as he waited for the sentry to clear his admittance. While Hussein sat comfortably secure in his concrete shelter below ground level, he expected his troops to defend their positions against an army that out numbered them and also had far superior weaponry. Abdel was regretting his return to Baghdad. He knew now he should have surrendered to the Americans. He undoubtedly would have received better treatment.

It was several minutes before the sentry returned with a security pass. "Follow me, Colonel." The sentry guard led Abdel down a long corridor to a stairway. Everything inside was constructed of concrete and reinforcing steel rods. The builders had been in such a hurry that a lot of the inside was not yet finished. They went down five levels before reaching the bottom. They went by Hussein's private quarters. That too was not finished and anything but plush. But Abdel did notice an emergency exit passage in the rear.

The sentry stopped outside of Gen. Ahmed Aziz's quarters and directed Abdel to enter. The sentry posted himself in the doorway while Gen. Aziz spoke briefly with Abdel.

"Col. Abdel, you were given orders to remain at your position and to defend it against all odds. Why did you not die defending Iraq against the American invasion? That would have been a more honorable way to die."

"General, our food and water was already being rationed. We could not have held the Americans for long without dying of hunger and thirst. I repeatedly requisitioned more food and water. Some of my soldiers had nothing to wear on their feet. All we had to repulse the American army with was small arms and a few anti-tank guns. They broke through the tank barricades and destroyed our tanks that were dug in. Their tanks are able to pinpoint a target and fire without stopping. Men alone cannot stop a wave like that.

"General, this is not the Iranians that we are fighting now. These troops are experienced and are heavily armed. We have nothing, Sir, that can stop them."

"Colonel, might I remind you that you were ordered to remain at your position and to defend it. Any delay at all would have bought us valuable time to finish building our first nuclear warhead and deploy it. You have cost us that precious time, Colonel!"

"General, how can I make you understand, we didn't have any choice. Even if we had stayed at our position, the Americans would have rolled over the top of us without stopping. We could not have delayed them at all.

"We captured an American fighter pilot, a captain. He was returning from Baghdad when his F-15 exploded. He is still with my company at the railway depot."

"Colonel, you are under arrest for desertion and cowardice. Saddam Hussein has already ordered your execution. Tomorrow morning you will be shot. Sentry, come here! Col. Abdel is under arrest. You will escort the colonel to the army depot guard house. Before you leave, tell Capt. Omar I want to see him."

* * * *

There was nothing more to be said. Col. Abdel ruefully followed the sentry guard. Capt. Omar was ordered to transport the American prisoner to Command headquarters and then to take command of Abdel's company and return to the front.

As Zack followed his escorts through the command center, everyone he encountered stopped whatever they were doing to stare reproachfully as if to say he was singly responsible for all the carnage left behind from the bombing. Gen. Aziz had assigned his aid Col. Sharif ibn Rushd to interrogate the American prisoner.

Zack was marshaled by two sentry guards to an empty room, except for a chair and a crude table. He was ordered to stand until Col. Rushd arrived. He stood waiting for two hours. The colonel sat in the chair and opened his briefcase on the table and took out a pad of paper and pen.

"Your name?"

"Capt. Zachary Breinstein."

Rushd looked up from his writing. "Ah, a Jew I see. How did you happen to be in Iraq?"

"My fighter malfunctioned and exploded. I was jettisoned from the wreckage."

"What were your orders that led you to Baghdad?"

"To destroy the airbase and take out any aircraft found on the ground."

"Then Captain—Jew! Why did you bomb school buildings and kill innocent children," Rushd screamed as he hit the crude table with his fist.

"I didn't," Zack retorted, "none of the fighters or B-52 commands were given orders to bomb anything except military installations."

"You lie, Jew!"

"No! If school buildings were bombed then it was because Hussein had tried to hide a military target there!" Zack answered.

Col. Rushd nodded his head and one of the sentry guards hit Zack between the shoulders with the butt of his rifle. Zack staggered and fell to the floor.

"How many Jews does the Ally Command have working for them?" Rushd demanded.

"I don't know. I'm not a Jew."

"Breinstein is your name isn't it? That's a Jew name!"

"It may indeed be a Hebrew name, but that doesn't make me a Jew."

"You talk so blatantly about the Allies bombing school buildings, but what about your own scud missiles that you send indiscriminately into Saudi Arabia and Israel? They're nothing more than an instrument of mass murders."

Again Zack was hit with the rifle butt. "Take this Jew away! Put him in one of the empty cells." He turned his attention back to Zack, "Later we will talk some more if you can keep a civil tongue in your mouth."

Zack was taken to the army depot and locked up in a crudely built stockade. The guards threw him forcibly to the floor. One of the guards walked over and kicked him in the stomach. "There Jew, perhaps if you're lucky you'll rot in this cell and die, before the people of Baghdad discover that we have captured one of the enemy pilots who has been bombing our schools and hospitals." The door was locked and the guards left.

Zack lay sprawled on the cold damp floor. His head hurt along with his back and stomach. And in particular what the guards had said about schools and hospitals being destroyed. Could it be possible? With all the Intelligence and high technology could there have been mistakes made? Or had they really been bombed and then Intelligence had purposely lied to cover it up? Telling him only what Intelligence wanted him to know or believe.

After agonizing hours of laying on the cold and damp floor, Zack composed himself enough to look around his cell. There was nothing there. No bed or toilet. Only himself, enclosed in a heavy cold steel cage. He was cold and in pain, and for the first time in his life he was so alone and afraid of what tomorrow might bring. Perhaps the guard was right. Perhaps it would be better to die, than what his future had in store for him. By now his family would have been told about the explosion and it would probably be assumed that he had been killed in action. No one would know that he was still alive.

For the rest of that day and the following night, Zack sat huddled in the corner holding onto his side. "Why won't they believe I'm not a Jew? Just because I have a Hebrew name! What difference would it make if my name was Smith or Jones?" Would he be only a POW then? These thoughts tormented him all night.

At sunrise Col. Rushd and two new guards opened the stockade door and walked down the long corridor to Zack's cell. Zack froze with horror, wondering what they would do to him now. One of the guards unlocked the cell door and Col. Rushd said, "Captain, this morning you will witness the discipline of the Iraqi Army." The guards pulled Zack to his feet and escorted him outside. There was a man standing alone with his hands tied behind him against a brick wall and about fifty yards away were six soldiers with rifles. This was going to be an execution. His probably, he thought.

Col. Rushd paraded the American captive between the executioners and the one to be executed. Zack turned to look at the poor soul and was surprised to recognize Col. Abdel. They exchanged looks and Zack could see the misunderstanding, the apathy in his expression, or the lack of it. In that fleeting instant Zack understood that Abdel was being condemned to die for a course of action he had taken, which he had had no reasonable option. Was this the norm for Hussein's reactions? Did he handle all his decisions like this? If he did, then why did the Iraqi people follow him so blindly?

"May Allah bestow you a better fate, Captain," Abdel said before he was blindfolded.

Zack watched the execution in disbelief. How could a civilized society be so brutal? Col. Abdel had undoubtedly saved the lives of his company when he ordered the retreat in front of the massive Allied forces. Could or should a man be condemned and executed for only reacting responsibly?

"Captain, you have witnessed the Iraqi Army's discipline. Do you American's discipline your own so rigorously?" When Zack didn't answer, the colonel added, "I thought not. You American's are weak. And you will be defeated by the Iraqi Army."

The colonel's next words were drowned out by a wing of B-52s overhead. Zack looked around and was surprised when no one ran for shelter. Everyone stopped and watched the huge bombers pass. These people had been conditioned not to fear the huge planes. They knew the bombs would not be dropped so near the city. Their targets were outside the city. *Probably Command Headquarters* Zack thought. These people had been told what to believe about schools and hospitals being bombed and that civilians were being massively murdered. But from the reactions of these people it was obvious they were only being programmed with what Hussein wanted his people to believe. Much like Intelligence was doing.

"There, Captain! How does it feel to stand beneath those huge bombers and listen to their deafening roar! They're on their way to kill more innocent people!" Rushd screamed.

Zack again didn't answer. He knew the B-52s were heading away from the city towards Command Headquarters.

Zack was taken back to his cell and for the rest of that day and the next he was left to himself. He figured the B-52s had probably penetrated at least part of Command Headquarters and in the confusion he had been forgotten, for the time being at least. He was hungry and needed food and water soon or he would surely die. He couldn't remember when his last meal had been. He wasn't even sure how many days had passed since he ejected from his F-15. His head and thoughts were in a turmoil. Northing was clear or for certain any longer.

Another day passed and still he sat in the corner of his cell; cold, thirsty and hungry. The only person he had seen besides Col. Rushd and his two guards was an old man who it seemed was responsible for cleaning the stockade building and cells. The old man would often walk by Zack's cell and peek in, as if Zack was a unique novelty. The old man seemed harmless enough, but considering his present circumstances he couldn't afford to trust anyone.

There were others locked away. They like Zack remained huddled in a corner of their cell. Dirty clothes nothing more than rags and obviously starving to death. Zack did notice that the old man didn't display the same curiosity towards the others as he had done with him. Probably because he was a captive American pilot and the others—who could guess what their crimes might have been.

At dusk one day the old man returned to Zack's cell and stood by the door staring at the huddled person in the corner. Zack felt his presence and when he looked up the old man walked off. An hour later he returned again and this time he was carrying something. "Captain, Captain are you hungry?"

Zack was mildly surprised to hear the old man speaking English and even more surprised to find him addressing him and asking if he was hungry. He pulled himself to his feet and stepped to the door where the old man was standing on the other side. The distance wasn't great but his body still racked with pain. "Who are you?" Zack asked, bewildered.

"Just an old man in charge of cleaning."

"What do you want with me?"

"I have brought you some food and fresh water."

Zack was awed by the old man's offering of food and water. He first thought that it might only be a savage trick. He asked, "Why do you bring me food and drink?"

The old man replied, "Is it so strange to offer one who is hungry a little food? Have you not at sometime or other offered someone some food?"

"Yes, but it seems all so strange. I am a prisoner of war in your country for dropping bombs on Hussein's military installations. And—and because of my name. Because my name is Hebrew, I'm automatically called a Jew."

"Ah, a Jew in the midst of an Islamic holy war. That is not good." The old man pushed the food and water under the cell door and left.

Zack stood by the door watching until he had disappeared. He couldn't form an opinion of the old man. He seemed to be neither for nor against him being a captive American pilot or that his name was Hebrew.

With nourishing food in his stomach he felt better. Stronger and more alert. But he had nothing to do but wait. *Wait for what?* Whenever he heard the roar of the B-52s or the screaming whine of fighters, he wished that one would drop a bomb on him and end his misery. Bombs were dropping all around him but for some reason the stockade was safely guarded from destruction.

The next morning guards escorted Zack back to Col. Rushd's office. He was made to stand before Rushd's desk. The guards remained in the room but at the door. "Captain, the war is beginning to turn now. Just last night the Elite Guard pushed an armored division back into Saudi Arabia. One of the new M-1 tanks was captured and one hundred troops were taken prisoner. Today even as we speak the Allies are slowly being pushed out of Kuwait. Everyday the Iraqi Army gets stronger. It'll only be a matter of days now and our work on the nuclear bomb will be completed. The first two bombs will be dropped on Israel and New York City."

"What do you think that'll gain for you? The second you release the first bomb President Bush will order Iraq to be taken out. There'll not be any more Iraq," Zack replied.

"But by then, Captain, Saddam will have united all the Arab nations, to help repel the scum from our lands. Then you—your President Bush—will have more to worry about than only Iraq.

"There will never be peace in the Middle East until you Jews are driven from this land. Your President Bush started a war he can never finish. This holy war has been going on ever since you Jews broke away from the original Islamic movement. You violated Muhammad's law. This is between Jews and Muslims. Bush should have stayed out of it. But then, how could he with the influence that Israel has over your country. He has brought a lot of misfortune to your people. When this is all over, we don't want anything from the United States except the right to exist as a free Islamic state and to rid the land of you Jews."

Zack tried to close his mind to Rushd's words. He couldn't believe that the Iraqis were pushing the Americans back. Or how could they have possibly captured one of the new M-1 tanks? This was only another form of brainwashing, trying to gain his submission and obedience. The whole world it seemed was trying to dominate someone else by forcing obedience and submission, by the telling of lies and untruths. Was there no place where he could find truth? Intelligence was doing the same to the Allied Troops and to the world.

"Captain, I'll ask you again; who sent you here to spy on Iraq? What were your orders once inside of Iraq's borders?"

"I had orders to destroy the airbase and as many aircraft as I could," Zack answered.

Col. Rushd jumped up from his chair and pounded on the top of the table with his fist and said, "I want to know who sent you here and what your orders were? Who are your associates? I will not allow any Jew to terrorize Arab people! Now—who sent you?"

Again Zack told Rushd he was sent to destroy the airbase. Rushd nodded to the guards and one of them stepped forward and using his rifle butt hit Zack in the head. He fell to the floor unconscious. "Take him back to his cell!"

When the guards were gone, Rushd sat back in his chair; a worried expression on his face. He knew the Americans had not been pushed back. In fact they were getting closer to Baghdad with each day. He hated the American pilot because he was a Jew. He wanted to beat him unmercifully. But when Hussein loses this war, and lose he would, Rushd was certain then he didn't want to be charged with atrocities to this Jew. Israel would air this as another holocaust against the Jews. Then he would be executed like he had executed Col. Abdel. How he wished he could desert Hussein's Army and his demented satanic thinking. If he had more courage he would try to assassinate Saddam himself. But if he failed. . .he didn't want to think about what Saddam would do to him.

*   *   *   *

Zack was thrown back into his cell and the cold iron bars vibrated when the door was closed and locked. That night he was brought a meager meal of rice and some water. Sleep was impossible. He was still hungry and concerned about his uncertain future. He sat against the iron walls and listened to the Allied planes flying overhead. Even though the roar of the huge B-52s was deafening, the noise was a welcome relief. It was the only tangible link he had, knowing that the United States had not lost to Saddam. That President Bush was still fighting the campaign to rid the Mid East of Saddam.

As he sat there listening, he couldn't help but notice, whenever the B-52s were overhead everything else fell silent. Everyone stopped what they were doing and either ran for shelter or stood in fear knowing that death was near. He wanted to laugh at their fears and shout out at them that they were cowards, but his head was still aching from the beating he had received in Rushd's office.

Behind the B-52s Zack heard the unmistakable crack and whine of fighters. He could hear their rockets exploding. The pilots were destroying specific targets and not random bombing. Precision destruction and not mass random murdering like Saddam's scud missiles. Eventually the bombing stopped and all was quiet, except for the nervous chatter of people as they returned from the safety of hidden shelters.

Once again Zack was left with the loneliness of his thoughts. However odd it seemed, there was a familiarity with everything that was happening. It was almost as if everything now was no more than a repeat of earlier events. He shook his head to clear his mind. "Must have been dreaming," he said aloud.

During the stillness of the rest of that night, Zack prayed for the return of the B-52s and the fighter jets. It was his only hold on security; knowing that the Americans had not given up. Without that one hold, he knew he would slip away and give up hope of ever returning to the green hills of home.

Zack heard a whispering sound near his cell door and looked up to find the old man, who had brought him food earlier, standing there with a sack of clean straw and a blanket. "Perhaps you will find this more comfortable to lie on, and I have for you a blanket too." The old man pushed the straw under the cell door and handed the blanket through the iron bars to Zack. Then he disappeared.

Zack was puzzled with the behavior of the old man. To the old man, he was only another unfortunate soul caught up in Hussein's demonic struggle for power. The old man provided the bare necessities that kept him alive though. A benefactor. But why? What was he to the old man?

Zack spread the straw on the floor and laid the clean blanket over it and lay down. The old man was deep in his thoughts as he drifted off to sleep. Before complete dissolution, Zack heard the echoing of the old man's words, "You have to do this for yourself." Before Zack could understand what was said or why, he had fallen asleep.

In the morning the old man returned to Zack's cell and woke him. "Captain, Captain I have brought you some food."

Zack rubbed the sleep from his eyes and stood by the cell door in disbelief. "Why do you do this old man? Aren't you afraid you'll be seen with me?"

"Why should I be afraid? No—there is more outside these walls to be afraid of. I bring you food because you must keep your strength up. Besides, I am only an old man and there's not much they can do to me. Come, eat."

Zack ate the bread and cheese and washed it down with goat's milk. "There is no fresh water in Baghdad now. Your American bombs have destroyed the electrical generators and the water pumps. There isn't much food left in the city at all. The embargo against Hussein is killing all of Iraq. Your President Bush hopes that once there is no more food or water that the Iraqi people will turn against Saddam Hussein; this will never happen."

"Why won't the Iraqi people turn against him, old man? Is everyone that much afraid of him?"

"Yes, and also because you do not understand Islamic law or traditions. The Muslim people are devoid of any imagination. They are not free to think for themselves. They are kept in a resigned submissive control by the tyrannous rulers. No matter how this war ends, the Iraqi people will honestly believe that they are victorious. So it doesn't matter if Hussein dies now or not. The final outcome will be the same. It has already been declared, long before even the threat of war. In a society as we have here in the Mid East, the people only know or believe what they are told. They cannot perceive anything other than what they are told. This was not Muhammad's intentions when he dictated the scriptures which became the Koran. The fault lies with the Muslim rulers who want complete obedience over their people.

"No, Captain, no one will assassinate Saddam Hussein. And until this conflict has finally ended there will be little food and fresh water."

"It's unbelievable that Hussein could have such complete control over his people. Even when they are faced with starvation, disease and the destruction of their homes. I just don't understand it," Zack replied shaking his head.

"Sad isn't it, Captain? A whole country suppressed to one individual's way of thinking." The old man didn't say anymore. He walked off leaving Zack to his own thoughts.

Zack sat down on his bed of straw and began to ruminate about what the old man had said. It was unbelievable that one man could have complete control over so many, especially in the circumstances of the Iraqi people. The Iraqis were not or could not think for themselves. They had to be told what to believe and how to think. They could no longer do for themselves. They were like little children playing a new game for the first time.

How was it possible for Hussein to have their loyalty? It couldn't possibly be through love. It had to be because of fear. The whole aspect was sickening. Zack couldn't imagine himself living under those conditions. Then he looked around him and began to laugh hysterically. He was now under Hussein's control; every aspect of his life. At least the Iraqi people were free to move about. "At least he'll never be able to control my mind," Zack said aloud in anger.

Later that day while still thinking about the old man, Zack began to wonder why the old man, when referring to the Iraqi people, kept saying they and not we. Apparently he was not considering himself as one of them, but if not, then who was he? And why was he so congenial? If it had not been for him, Zack probably would have died from starvation already.

The skies over Baghdad were quiet that day. No bombs exploded around the city. People crawled out of what shelter they had found and looked nervously to the skies. Wondering when the awesome B-52s would reappear.

Zack lay on his bed of straw wondering almost the same. Why hadn't the bombers returned today? Had Col. Rushd been right all along? Were the Allies being pushed back, out of Iraq and Kuwait?

CHAPTER EIGHT

The universe began to resonate with a deep guttural roar. The melodious humming gone. The land began to quake and trees trembled. Brahm was laughing "Ha, ha, ha, Old One! Looks like your special pupil can't help himself. He forgot everything you tried to teach him. He sits behind iron bars and feels sorry for himself! He's a weakling, Old One! Give up on him! Admit that you made a mistake with this one. Say the word, Old One, and I'll have the physical body destroyed and he can return to My village. There he can live as before. All memories of you and your teachings will be erased from his memory." Brahm had spoken.

"Brahm, oh Great One, would life under your guardianship be any different than where my young friend is presently? You may not be as cruel, Great One, but then no less kinder for demanding his complete devotion and obedience."

Brahm had been rebuked again. He let out a gasp of air in disgust and a mighty wind blew across the land. "Why do you continue to waste your time, Old One? Isn't it obvious that this one can not remember anything you have taught him? He continues to see only what is in front of him. He will soon die before the lessons are remembered!"

"My Lord, you seem to evade adroitly the fact that you sent my young friend into the worse situation possible. I will admit that at present he seems to be beset with worries and can not yet grasp the lessons which would pull him out of this mess. But this is a test, My Lord, and Zvi has not failed yet. He is only momentarily experiencing the darker side of life. And don't forget, that any memories of me or your world Brahm, will for the present only seem like shattered fragments of a dream. In time he will remember the lessons and then he will discover truth and a way to free himself from his captives and then he will return here. A stronger and wiser being than before."

"Perhaps you're right, Old One. This is a test, but your pupil so far hasn't even begun to read the questions. Why are you so sure of him, Old One?" Brahm's voice echoed throughout the valley.

"Because his quest is for truth, and he is sincere. And that is all that he is searching for. Or you would not have placed him in such a precarious situation. The severity of his test exemplifies his distinction."

Brahm grumbled and the land shook. The animals stopped to listen and the birds stopped their singing.

"If anyone else had talked to me in the manner that you have. . .well My wrath would have befallen them. Only you, Old One, can get away with rebuking me. Why do I consistently let you get away with it?"

The Old One smiled before answering, "Perhaps because you know that I am right. And besides, My Lord, I am as old as you."

Brahm laughed and said, "Yes, Old One, you are the only being who could get away with such indignities and escape My Wrath." Brahm laughed again as his essence faded. Once again the birds sang and the animals went about their pleasure. The Old One was showing signs of consternation in his face. Brahm had dealt Zvi a tough hand indeed.

CHAPTER NINE

Zack was sinking deeper everyday into depression. The American bombers no longer flew over Baghdad. No bombs exploded that he could hear. His only tenure with the war now was these two facets and they both were silent. It had been several days since the old man had come to talk or bring him some food. One guard did bring some water. But that was tainted and discolored, "Sorry," said the guard, "there is no more clean water in the city. And our food is almost gone. What is left goes to Saddam's troops." The guard left the pail of water and left Zack to himself again.

In the quietude Zack supplicated all sorts of reasons why the B-52s no longer flew over the city and dropped their bombs. But every reason was inconsistent with what he knew was happening. Which was precious little.

Four days passed and the old man quietly appeared next to his cell door, and handed him a loaf of bread, cheese and fresh goats milk. Excitedly Zack asked, "Where have you been old man? I thought you had deserted me."

"I had to make a small journey and talk with an old acquaintance."

"What's happening with the war? I don't hear the bombers anymore. Has Hussein been defeated?"

"I don't know how goes the war. As I said I have been on a small journey. Away from this troubled area. There is still considerable turmoil about the city streets. There is little food and no clean water."

The old man walked quietly away while Zack ate his food. That was the last that he would ever see of his benevolent benefactor. Not long after he had finished eating Col. Rushd appeared, escorted by four young men dressed in civilian clothes. "Captain, you Americans have lost the war. Kuwait is once again in our control and we have pushed the Allied vermin from Iraqi soil and will soon have removed all presence from all our soils."

"Then as a prisoner of war you'll have to release me," Zack replied.

Rushd spit on the cell floor by Zack's feet. "If you were a prisoner of war that would be true. But you are a Jew infidel. A conspirator against the Islamic Jihad. No, Captain, you are no longer a prisoner of war, but a prisoner of Iraq. You will remain as a hostage until such time that Israel will agree to release some of our captives."

Zack's nerves were crumbling. Any hope of release was now gone. He could see himself being held in a locked room somewhere for years while Israel waited to make up its mind about meeting Iraq's demand. How he wished he could just wake up from this nightmare and—and what? As he thought about it in that fleeting instant, everything seemed like a dream, a terrible nightmare, ever since he had taken that stroll in the hills behind his house in Vermont. If all this was only a bad dream then what would he awaken to?

These thoughts were interrupted as two of the young men grabbed him and tied his hands behind him. Rushd motioned for them to leave. A blindfold was placed over Zack's eyes and they left the prison barracks at the army depot. There was loud confusion in the streets everywhere and the stench of open sewers and decaying meat was overwhelming. Rocks and bottles were thrown at Zack as he was escorted along debris filled streets. Most of the refuse was caused by the Iraqis themselves, from looting, in search of food. Store windows and doors were broken and any food inside was soon scavenged. Garbage was just thrown into the streets.

*   *   *   *

Zack's new abode was on the other side of the city next to the hospital, in a cramped two-story house, reasonably safe from attack by the American B-52s, because the Allies had sworn no indiscriminate bombing of residential areas or hospital zones. Hidden away in a residential dwelling, the Americans would be less likely to inspect the premises and discover their captive: the air force captain. The army depot was certain to be inspected once the American ground troops took control of Baghdad.

But Zack was not told this. He was only informed that he would be a hostage for future use. Rushd had made it clear that Iraq had defeated the American invasion; and during Zack's captivity that's all he would be told.

Once inside the two story building Zack's blindfold was removed and his hands untied. A door was opened and then he was pushed inside and the door closed and locked. Benignly Zack looked at his new home. He was rather pleased with his new surroundings. There was a crude bed, not straw on a concrete floor, a wash basin and his own toilet—some improvement over the soiled conditions back at the army depot. But what about the old man, what had become of him? In days to come Zack would give anything to have a meaningful conversation with him again.

There had been a window in the room at one time, but it had been boarded over and now only a vent to let in fresh air. Zack turned slowly around looking at his new home. Even though an improvement over the iron cell, he still felt like a caged animal. Only now was he beginning to appreciate his freedom that he had taken for granted all his life. Here he wasn't free to move or walk where he chose or to know the true state of affairs. He would be told only what his captors wanted him to know and believe.

Zack sat down on the bed and folded his hands in his lap and stared helplessly at the floor. His four captors were in the adjoining room arguing about something.

There would be a knock on the door and new voices heard in the other room and then the visitor would leave again. This occurred quite regularly. Once he thought he could distinguish Col. Rushd's voice. When he left, three of his captors, whom Zack would refer to in his own mind as jailors, left with the colonel.

Zack laid back on his bed, and was enjoying the quiet. The person left to guard him was pacing back and forth in the other room. Zack laid still, listening to him, wondering if something had gone wrong and if his life might be in jeopardy. The pacing stopped and the lock was being moved. Zack sat up and the door opened. The youngest of the four swung the door open and stood in the doorway staring at him. Zack estimated his age to be about twenty. The one called Kalidasa.

There was anger and rage in his expression. "You Jew pig! You bombed our city! Killed our young, sick and old! You destroyed our drinking water and cut off our food supplies from the west! Why should you live Jew, when you have killed so many?"

Zack's reply was so clear and precise that at first Kalidasa was lost for words. "I am not a Jew and neither did I start this war. Perhaps you should question your insane leader, Hussein."

When Kalidasa had recovered from being rebuked so clearly, he stepped forward and drove his foot into Zack's stomach, sending him sprawling to the floor. With painful effort Zack rolled onto his side and pulled himself up to his bed. He sat on the edge facing his attacker and said, "That only demonstrates your cowardly belligerence. Is that how all Iraqis behave? Anger and brutality. Is that the percepts of Islam?" Zack had probably provoked Kalidasa too far. But he was tired of being hit and kicked.

Anger was building in Kalidasa and Zack knew he would be beaten again. Kalidasa came at him with both fists clenched like pieces of stone. In deliberate slow motion he raised his left arm and pulled his shoulder back. But before he could deliver his attack, his two companions burst into the outer room. Kalidasa sneered at Zack and said, "Another day." Then he left the room and closed the door.

Each day passed with the same antagonism. If Zack didn't agree with what was said and instead offered an opposed opinion he was beaten. Zack knew in order to stop the beatings all he had to do was surrender his will and believe as his captors wanted. But he would not do that. Not as long as he was alive, no one was going to forcefully coerce his thinking. He was a human being capable of thinking for himself and no amount of beatings were going to change that. At the same time he had decided that if he ever got out of this situation in Baghdad and returned home, he was never again going to let another individual control his every action or tell him what he could believe or not believe. Not intelligence or the American Government. He would decide things on his own.

Javier enjoyed the attacks against Zack. Though the attacks were not as harsh as Jinnah's, he sadistically enjoyed torturing him though. Kalidasa and Jinnah expressed more anger and their attacks were swift and brutal. Javier wanted to toy and play with his victim like a cat with a mouse, before it decided to kill and eat it.

Zack was fed regularly, with little water, and none to bathe with. There was no extra water anywhere in the city for such a luxury. No one from higher command ever came to inquire about him. There were no visitors at all. Zack was beginning to believe that his captivity was probably being kept secret. But why? Then it occurred to him! The Americans had not been defeated. In fact he guessed that the war was probably over. That would explain why the bombers no longer flew over the city. And probably the Americans or a delegation were in the city and that would explain why he had been moved and why his captivity was being kept secret.

Then his spirits fell. He understood then the impact of "hostage." He, as Col. Rushd had said earlier, was no longer a prisoner of war but a hostage. A hostage held by defeat. For what purpose? Would he remain in Baghdad like so many other hostages held by other Muslim factions? Would he be used to bargain for the release of an Islamic Terrorist? Someone who had indiscriminately killed and maimed innocent people. The thought sickened him.

*   *   *   *

Zack sat on the floor, not on his bed, in the corner of his room. He had perceived the unmitigated truth about the end to the Gulf War and he was slowly sinking into a state of depression with the awful realization of his unpredictable future.

He had flown his F-15 as directed. Fought President Bush's war; destroying key installations and had lost his fighter over Iraq and then captured. No one knew he was alive. His family would go on with their own lives, slowly forgetting about him. And the United States Air Force—did the Pentagon or Intelligence even care if he had ejected safely and was lying in some Iraqi hell hole, a prisoner or better yet a hostage. To the rest of the world he was already dead. If he was ever going to get out of Iraq and return to his family, he would have to do it without any outside help. The initiative would have to be his alone. And the more he thought about the impossibilities of escape the more depressed he became.

His captors continued their assertive tactics. When Zack remained seated on the floor staring at his hands and not responding verbally, as he had done so unambiguously, earlier, the three Iraqi captors assumed they had subjugated his will.

Their assumptions were wrong. Zack still resisted their pliant strategy of dominating his individuality and his thinking, but he was buried so deep in his own self pity that he was not actually conscious of his captors and not paying any attention to them. Eventually the three Iraqis left him alone; huddled in the corner of his room.

For days Zack remained huddled in the corner. His back to the wall, his knees pulled up under his chin. He was oblivious to his three captors whenever they entered his room; he would focus his attention on a protective mental barrier he had placed between himself and them. That way he would not be disturbed as he wallowed in his own pity. How could life be so cruel and unfair, to forsake him and leave him so helpless?

Day after day he would dwell on this piteous thinking. And with each passing day he receded deeper within himself. Even his captors became concerned. Col. Rushd had said to keep the Jew alive. 'He's no good to us if he dies.' Kalidasa even in his earlier anger showed more concern now. He brought Zack more food and cleaner water. But it went untouched. He tried to feed him. Zack had traveled so far within himself that he was not cognizant of either the food or Kalidasa. Finally Kalidasa left him alone too.

*   *   *   *

Zack had withdrawn so far within himself, for a short time he was living in another world. One of peace and serenity. There were no wars. No jails or oppression. He didn't know where he was, only that life here was one of quietude and joy. There was no one else there. Only himself. And he saw nothing that sparked a familiarity. He was sure he had never been here before. There were no animals either, or trees or flowers. Only light. A beautiful array of soft pastel colors. It was a strangely beautiful place that he found himself in and somehow he found a renewed sense of strength and courage and was filled with new wisdom.

Somehow he knew he could not stay here for long. There was something that had to be done. He wasn't sure just what it was, only that there seemed to be an utmost urgency to complete whatever task was at hand.

CHAPTER TEN

Zack found himself in the middle of a bad dream. He was falling helplessly into a black void. He couldn't touch anything or even feel the air around him as he fell, but he was experiencing the sick nauseating feeling of spiraling downward like a plane.

He began to retch. He turned over to what he presumed was downward so the vomit would not choke him. He retched from the pit of his stomach. Over and over until his stomach muscles were too sore to retch again.

The spiraling stopped. Zack opened his eyes and discovered he was lying on the floor of his room, covered with his own vomit. The spinning sensation had stopped, but he was sick to his stomach and dizzy.

Kalidasa heard the commotion and rushed in to see what had happened. "It is not surprising to see that you are sick Jew, you have not eaten for several days. We thought perhaps you might be trying to starve yourself." Zack made no comment, only groaned and tried to pull himself up. Once he had seated himself on the edge of his bed Kalidasa left him alone. He closed and locked the door.

Zack rubbed his face and ran his fingers through his hair. There was some food on the stand and a pitcher of water. Later Zack laid back on his bed and thought about the strange world he had seen in his dream. How very real it had seemed at the time.

As he lay there, he became aware of a new awakening. One that perhaps even had a future to it. He couldn't describe the sudden feeling, but it was real and it gave him hope. He fell asleep and for the first time since being captured, he slept well. He had a long way to go to recover from his unconscious state and his depression. He didn't know for how many days he had remained huddled in the corner of his room, but for the first time, he was now feeling better about his situation.

It took several days to regain his strength, especially with the poor food he was given. His progress was slow, but with each day he regained lost strength and awareness. But even with his physical strength recouped, he knew escape would be impossible unless he was also mentally prepared.

Somewhere he could vaguely remember someone saying that to accomplish a difficult task, the mind must be as alert as the body is strong. Wherever he had heard it, it now seemed so far away. But he knew, he must sharpen his wits and awareness. First though, he had to strengthen his muscles. This would be difficult cooped up in a small room. And he would have to be especially careful not to alert his captors.

During the next several weeks while his captors slept, Zack would do a variety of exercises to loosen and tone unused muscles. Whenever one of the three entered his room he would purposely act like a lifeless doll. Drained of his previous energy and determination.

Jinnah and Javier had lost interest in Zack. There were more and bigger problems outside the house to deal with. But Kalidasa for some unknown reason was drawn to his American pilot prisoner. He scorned him because he was Jewish, but at the same time, he listened openly when Zack talked with him. It wasn't as much a friendship as it was a curiosity.

*   *   *   *

One day while Jinnah and Javier were away Kalidasa unbolted Zack's door. "Hey Jew, what was that noise I heard?"

"Nothing. Saw a mouse run under the bed and I tried

to catch it," he lied, hoping Kalidasa would not learn of his exercising.

"How does it feel to be alone—none of your Jew friends to help you? You Jews are infamous for helping another Jew, but if a beggar who wasn't a Jew asked for bread to fill his hungry stomach, you Jews would kick the beggar in the stomach instead. But if he was one of your own, you would give him more bread than he had asked for. You'll help each other but not someone who isn't a Jew," Kalidasa exclaimed.

"I am not a Jew," Zack replied flatly.

Kalidasa grunted and then said, "Your name is Breinstein, isn't it? That's a Jew name."

"No it isn't!" Zack retorted. "The name is Hebrew and that doesn't necessarily make me a Jew. Being Jew is practicing the religious concepts. I don't and never have followed the Jewish teachings. Therefore I have never considered myself a Jew.

"If your last name was LaBried, a French name, would that automatically make you a Catholic? Perhaps you might even have decided to follow the Protestant Teachings. Or the Eastern cultures! Just because you're French wouldn't automatically make you anymore Catholic than I am a Jew!"

"But anyone not born a Jew is not likely to ever be accepted as a Jew even if he wanted to change religions. But a Catholic, Protestant or Muslim is free to belong to whatever teaching he wants and would be readily accepted. But not the Jews!" Kalidasa snapped back.

It was useless to argue the point any further. Kalidasa hadn't answered his question and only offered an excuse that was too removed from the point to argue. Kalidasa didn't want to discuss it any further either and he stalked out of the room and drew the bolt closed. Zack sat back and smiled wily to himself. He waited until night when the three had gone to sleep before continuing his exercises.

Along with the strengthening of his muscles Zack also saw a new awakening of his consciousness. He was more perceptive and he understood things more clearly. Now he wished he could see the old beggar again. The old man could easily inspire him and it was a joy to talk with someone who had such wisdom. The old beggar reminded him of someone else. Someone in his past. He tried to think who it could be. He couldn't remember. "Perhaps it had only been a dream."

*   *   *   *

Outside of the walls that imprisoned Zack, life was in turmoil. Hussein was still in power, declaring that his Iraqi troops had been victorious. And surprisingly few doubted his claims of victory. Those that did, didn't do it openly. He still controlled the minds and the will of the people. He had established himself provider of his people; as long as the people were in complete obedience and submitted to Hussein's proclamations and his principles. If one chose disobedience then his fate and his future were both questionable.

Disease was running unchecked through the streets of Baghdad. Any medicine that had been in the hospitals had been confiscated by Hussein for his troops. The hospitals and clinics were full and people were being turned away to die quietly, alone. The embargo against Iraq had not been lifted yet and their food supplies were almost non-existent. The Tigris River was filling rapidly with sewage and human excretions. But Hussein had implored his people to start rebuilding the roads, bridges and generation stations.

Everyone was suspicious though and tempers flared and in general, morale was poor. And it showed one day when Jinnah and Javier returned from a meeting with Col. Rushd. Rushd had informed Javier that his wife had died from an infection of a wound when the generation station had been destroyed. Some debris had blown away and hit her in the legs. There was no medicine and the infection had gotten worse and worse. Now Javier was solely blaming the American pilot and wanted his life to avenge his wife's. Jinnah could not restrain him. He bolted into the room and savagely attacked Zack. Kalidasa and Jinnah together were able to pull him away. He was screaming in Arabic and tears ran down his face.

Zack had not been hurt and he now looked at Javier with sympathy. In his mind Zack wondered if Javier would continue to support Hussein. Surely now that tragedy from the war had taken his wife, Hussein's holy war, a misguided invasion of Kuwait and against the Allied Forces—Javier would see the fallacy of Hussein and his ill fated oppression. But in the following days Javier grew more bitter and a stronger supporter of Hussein.

Kalidasa and Jinnah had agreed not to let Javier alone with the American. One of them would always have to be with him.

That night Javier didn't return to the house. While Jinnah went searching for him Kalidasa brought some food and water to Zack. "This morning my friend was told his wife had died from an injury when the generation station was bombed. He was upset and wanted your life to avenge her death."

Zack didn't tell him that it could have been one of his bombs that had ultimately caused the death of Javier's wife. Instead he replied, "His anguish is understandable."

"That's a typical reply coming from a Jew. You people always act so virtuous and so smug."

"Kalidasa—what is it about the Jews that really upsets you so?" Zack asked.

"Your smugness. You're always so content with your own accomplishments; never giving credit to anyone else for doing something of equal importance. You Jews seem to think that God follows in your footsteps. Not that you actually follow in His. You identify God in the likeness of yourself, not you in the likeness of God. You bring God down to your own level, instead of raising your consciousness to meet His. You're abrasive and pushy. Whether it's a business transaction or your conquest for expansion. Israel continually says you only want peace, but you constantly wage war on the East Bank, which does not belong to you!"

"Oh and perhaps you think that Hussein's annexation of Kuwait was too trifle to notice!" Zack exclaimed. "Isn't that the same as what you say Israel is doing?"

"No it is not the same!" Kalidasa spoke with obvious anger in his voice. "No it is not the same. Kuwait belongs to Iraq. At one time Kuwait was an integral part of Iraq. At the turn of the century when Germany sought to extend the Berlin-Baghdad Railway to Kuwait, Great Britain, fearful of losing Mid East support, established an agreement with the ruling Kuwait Sheikh to assume control of Kuwait's affairs and then later a protectorate over Kuwait and then only thirty years ago Britain helped Kuwait with its independence. This was done to keep Iraq suppressed and dependent on the rest of the world! And because of Kuwait's oil. No, Captain, it is not the same. Israel has no legal claim to the East bank.

"Does that explain your question, why Iraq hates you Jews?"

"Is that a formula answer, expressing *whose* viewpoint? Yours, Kalidasa? Hussein's? Or all Muslims?"

"It's the truth! Israel only wants to repress Iraq because our religious views are different."

"Can't that also be said about Islam and your holy war?" Zack asked. "Doesn't the Islamic movement want to repress Judaism and all other religions? And to do that you wage war against your neighbors—sometimes even your own brother."

Kalidasa had heard enough. He glared at Zack and then left his room and bolted the door. Zack sat on his bed for a long time, thinking about what Kalidasa had said about Kuwait actually belonging to Iraq. He had never studied history in that part of the world. He was totally absent of any concept of the problems of the Arab nations in the Mid East or their difficulties existing next door to a country whose religions were so different than their own. An exact opposite. How could one small Jewish state like Israel cause so many problems with all of the Muslim nations around her border?

That baffled Zack. How one small country could cause so many problems? How has Israel gotten such a strong hold in the Mid East? The only answer Zack could find was the support from Great Britain and the United States. A buffer state controlled by Intelligence, both English and American.

Zack's mind was running rampant. Surely Intelligence must have known about Kuwait being an integral part of Iraq before Great Britain's involvement. Had Hussein done anything different than the United Stated had done in the past? Or other countries? This was leading Zack to believe that the war was fought over something else besides Iraq's annexation of Kuwait. But why was Intelligence keeping it so secretive. What did Intelligence know that the rest of the world didn't? Had Intelligence so cleverly masked its real intention only to further repress Iraq? Or was it after all only because the Arab nations were Muslims? And Intelligence was trying to suppress Muslims world over?

Zack was being torn to shreds. His last values of the country he fought for were beginning to be meaningless. How many more times in the past had Intelligence beguiled the American people and lied, in order to further its own desires and control the mass populations. What actually happened at Grenada, Panama, Cuba, Honduras, Vietnam, Korea? Were the battles to liberate an enslaved populace, or only to cover up a mistake made by Intelligence? Did Watergate happen only to rid President Nixon from Intelligence? Did President Kennedy die because he stood up against Intelligence and wanted to end the fighting in Vietnam? Did Intelligence allow the bombing of Pearl Harbor so the Americans would unite and destroy the Axis Powers, so Intelligence could dominate the globe?

How much more had Intelligence been involved with that had never surfaced as being suspicious? How little of his own life did he truly control?

What Hussein was doing to the Iraqi people was no different than what Intelligence had done in the past and was still currently doing to the American people. Only his methods were more noticeable and the consequences more severe if obedience was not obtained. He did not yet have the refined subtleties of Intelligence.

Zack wondered just how much freedom the Iraqis had or the Muslims in general. It seemed to him that every phase of a Muslim's life was controlled by another. The Muslim surely did not have the freedom that he had. Zack burst out laughing then. He looked around him at his present world. Not much, not as much freedom as his Muslim captors had.

The big difference he found was that in America under a democratic society, everyone was free to choose whatever religious following he wanted. Then he paused a minute with that line of thinking. He reflected on the religious foundations in his own country. They were not so different than Islam, here in the Mid East. Again more subtle and the consequences for non-compliance of the church structure of disobedience with religious regulations were not as noticeably severe.

Even in his own country the grand United States of the Americas, people were being led by the nose. Told what to believe and what not to believe, what was best for them and how to act towards another religious belief. It was the same everywhere, only more subtle in some places than others. No one was really in control of their own destiny. Or were they?

It was not surprising then, living under such stultifying conditions, to find no imagination. The religious establishments were afraid someone might someday imagine that there was a whole lot more to life and existence and God, than what was being told. The masses had to be restrained and suppressed or those in control would soon lose that control.

Intelligence was the same. The people were kept in the dark about certain causes around the world and the actual reasons for going to war; for if the people knew the "TRUTH", they would rebel against those trying to influence their thinking, their beliefs, and those trying to obscure the truth.

Zack started to think about imagination. That's all he had to do—think. It was a lonely, devastating companion. Without an imaginative faculty there can be no progress. How could the wheel or the lever ever have been discovered, if first the idea had not been imagined? How can one or a nation better itself, if it first cannot imagine that things could be better or different? Or dare to challenge propaganda. Without it, people would live in a very repressed society.

If the Iraqi people were not afraid to use their imagination, then the country as a whole would not be as repressed or so poorly developed. But then Hussein would lose his control of his people and once they had discovered how much they had been deceived then they would have rebelled against his abusive control.

The reflection on imagination and its threatened use of, started a series of images into motion in Zack's inner vision. It was so peculiar. He was sure he had already experienced this concept. Or one so very similar. He tried to hold the images he could see on his inner screen, but they vanished. But in that brief moment the images instilled a feeling of delectation and enlightened his awareness evermore.

*   *   *   *

In the following days Zack tried to forget about the images he had seen in his inner vision. They were disturbing. Not so much that the images had reminded him that he had dared to challenge some authority, but where had he been? Whose authority had he challenged? It all seemed so far away. In another world perhaps. He didn't know, but all the same, he was left with a disturbing feeling that there was more to what he had been shown. Only if he could have seen more. Perhaps then he could have had a better understanding what the images had represented.

Javier was spending more and more time away. In the wake of his wife's death Col. Rushd was training him for terrorist activities abroad.

Jinnah was usually busy finding food and water and the only time he spent at the house was at night to sleep. Kalidasa was left behind to guard the American captain. It was appalling. He had a radio, but there was but one station. And day after day the broadcast was the same; the Americans had inflicted so much pain upon the Iraqi people. That Hussein had only been used as a pawn, an excuse to destroy Iraq and put down the Islamic movement. That the war had been against Muslims and not against Hussein. That Hussein cared about his people and he would provide for them.

If there had been anything new on the radio, he would have listened, but he was getting tired of listening to the same old propaganda every day. Perhaps that's why he so often chose to talk with Zack. At least he offered new views, even if they were opposing.

"You Americans with all of your high technology and your superior arms and overwhelming numbers, still did not show the ferocity or the stamina that our Elite Guard showed. Our weapons were primitive compared to yours. But we stood up to you. The world feared our troops. There are none like them in all the world. If the American troops had been equipped with the same weaponry that we had, you would never have gotten into Kuwait or across our borders. You do not have the superior fighting attitude that we Iraqis have. That only comes with generations of warfare in the deserts and the mountains with untold hardships.

"What was your fighting schedule, Captain? Did you fly for eight hours each day then return to a clean house and clean sheets and a hot meal? Did you ever see the destruction your bombs caused? Did you ever hear women and children screaming or watch a friend bleed to death while trapped under a wall of concrete? Did you, Captain?"

159

Zack thought about what he said. *It was true*. After he was done for the day, he ate a hot meal and slept in clean sheets. He had seen some of the destruction in Baghdad from bombs, but he had never seen the innocent victims of his bombs. In part Kalidasa was right. He didn't answer.

"I thought not, Captain. To you the war is nothing more than a fast ride in a plane. Blue sky and sunshine! You do not understand the terror of facing an army with overwhelming odds."

Zack wasn't listening. His full attention was focused on images passing across his inner vision. They were clear and precise images of a beautiful land. Too beautiful in fact to be found on Earth. The colors were excitingly different and vibrant. Green grass grew like a thick piled carpet that blanketed a vast valley. The atmosphere was filled with a melodious humming. Within the humming was a voice. It was his own. The voice was telling him to go within. To look for his answers within himself.

Before Zack could fully understand what the voice was implying, Kalidasa's angry shouting brought him back to his present situation.

"Do you hear me, Captain? You Americans are cowards! You don't know what the word bravery implies."

"So you think that the Iraqis, or is it Muslims, that are so much more valiant and fearful than Americans, which is it Kalidasa? Iraqis or Iraqis because your Muslim?" Zack answered.

"Both! Iraqis because we have never known anything but war. And because we are Muslim, we are destined to fight the Jihad. To drive out the infidels and stop the worshiping of idols."

"Oh, so Muslims are against everyone that does not believe as Muslims do. So you're not against just the Jew. It's the whole world, whoever happens to belong to another religion. Is that the whole premise of your religious beliefs?"

"We are against the Jews because they won't let us live in peace. They keep trying to take land that isn't theirs. They keep pushing and pushing. And their God, I don't think is actually a God at all. It's more of a super human deity that they have created in their own image. They will not give the same courtesy to one outside their religion as they will one of their own.

"Their God exists separate of the universes instead of the universes being an integral part of God," Kalidasa said, some of his earlier anger now gone.

"Where does your God or Allah exist?" Zack asked.

"If you can tell me where your soul is, then I'll tell you where Allah can be found."

"God rests at the heart of every living thing, so therefore, also soul sits," Zack replied.

Kalidasa's bluff had been called and answered. He didn't know how to respond now. He didn't know where to look for Allah, and he had never heard of Zack's response. It was not typical of a Jew. Because most Jews didn't know where their soul was, if indeed there was one.

"I have never heard of that before. The Jews I know wouldn't know where to find their soul, let alone Allah. And to be honest, I didn't know where to find Allah either. How do you know Allah and soul both sit at the heart of Man? That's not a Jewish concept."

"I've been telling you and Col. Rushd right along that I'm not Jewish. And I just know that both God and soul are at the heart and center of everything. I don't think I can explain it. It's just something I know."

"I can't accept that so readily. How can a simple man tell me where to find my soul. You tell me Allah is inside me, at my heart, but what proof do you have. None! How can you know more about Allah than our own leaders and holy-men. Saddam would have you executed for saying such blasphemy.

"You are trying to ridicule me and you make a mockery of Islam. You Jew, only a coward would try to mock another's religion and his God! That's all you Jews know how to do!"

Zack noticed that now Kalidasa had switched back to

calling him a Jew again. There was a moment, while his mind was trying to accept the concept of God and soul being within man that he spoke of the Jews as "They."

"You speak freely about cowards," Zack said. "What about Iraq's terrorist activities? There's nothing more cowardly than that. Only women, children, old people and the innocent are the victims. And what good does it do? None! It only attracts more attention to yourself and people alienate themselves against your cause. Even if the cause should be for the good. It's a despicable excuse for vengeance. Regardless of what you call it, it's nothing more than brutal murder."

"Sometimes it's the only way out we have. I don't expect you to understand," Kalidasa said.

"There's no excuse for murdering innocent people. If you think it'll further your cause—you're dead wrong. You only make it harder for your own countrymen. You only generate hatred and disgust for yourself, your religious beliefs and your people. There's no possible good that could ever come from any terrorist activity."

Kalidasa remained silent. Zack didn't know why, but he felt an unexplainable urge to push a little further. "When Hussein ordered the scud missiles to be fired at Israel, what possible advantage could he hope for? There was no precision targeting. The scud missile is nothing more than a mad dog at large. Uncontrollable, there were never any military targets; only a wild frenzy to kill. To murder innocent people. It turned the whole world against Iraq."

"It was done with the intention of uniting the Arab nations together!" Kalidasa demanded.

"How was bombing Israel going to unite the Arab nations?" Zack asked.

"Israel could not stand by idly, while Iraq bombed her. The Jew holds to the belief of an eye for an eye. They would have to retaliate to save honor with all Jews. If nothing else than to show the world that Jews are not cowards. If Israel had retaliated against a Muslim state then all Muslims would have come to the aid of Iraq."

"That's a sick, manipulative, inhumane idea. Hussein was willing to sacrifice the lives of thousands of his own people, hoping to unite Arab support? That's revolting. Only a deranged madman would do that to his own country. His own people.

"And what's even more sickening is the fact that you—you Iraqis let him get away with it! You keep right on supporting him.

"Did you ever once stop and think about how much worldly support you'd get if Iraq rebelled against Hussein's politics and his exaggerated sense of self-importance?"

"It's not that easy. You don't understand Islamic basic cultures. We not only would rebel against Hussein, but our Holy establishment as well.

"Perhaps Hussein was wrong to bomb Israel. His plan did not work however. And the Jews will forever wave the flag in our face and mock us. And they'll exaggerate the number of scuds deployed as well as the numbers killed and injured. Just like they have waved the flag of the holocaust in Germany during World War II, trying to keep alive the deaths of six million Jews. For nearly fifty years they have been screaming about the injustices. And why do they persist? I'll tell you why! So they can get sympathy from your country, Captain, and the English. Israel has been bleeding both countries ever since the lot of them were relocated after the war. The louder Israel screams, the more money your President and the Queen gives the Jews.

"Instead of letting the memories of the holocaust die, if indeed six million Jews did die which I doubt, Israel keeps reminding the world, trying to stir-up trouble and new problems. And I'll guarantee Israel will do the same with the scud missile attacks. Years from now they'll still be waving the flag and using it as an excuse for their aggression!

"You look doubtful, Captain," Kalidasa said in a softened voice. "Perhaps if you had had spent any time here in the Mid-

163

East and viewed the problems first hand, you would not be the skeptic."

"Maybe instead of fighting each other all the time, Muslims and Jews should try to work out their differences peacefully," Zack said.

Kalidasa stood up and started to pace back and forth in the small room. Zack knew he had hit upon a sensitive nerve. Finally Kalidasa stopped with his back to Zack and in a low voice, absent of the earlier hostility replied, "That would of course be the sensible thing to do. But there is a preeminent difficulty and it lies within Islamic laws and beliefs and those who proclaim to be the virtuous and the true disciples of Muhammad. Those who proclaim to be the Islamic leaders; the holy-men, have misinterpreted the Koran for their own desires, power and the influence over Muslims everywhere. Even in your own grand country, Captain." He turned back to Zack and continued, "It puzzles you to hear me speak about my own religion does it not, Captain?"

"Yes it does."

"When Muhammad died, his successor, the first Khalifah and those that followed his succession have misinterpreted and misused some of the basic percepts, like the holy war, Jihad. The true Jihad had two facets, the lesser and the greater. The lesser, which is demonstrated through battle, purifying the land of idols and idol worshipers. It was so revealed by Muhammad that who-so-ever died in battle while fighting Jihad, then the spirit of the warrior would be guaranteed a place in Empyrean with riches and eternity.

"The greater Jihad, the one I believe Muhammad wanted his people to fight as warriors was a battle by the individual. Man had to learn to discipline his soul as he immersed himself in the world. Achieving a balanced enlightenment. Purifying his aggression and perversions of the mind and body.

"Today the greater Jihad is almost lost and forgotten, while the lesser, misinterpreted and misused, is used to loot, plunder and an excuse for our leaders today to declare war on our neighbors, instead of spending the time in useful contemplation." Kalidasa left the room without saying anything more. Zack actually felt sorry for him. Unlike himself, Kalidasa had viewed his world objectively—had seen the truth.

*   *   *   *

Zack sat on the edge of his bed and wondered if he could have been as honest as Kalidasa had been, about his own country and his religion. What was his religion? He didn't follow any organized following. He just believed—no he didn't believe, he knew there was a God; there was that difference.

He thought about what Kalidasa had said about the holocaust, and how the Jews were trying to keep the memories alive. Wasn't the United States doing the same with Pearl Harbor? Every year around the first of December there would be a lot of flag waving about the holocaust at Pearl Harbor. Why couldn't the United States bury the incident at Pearl Harbor once and for all? Let the memory of that tragedy die. The Japanese had been defeated as Germany had and those responsible were held accountable for their actions. Was it Intelligence again, waving the flag to stir up trouble and keep the abomination alive?

Zack decided there could never be peace among nations; whether they were of different religious beliefs or not, as long as Intelligence kept the truth from the people. Or peace within his own country, as long as Intelligence continued to deceive the people and keep different factions fighting each other. If there was peace, then Intelligence would be out of a job. *How laughable*. He laughed out loud.

The next day Zack heard several voices in the next room. One voice sounded like Col. Rushd. Whoever it was, was excited about something. There was another unfamiliar voice, one that sounded of contempt and cruelty.

After what seemed to be about two hours, Rushd left.

165

The new voice and Kalidasa were busy. They were in a hurry. The door opened and again Zack was dealt another blow of Islamic vengeance and pugnacity. Raoshan stepped into Zack's room and glared at him. "You murdering Jew! You drop your bombs on Baghdad killing innocent people! Sick people in hospitals and children sitting in their classrooms! If it was up to me I would kill you here! Saddam must have a useful purpose for you or you would not have lived this long."

Zack was thinking to himself that the intimidations, beatings and suffering were about to repeat themselves. The lies now were more open and not as subtle. Raoshan beat Zack about the face until he fell to the floor and then kicked him in the stomach. Kalidasa didn't come to his rescue this time.

When Zack regained consciousness he was dressed in a black robe and sandals. His air force flight suit and boots had been removed. He was blind folded and led down stairs to a van. He was being moved to a new location. Why all the secrecy unless there were allies in the city. And he wouldn't be moved unless his disclosure might be discovered. These thoughts gave him a slight ray of hope. He was beginning to perceive truth without actually seeing or hearing it. Who was it that had told him to learn to perceive. He couldn't remember. It seemed like an eternity ago. Probably only a dream. He dismissed it.

*   *   *   *

Zack was moved to a safer location. One that had already been searched by officials from the British Red Cross and a team of U.N. mediators. He had perceived correctly. Where was he now? He couldn't hear any noise and there were no windows in what seemed to be the basement of a house. At least it was cool.

Jinnah wasn't around much. He was there in the late evenings and spent the night and then gone again the next day. His behavior seemed to be similar to Javier's. Kalidasa became moody, quiet. Raoshan seemed to be in control now. There was still no news from the outside world. His only contacts were Raoshan and Kalidasa.

Zack began to withdraw again, forgetting completely about the slight ray of hope when he had perceived the presence of Allied personnel. He refused the meager meals, pushing them aside. He was searching for answers. And to find those, he knew for some unexplainable reason he would have to look within himself. He sat for days with his back against the wall. Drinking only sparingly and eating nothing at all, he subsided into a mournful state of sadness. Guilt weighed heavily over him. Was it just the oppressive treatment from his captors or was he actually feeling partially responsible for the destruction of so many lives. The space around him was darkening, like thunder clouds gathering before the storm, as he slipped deeper into a passive state of inertia. He needed something, a push from outside perhaps, to get him started.

The answer he knew was there, right at the surface. If only he could recognize it and grasp it. The more he dwelled on it, the further away it became. He looked deeper into the void that was in front of him. He thought he was falling, but he couldn't feel the air passing around him. He let go and decided to see where he would land, if indeed he was falling. The void was a bottomless pit. He kept falling and falling. Nothing changed. Was he finally loosing his mind and only imagining he was falling?

There was a voice, he thought. Speaking to him from somewhere outside the void. He strained, trying to hear it again. He tried to speak out and ask who was there, but no sound would come from his lips. He tried again. Nothing. He gave up. Then the voice was inside his head. This time he listened. The voice was his own, telling him to discipline his mind and body. He had to awaken his consciousness and get himself out of this mess.

As soon as he came to this realization he stopped falling. Slowly he came back to his present situation. He was hungry and looked about for some food. He had no idea how many days had passed. During the days that followed he busied himself with exercising and focusing his attention on more pleasant things. He tried to forget where he was and of his uncertain future.

In no time he was feeling better. His muscle tissues tightened and the skin on his face no longer sagged. This time he would win. He would find a way of escape. To exercise his mind and to keep from thinking about his captivity, he started to conjure up in his mind mathematical equations and formulas and then solve them. At first it was slow; frustrating. But he kept at it, each day finding a new equation, making it more difficult. It wasn't long before he completely forgot about his captors. He was too engrossed in solving mathematical equations. And through the process of exercising his mind, his alertness and awareness were sharpened.

*　　*　　*　　*

The morning sun rose and then set again. But Zack was never aware of the daylight. He was kept in the basement without ever seeing the outside. Lights were kept on so he was never in darkness. Once a day food was brought down with some water. Kalidasa would set the tray and the water pitcher down and then leave. He no longer lingered behind to talk. Since Raoshan's arrival a lot had changed. Zack supposed that Raoshan was now the leader. He seemed to be more militant than Kalidasa and he was emphatic about Iraq's or Hussein's cause.

There always seemed to be people coming and leaving all hours of the day. He couldn't hear doors opening and closing, only the footsteps on the floor above him. There were times when several people were moving about. Zack wondered what was happening up there. Was it some kind of headquarters?

The next day Zack would see for himself. Early in the morning Kalidasa came down and said, "Come with me, Captain."

"What's going on up there, Kalidasa?"

"Just come with me. There are those who want to ask you some questions."

Zack couldn't help but notice the apathy on Kalidasa's face and the lack of expression in his voice. He had changed. He no longer agreed with what he was told to do. His views had changed, Zack was sure of this, without Kalidasa having to say anything about it. What had happened to change him? Was it his discovery of the truth he had found? Perhaps. And that would also explain Raoshan's appearance and his control.

Zack followed Kalidasa up the stairs. "Captain, I advise you to tell them what they want to know. Do not argue. Your life could be in danger if you do."

Before Zack could answer, the door at the top of the stairs opened. Two armed guards were waiting. Jinnah and Raoshan. He was escorted into another room and the three waited, standing in the center of the room before an empty table. There were seven chairs. Probably a military inquisition. Behind the table was a large picture of Saddam Hussein. He looked like he was sneering at the rest of the world, mocking others' individuality.

The idea of this hideous man using his own countrymen as hostages and they supporting him in turn, was sickening. He wanted to laugh out loud and scream out what he was thinking.

While they waited, Zack thought about Kalidasa's advice to tell them what they wanted to know. *Who were they? And what had he meant by—tell them what they wanted to know.* Was he supposed to make up lies or tell them the truth? *Did they want the truth or as Kalidasa had said—what they want to know.*

Zack had already made up his mind. He would not bow before them, even if it meant a beating. He wouldn't be defiant, but at the same time he would not be intimidated by them either. He would not lie, he decided. He would tell it as it is, whether that's what they wanted to hear or not. Let it be.

Jinnah and Raoshan had stern expressions, unlike Kalidasa's unassuming expression. They were aggressive and they undecidedly believed in what they were doing. They probably would be capable of terrorist activities; killing and maiming innocent people without giving it a second thought or caring.

Zack's thoughts were interrupted then. The door behind the empty table opened and seven military officers seated themselves at the table without speaking or looking at Zack. They shuffled through some papers making notes and talking with each other.

Zack recognized Col. Rushd immediately. The others he had never seen. Rushd looked at Zack with contempt. He stared back with intentness. The look of a boxer, as he meets his opponent in the center ring. After the others were settled Rushd asked, "State your full name and rank."

"Capt. Zachary Breinstein, U.S. Air Force."

"What was your position, Captain?"

"Fighter pilot," Zack replied, cutting the explanation short.

"Then why were you found in the desert? Isn't it true, Captain, that you were sent here as a spy? To gather information about your bombing raids and to terrorize Iraqi people!"

"No, it is not true. If I were indeed a spy, do you think that I would be dressed in a U. S. Air Force flight suit?" Zack replied.

No sooner had Zack answered and Jinnah hit him in the back with his rifle butt. "I'll ask you again, Captain, isn't it true that you were sent here to spy on Saddam and the Iraqi Troops?"

"No."

"I'll ask you again, Captain. What were you doing in the desert?"

"I was returning to Riyadh and I had engine trouble. When I couldn't correct the problem, I ejected and the plane exploded."

"You were returning to Riyadh from where?" Rushd asked.

"Baghdad," Zack replied.

"What was your target, Captain?"

"The air base. We were to take out as many aircraft as we could."

"If your fighter had exploded as you say, then why couldn't my troops find any wreckage near the area where you were found?"

"I had been in the desert for several days. I had been following the Euphrates River. Your troops found me after I left the river."

"And you expect us to believe that you were going to walk across the desert back to Riyadh?"

"What other choice did I have?" Again Zack was hit with the rifle butt. He staggered but he would not fall to the floor.

"How long had you been stationed at Riyadh?"

"Since the last part of the summer," Zack replied, his back and shoulders aching.

"What were your assigned duties after your arrival?"

"Routine recon-flights over Iraq and Kuwait."

"What were you looking for?" Rushd asked.

"Intelligence never confided in the pilots. We opened our orders after takeoff each day. At the end of each flight our flight recorders were turned over to Intelligence. They never said what they were looking for."

"You must have been curious, Captain. What did you think you were looking for?"

"Military targets and the movement of your troops."

"Where were you stationed before Riyadh?"

"Upstate New York, Plattsburgh Air Base."

"Where is your home, Captain?"

"Iowa," Zack lied. He saw the trap. He would not endanger his wife and daughter. What would prevent Hussein from ordering a terrorist attack on his family? No, he would be cautious.

"Where in Iowa?"

"Near Offutt Air Base."

"What did you do there?"

"My folks had a small farm. They have both died since."

"You play your role well, Captain. It is after all a

171

believable story. Except there is no wreckage from your plane! I believe you were ordered to Iraq to spy on Hussein's troops and to gather information. Your flight suit was only a clever ploy, if you were caught.

"Now, Captain, tell us the real reason you were found in the desert."

"I told you already." Again he was hit. In the stomach this time. After he caught his breath again, he straightened up and looked squarely at Col. Rushd. A look that said, "I will not be subdued." Rushd shifted nervously in his chair.

"I believe you were ordered here by Israel. Isn't that so, Captain?"

"No."

"Who do you answer to?"

"Col. Lowell Davis, U.S. Air Force, Wing Commander. He is my immediate supervisor."

Col. Rushd asked the same questions over and over, and always accusing him of spying for Israel. That's what he wanted to hear. And that was what Kalidasa had tried to warn him about. The inquisition was taking all day. Undoubtedly it had been planned that way to wear Zack's resistance down. He was tired; tired of standing and he ached from the rifle blows.

"Breinstein—that's a Jew name." Rushd knew this already from their first encounter when Zack had been Col. Abdel's prisoner. He was only toying with Zack now. "Again, perhaps you were sent here by Israel to spy. That is a Jew name is it not, Captain?"

"The name is Hebrew. That does not make me a Jew. I have never followed the Jewish teachings."

"And why is that, Captain?" Rushd asked mockingly.

"There is no particular reason. My parents were not strict believers of Judaism. They were too busy trying to etch a living from farming. And I never found the teachings particularly interesting."

"Then you are an atheist?"

"No. I believe in one God, the same as you," Zack said.

"Then what religion do you follow, Captain?"

"I don't follow any organized teaching. I believe in the truth, as I find it."

"We will continue this discussion until another day. Until then, Captain, you will be treated as an Israeli spy. Unless you can convince us otherwise," Rushd said as he stood up and moved away from the table.

"Colonel," Zack rebutted, "I don't have to convince anyone of anything."

Col. Rushd stopped and looked at Zack, but couldn't find anything appropriate to say. He left the inquisition without saying anything else.

Jinnah and Raoshan took Zack back to the basement. Jinnah opened the door and Raoshan pushed him through the doorway and down the stairs.

Zack lay in a heap at the bottom. His legs hurt. His back felt like it was broken from the beatings and he was disheartened. The inquisition was designed only to break his spirit and to coerce him into admitting he was an Israeli spy. There was absolutely nothing new discovered about him that Rushd did not already know.

After several minutes he managed to stand and limp to his bed. All that night Zack laid on his back staring at the floor above him. The beatings were getting worse. He didn't know for how much more of the beatings he could take. His bones were becoming brittle from the lack of calcium in his diet. It took longer and longer to recover from the beatings. But he would not submit to their beatings or intimidations. He would not allow them to deter him from the truth.

Perhaps he would die unless he was willing to abandon truth and submit to their cunning manipulations. Zack wasn't afraid of death. What was death but an awakening to a new life? A life that had to be better than what he was now experiencing. For some inexplicable reason this idea brought with it a comforting warmth that surrounded his body and let him, for a moment, forget his anguish and discomfort.

For the first time, since his captivity, he began thinking of more pleasant reflections. He had been so concerned about his well-being that he had forgotten about his wife and daughter and the anguish they must be feeling. To them he was already dead. How could they possibly know that he was alive and rotting in a basement in Baghdad? He wondered what they were doing. How had they changed? How much had Becky grown? Was she still a happy little girl? He thought about Rachel's warm touch and how pretty her smile was. How had they grown so far apart in so short a time?

He thought about the walks he took in the hills behind their house. There he could leave the rest of the world and the world's problems behind and for a while escape into his own private world. One that seemed to be more real than the world he was now living. In his world he could not remember of so much hatred and pain. This world, with all its pain and suffering, was a nightmare, compared to his world.

*　　*　　*　　*

The days passed since the inquisition, and since that day the noise and activity sounding on the floor above him had lessened. Kalidasa still brought him his meals but never stayed to talk. Jinnah and Raoshan were never there and the other officers at the inquisition had not returned. Something of major importance must have happened. But what, Zack asked himself.

One evening as Kalidasa was setting the food tray down Zack asked, "Kalidasa, why is it so quiet here now? Has something happened?'

Kalidasa turned away and started up the stairs, then stopped. "A United Nations Commission is in Baghdad."

Zack reached for a ray of hope, "Are they looking for hostages and prisoners of war? Those reported missing in action?"

"No. They're searching for nuclear weapons, laboratories and papers that Hussein has."

Kalidasa left and Zack sat back on his bed, "So he had nuclear capabilities after all."

The days continued to pass with the only footsteps above him were Kalidasa's. There was something more happening other than the U.N. Commission looking for nuclear weapons. Col. Rushd, Raoshan and Jinnah were always away. Busy doing something. But what? Organizing new terrorist activities? Perhaps. Their absence was actually a welcomed relief. When the three were in the building beatings became imminent. They vented their anger and frustrations on Zack.

The basement walls were made of concrete and rocks. There was no possible way of finding escape through it. There were no openings at all, except for the one door at the top of the stairs. That was always locked and bolted. If he tried to break it down, the noise would alarm his captors. There was nothing to do but wait and watch for that moment to escape. Zack had already made up his mind. He would not be just another hostage statistic, like those being held in Iran and Lebanon. If he was to die, then he would die fighting for his freedom.

Col. Rushd, Raoshan and Jinnah returned the next morning and at noon Zack was summoned again to the floor above to continue with the inquisition. This time Rushd sat alone at the table. "We did not learn much of anything useful last time, Captain. I hope you will be more cooperative today."

"I believe we determined that you are an Israeli spy; cleverly disguised. We did not learn what your orders were once you had infiltrated your target area. Now, Captain, let us waste no more time. What was your purpose, your orders, once you were in Iraq?"

Zack started to laugh. Then Raoshan hit him in the back with his rifle butt. "Colonel, do you actually believe that if I were an Israeli spy that I would come into Iraq with a name like Breinstein? It would be suicidal. Come on, Colonel, use a little common sense." He was hit in the back again. Rushd had been rebutted and his bluff called. His prisoner now knew the fallacy of this line of questioning. He would have to find a different approach.

"Captain, why did you choose to fight in a battle that was so far away from your own country, your own home? Surely you could not have felt threatened."

"I am a fighter pilot in the U.S. Air Force. When I received orders to fly my plane to Saudi Arabia, I did not think to challenge or question the orders. I did as I was instructed. When I received orders to fly recon missions over Iraq, I followed orders. When I was ordered to take out a particular military installation, I followed orders again. Surely, Colonel, as a military person you can understand that. Perhaps if I had had all of the information gathered by Intelligence, then I might have had a better understanding of what was occurring. Since I did not, Colonel, I followed orders."

"Your President, Captain, lied to the world. He told you one reason why he was invading Iraq, but he did so for a completely separate reason. He convinced the whole world that he was sending U.S. forces to invade Iraq to liberate Kuwait and recover Kuwait's rich oil fields. Those were only lies, Captain. Only an excuse for doing what he did to Saddam and the Iraqi people. When he could no longer justify moving the Allied Troops closer to Baghdad, he cleverly incited the Kurds to revolt and assassinate Saddam Hussein. To do his dirty work, so the truth would never be known."

Zack remained quiet. Perhaps Rushd would come out with it. The real reason for invading Iraq as he too had suspected for so long. When he didn't comment, Rushd continued. "You simpleton! You don't know, do you? It was over nuclear capability. Which your government helped us to build."

There it was. As he had suspected. The real reason for fighting the Iraqis was over nuclear weapons.

"We sent our best engineers to a seminar in your country,

Captain. When they returned, they brought with them the knowledge and papers to build a nuclear bomb." Now it was Rushd who was laughing. "You Americans helped us to build the bomb and when you discovered what you had done, you fabricated a war to crush Iraq, Saddam and steal our nuclear plans. You didn't care at all about the fate of Kuwait or their oil fields. It was Saddam and the bomb you were after from the beginning."

Zack could see it all now, in his mind. It was very probable that Saddam had sent his nuclear engineers to a seminar in the United States and that Iraq had progressed far enough with the development of the bomb to be a threatening aspect to peace in the Mid-East. He had proven to the world in the past that he would use any weapon he had against any enemy. Even his own people. "What you have said, Colonel, is probably true. But still, Hussein had to be stopped. He is a sadistic murderer. He would have used the bomb, if only to demonstrate his power." Jinnah and Raoshan both beat him with their rifle butts until he collapsed to the floor.

Kalidasa watched with horror as the two beat Zack. Why had he done it? He must have known he would be beaten. But Kalidasa also appreciated the courage and fortitude Zack showed by standing up and telling Rushd what he thought. And Zack was correct, Saddam had to be stopped.

Zack managed to stand, but with difficulty. It was obvious he was hurting. Kalidasa was saying to himself to stay on the floor. But he knew Zack would stand, and defy Col. Rushd again, and again. He would be beaten, only to stand again if he was able. To stand and defy and be beaten.

"Is this how Muslims show their courage and gallantry? The cruelty of these two with rifles. Is this part of your precious Jihad, Colonel? You think that fighting under the name of Jihad that that will excuse your cowardly behavior or your forceful domination of others! Whatever became of the greater Jihad, where Muslims practiced enlightening of the inner self? Have your holy wars or battles erased everything good that Islam has ever stood for? Is this how Muhammad expected the "five pillars" of Islam to be administrated? I don't believe so. You have desecrated and shamed the fundamentals of Islam and the true meaning of Jihad?

"Today's Jihad or holy war is nothing more than an excuse for spiritual warfare to plunder, loot and rape! Yes, Saddam had to be stopped! A nuclear weapon in his grasp is unconscionable!"

Kalidasa froze with horror. Even though Zack had spoken the truth, he would probably be beaten to death. He looked at Zack with empathy and compassion. He stood there defiant and staunchly more superior than his captors about the basic tenants of life and spiritual truth. He wished he had some of Zack's understanding and fortitude.

Col. Rushd nodded his head. Raoshan and Jinnah pinned Zack's arms behind him and started to escort him out of the room. Much to everyone's surprise, especially to Kalidasa. Zack twisted sharply to one side freeing his arms and turned to face Rushd once more. "Colonel," Zack said in a low, smooth voice, "True Islam is a loving, compassionate religion. Does not your Koran urge all Muslims to respect their fellowman, as all human beings, even Jews, are equal in God's eye? But the modern day teachings of Islam have their basic percepts cemented with lies and mistruths. You surely do not treat your women as equals. They have become nothing more than chattel.

"You have these two beat me every time I speak the truth. Does truth disturb you that much, Colonel? Does truth upset you that much?"

Rushd jumped to his feet and over turned the table in front of him. His face was reddened with anger and his eyes shot daggers of fire. "Take him away! Get him out of here!" he bellowed.

On the way back to the basement Zack knew he would be beaten again. This time it would be more severe. He had already made up his mind to fight back. No longer was he going to remain passive while two thugs beat him nearly to death. No, this time he would fight back. He'd wait until they were in the basement alone. Just he, Raoshan and Jinnah. If he was to win the fight, then he had no alternative; he had to try and escape. Raoshan carried with him the keys to the building. If he lost, well then he probably would die.

Kalidasa watched as his two comrades escorted Zack out of the room to the basement below. He also knew that this would probably be Zack's death sentence. Raoshan and Jinnah would beat him until he collapsed and had drawn his last breath.

Raoshan opened the door to the basement. As he was pushing the door open, Zack saw his opportunity. Raoshan was off balance, trying to hold on to his arm and swing the door open at the same time. With lightening speed Zack pulled together all the remaining strength he had. He jerked his arm free from Raoshan and leaned his body back against Jinnah for support. At the same instant he lashed out and up with both feet and caught Raoshan on the side of his chest sending him down the stairs. He laid at the bottom, motionless.

As soon as Jinnah had realized what had happened, he knocked Zack down the stairs and he landed on top of Raoshan, breaking his fall. Jinnah came running down the steps after him. Zack crawled over Raoshan and stood back. Jinnah stopped to check why Raoshan was not moving. He turned him over and it became obvious. His neck was broken. Jinnah looked at Zack. Hatred glared in his eyes. He didn't speak, he only glared and came towards Zack with slow methodical steps. Like a tiger approaching an enemy. Both fists were doubled into hard knots. He took another step and then another.

From somewhere deep within him, Zack was able to tap into his subconscious. He saw himself using a style of Shao-Lin self defense. The image was strange because he wasn't fighting an opponent. But only using the exercise to bring his mind in harmony with his body; enlightening his awareness.

179

Jinnah took another step and when he did, Zack in one swift fluid movement jumped into the air and kicked out with his right leg. The edge of his right foot caught Jinnah under the chin sending him backwards. Zack landed on both feet and turned to face Jinnah. His left foot was slightly ahead. Jinnah looked at Zack. His teeth were clenched and he was furious. He lunged at Zack and when he did, Zack took one step forward, turned completely around on the ball of his left foot and kicked out with his right. He hit Jinnah in the side again and broke two ribs. He could hear the bones snap. He rushed at Zack again. Zack took a step forward and met him with a closed fist in his throat. Jinnah fell back to the floor. His windpipe crushed, soon he was as silent and motionless as Raoshan.

The floor above was quiet. Apparently everybody had left. Whatever he was going to do, he had to do it now. As soon as these two were missing, someone would come looking. He went through Raoshan's clothing for the keys. As he was removing the keys he heard a movement on the stairs above. Kalidasa was standing there. He had closed the door. For some inexplicable reason Zack understood he didn't present any immediate threat.

He held the keys in his hand and backed away from the crumbled body. Kalidasa looked the body over and then looked over at Jinnah. Zack said, "He is dead also."

Kalidasa's statement took Zack by surprise. "What are your intentions now? I won't try to stop you."

"I must get out of here. Out of Baghdad and away from Iraq. There is nothing here but lies and untruths." Zack started to walk towards the stairs.

"There is no need to leave just yet. In fact it would be safer and easier to wait for darkness."

"Aren't the others apt to return? Or is that your intention? To trap me," Zack replied.

"No. Col. Rushd has taken a terrorist unit into the hills next to Turkey's border. Saddam wants to start the Kurds bickering and fighting amongst themselves, so they will return.

Col. Rushd and his men are to stop them from growing stronger. That means they will murder the Kurd leaders, if it becomes necessary.

"I am the only guard here now. You have killed the others. We were to stay here until Col. Rushd returned. Then you would be moved to another location. If you were still alive.

"So you see, time is on your side."

"How can I possibly trust you?" Zack asked.

"Because when you leave, I shall also leave. You have made me see the truth about what has been happening here. More than you'll ever know."

"If the Kurds return, what will happen to them?" Zack asked.

"It would be my guess that Saddam will have them executed," Kalidasa replied.

"Then I guess I have no choice. I believe you, Kalidasa. But if you turn against me—well, you'll end up like those two.

"Wouldn't it be wiser if you stayed upstairs, just in case someone comes in?"

"There's no chance of that. Besides I'd rather stay here and talk. Seven weeks ago Col. Rushd had my mother and father executed. He warned me that if I showed any disobedience to Saddam, my brother would also be executed. Since then I haven't felt like talking to anyone."

"I noticed the change. Where do we go once we leave here?" Zack asked.

"The U.N. Commission is in Ar-Ramadi. We got word this morning that the commission found some papers hidden there."

"What kind of papers?" Zack asked.

"Blueprints for the nuclear bomb. We've got two days to get there." It was obvious Kalidasa had no regrets about leaving Baghdad or Hussein's madness. In fact he was more enthusiastic than Zack. Zack still had his doubts about getting free of Baghdad and Hussein's talons. Kalidasa had no doubts at all.

"I never expected you to over power Jinnah and Raoshan. I thought they would beat you to death for what you said to Col. Rushd. How did you do it?"

"I'm not sure for certain. A sudden burst of energy perhaps."

"As you were lashing out at Col. Rushd, I started to remember the last time we talked, before you were moved here, about lesser and greater Jihad. I had forgotten our conversation until then. But you are correct, our corrupt leaders have set the importance of the lesser Jihad above the greater. We should not be so concerned about another's beliefs as to enlightening our own inner being. I think most Muslims would prefer to do this, but through the years we have been prevailed upon to put too much importance on fighting other religions."

"Will you leave Islam?" Zack asked.

"No. Even though I can now see the fallacy of the modern movement, Islam and Muhammad's teachings are still very important to me. The teachings are good. I would like to help others see the truth."

"How does Hussein keep such loyalty? Surely there are others who do not agree with what his is doing."

"Fear. He demands their obedience and promises to provide for the people. If anyone dares to challenge him, then he is apt to be shot and his execution publicized. He stays in control by controlling the minds of the masses."

Zack sat there in wonder. Somewhere he knew he had heard the same thing. Exactly where, had he heard it before? Had it only been a dream? He couldn't remember and he tried to push it aside. But the idea stayed with him, he couldn't just push it aside. For whatever reason, he knew that the concept must be important.

"What will you do once we get to the U.N. Commission in Ar-Ramadi?" Kalidasa asked.

"I'm not sure. I've had my fill of the Air Force. I like flying and I still think Hussein has to be stopped from further development of the nuclear bomb. But I don't like being deceived or lied to. I was nothing more than a piece of programmable machinery. Like you Kalidasa, Intelligence used me and lied to me in order to get me to do their dirty work. Why is truth so difficult for people, Kalidasa?"

"I don't know, but it is the same no matter where you go."

They talked for hours while waiting for darkness. Each one never forgetting that the other had been an enemy. Now they had been brought together by a common desire for truth. Kalidasa wanted to help the Islam movement towards working for the greater Jihad and stop warring against neighboring countries of different beliefs. He would have to leave Iraq now, because after helping Zack to escape he would be branded a traitor and executed without a trial. He also needed to get away from the immediate influence of a heavy Muslim culture. He needed space to sort things out and decide what he was going to do.

Darkness finally came. Kalidasa went to the rear of the house and opened a window leading to a back alley. "Come, we must go now," Kalidasa said.

As Zack was climbing through the window he experienced a warming happiness. A good feeling, free of worries and anxiety. He had started his long journey home. But it was more than that. More than just returning to his home in Vermont. A tremendous weight had been lifted. There was a familiar echo—vibrations of soft music beckoning him to follow. He knew in his heart and in his inner most being, that he was on his way to a place more splendid and glorious than anything he had ever seen or experienced before.

*   *   *   *

Once outside the building Kalidasa led the way. "You are my brother, Zack. If we are stopped you are sick and unable to talk." The streets were still busy. People hard at work, desperately trying to put their lives back together. Because the city's generators had not been completely repaired, most of the streets were not lit.

Kalidasa wound his way through the crowds. In and out of streets until he came to the main highway that led to Jordan and Syria. He hailed a truck and asked the driver, "Do you have any room. My brother and I are going to Ar-Ramadi?"

"Get in the back," the driver replied.

It was a slow ride. The highway was busy with transports carrying supplies from Jordan. Zack sat with his back to the side of the truck and watched the stars above. Never before, until this moment, had he realized just how precious freedom really was. Kalidasa slept most of the way, but Zack was too excited to sleep. He wanted to breathe the fresh air and enjoy in his regained freedom. On the outside Zack displayed a rather normal countenance. But on the inside, he was having a joyous reunion. Again he was aware of that peculiar warming glow. But only now, he could feel it surround his entire body.

In Ar-Ramadi the driver stopped for fuel. "You'll have to get off here," the driver said.

Kalidasa thanked the driver and the two disappeared in the darkness. "Do you know where to find the U.N. Commission?" Zack asked.

"No. But I know what they search for and where the laboratory is hidden. It would be best to go there and wait until the Commission arrives."

The sun was beginning to illuminate the eastern horizon and already the air was getting warmer. It was late summer and temperatures could rise as high as 110 degrees. Zack had completely forgotten about the arid heat. Locked away in the basement where it was always cool, he had never thought about the extreme heat at this time of year. After about an hour Kalidasa stopped outside the security gate at Ar-Ramadi's hospital. "Is this the laboratory, Kalidasa?"

"Yes, below ground level. Anything of military importance Saddam had hidden away in buildings like this. He knew you

Americans would not bomb these facilities. The laboratory is below ground level. If the hospital had been targeted, your bombs would not have reached the laboratories. They had been sealed in concrete."

"When the Commission arrives how do we get through the security gate?" Zack asked.

"I'm not sure. We'll have to find a way."

They found some shrubs nearby where they could watch the gate. "Perhaps if we waited until the Commission was through and then approach them as they come out through the gate," Kalidasa suggested.

"Kalidasa,"

"Yes,"

"Last night you asked what I would do once I was out of Iraq."

"And?"

"I'm going to retire from the Air Force and tell people the truth about what happened over here. I mean how Intelligence had purposely misled the whole world about why it became so important to push Hussein out of Kuwait and invade Iraq. I think it's time. Don't you?"

"Yes, but will anyone want to hear the truth. The war is over and all of your troops have been honored back in your country. Your countrymen are still singing "The Hero's Song." Even if you are believed, will anyone want to listen?"

"Maybe not. But I have to try. People everywhere have the right to know how Intelligence misconstrued the facts and intentionally went after Hussein and his nuclear capability, using Kuwait only as an excuse."

"But, Captain, he had to be stopped, did he not?"

"Yes, but why did we have to be lied to? Why is the truth so difficult, and abused?"

"Perhaps people everywhere would rather not know the truth. There are those who would rather remain ignorant than have to assume some responsibility. There are people, Captain, who can not accept truth," Kalidasa said.

It was daylight now and traffic had started through the security gate. No sign yet of any U.N. vehicles. Zack leaned back against a shrub and watched the vehicles as they passed through the gate. Neither one said anything until finally a gray colored van stopped at the gate. The only identification was the U.N. insignia on the license plate. Zack started to get up but Kalidasa coaxed him to wait. "Not yet. We will have to wait until they leave the building and come back through the gate later. Then we must have a plan to stop them and get you aboard."

"How do we do that Kalidasa?"

"Perhaps I could create a disturbance while you approach the van. Let's hope they do not come back through until after darkness," Kalidasa said.

Zack relaxed and they resumed the exchange of ideas and information. "Islam is the only religion I have ever heard of that preaches disciplining the soul or the inner self. What you call the greater Jihad. Is this what Muhammad had originally stressed and not the fighting of other beliefs?" Zack asked.

"This is what I hope to discover, and work towards returning all Muslims to this understanding."

"From what I have learned about Islam since I have been in the Mid-East, it sounds like a very compassionate and direct teaching."

Kalidasa smiled and said, "It is. Perhaps you would like to join me in my fight against the direction Islam is now taking?" They both laughed.

On a more serious note, "I don't think so, Kalidasa. I must find my own way home. When this is finally all behind me—well, lately I have noticed that there is something guiding me towards a definite awakening. There are times when I start to grasp it and then it fades away again. It's there. It's real and it is guiding me towards something."

Kalidasa thought about this for a moment then replied, "If you don't know what this something is, then will you recognize it when you find it?"

"Yes."

The day was already hot and promising to get hotter. The wind was from the south, bringing with it dry desert heat. Kalidasa and Zack decided to conserve their energy and just watch in silence. Neither had had any food or water since leaving Baghdad. Zack stretched out his legs and closed his eyes. His was tired and malnourished from his long months of captivity. He was soon asleep.

*   *   *   *

While Zack slept soundly, hidden in the shrubbery, he also awoke in a dream. A dream he had had before. He had been here before, a land that was so peaceful and tranquil that it almost seemed unreal. Again, he was alone in this strange and beautiful world, only the resplendent deep sonorous music that filled the air and made him vibrate with life. He called out "HELLO!" Again, no answer. He sat there motionless, listening to the music and wondering why he was alone. How could he possibly be alone in a land that was so beautiful? It was just not imaginable that there was no one else in this magnificent land. He knew there had to be. He wouldn't accept the idea. "No, there has to be an answer. I will not accept it," he thought. It was absurd. It couldn't be. He would not believe it.

Then the scenery, or images, started to change before him. He could see a small pleasant village on the seashore. But he was not part of the scene. He was viewing it from outside. This can not be either. "Hello!" he shouted. No one answered. Again he challenged what was before him. It was still too absurd to believe. "No, there has to be more! Nobody here has their individuality, their own mind or purpose."

Zack watched as the inhabitants went about their collective efforts. Everything was done the same. No imagination. He didn't want to be a part of this world. Then he realized that he wasn't, that he was standing outside of the apparition. Only an observer. There has to be something of more notable worth. Something more real. Reality!

The scene started to change again. The sky darkened and the atmosphere became gray. The scene continued to change and now he was looking at a strange valley. It was somehow familiar, but he couldn't remember being here before. The valley stretched into infinity it seemed. The wonderful music was still present in spite of the darkened sky and the dispirited atmosphere. He knew the answers lay at the far distant end of the valley. The answers to this strange and enchanting land.

*   *   *   *

Most of the day had passed while Zack slept. Kalidasa kept a close watch of the security gate. He decided there was no need to awaken Zack. He had been through a rough ordeal. The sun was beginning to set by the time Zack awoke. The dream of that strange land soon faded back into the invisible world. "What time is it?" Zack asked.

"Almost night, the sun is setting," Kalidasa replied.

"Have you seen anything of the van?"

"No, they are still inside. That is good. It'll be easier for us in the darkness."

Zack sat up beside Kalidasa. "Where will you go, once this is over? You said you wanted to help bring to the surface of Islam, the idea of the greater Jihad, but where will you go to do that?"

Kalidasa grinned, "To do that I'll have to go to a country where society will not suppress one's religious beliefs. The freest country in the world my friend: your United States."

"Won't that be a problem for you? How will you ever expect to get a visa? I mean, let's be honest, you are an Iraqi and right now I don't think any Iraqi would be accepted in many countries. Least of all, the United States."

Kalidasa laughed softly. "I will be there before you."

Zack looked doubtful and Kalidasa interpreted the expression. "It is no big problem to enter your country. It is one of the easiest in the world to enter. We have been doing it for a long time."

"But—," the rest of the question went unasked. The gray van was stopping at the gate.

"How will we do this?" Zack asked.

"I will create a distraction. You then talk to those inside. Force yourself in, if necessary. But get in at all cost. If the guards are alerted, the van will be stopped and searched. If your escape has been found and I believe that it probably has, all military personnel will have already been alerted. If you are found, you will be recaptured."

"But the U.N. officials surely will prevent that from happening."

"Look how you are dressed," Kalidasa said. "To them, their first impression of you will be an Arab. One who speaks English. You'll have to have time to convince them. That's why I said to force your way into the van if it becomes necessary. Do you understand now?"

"Yes," Zack replied. "What about you?"

"Don't worry about me, I'll be fine. You are the one in danger. Remember what I have said."

There was no time to reply. The van was leaving the gate. "Come," Kalidasa commanded, "follow me."

Zack crawled out of the shrubs behind Kalidasa and followed him across the road to where the van would be coming. They walked across the road as the van was coming towards them. Kalidasa stopped as if to let the van pass. Zack wondered if he had changed his mind. Just as the van was about to go by, Kalidasa stepped out in front and the front corner of the van hit him. He turned to roll aside and fell to the ground.

The van swerved and then stopped just beyond Kalidasa. Zack knelt down and asked, "Are you all right?"

Kalidasa looked up and said, "Go on, get out of here. This is your only chance."

Zack stood up and looked at his friend. There were no words to tell him what he was feeling. He turned and ran over to the passenger's door.

People were getting out to see if the man was injured. Kalidasa saw one walking towards him and started a verbal assault up on him. This gave Zack the precious time he needed. The passenger door opened, but before he could get out Zack held the door closed. "Excuse me! My name is Capt. Zachary Breinstein, U.S. Air Force, stationed at Riyadh. I was forced to eject from my F 15 when it exploded. I was captured by Iraqi troops and have been held hostage in Baghdad ever since. I need your help to get out of Iraq. Can you help me?"

The man just sat there stupefied. "Do you hear me?" Zack said in desperation. "I'm an American fighter pilot and have been held hostage in Baghdad since the end of January!"

The man finally responded, "That's preposterous! We were never informed that the Iraqis had held any prisoners. They had all been released. Besides, your name was never on the prisoner list."

"Listen you stupid bastard, my name was never on the list because my own squadron probably assumed I was killed in the explosion!"

"You don't look like an American. Although I must say your attitude is surely consistent with that of an American," the man said.

"Look, I haven't much time to convince you who I am. I don't have anything to lose if I was to haul your fat carcass out of that seat and leave you here. Since January I've been starved, beaten and battered. I killed two Iraqis while escaping. If I don't leave here now with you, I will be killed, so I have nothing to lose if I haul you out of there."

Zack looked back towards the security gate. Someone was running towards them. Kalidasa was standing and apparently okay. The driver was walking back to the van. Zack opened the door wide and grabbed the man by his clothes and started to drag him from the vehicle.

"That won't be necessary," the driver said. "Open the side door Herman, and let the Captain in. I believe him." The door opened and Zack climbed in. He turned to look at Kalidasa, but he had already disappeared.

"Shut the door!" the driver said, "Let's go!"

*　　*　　*　　*

The U.N. Commission met a transport helicopter outside the city limits. On the way there Zack was confronted with a multitude of questions, "Why are you wearing that awful black robe?" Herman asked him.

"When I was relocated from the army base my flight suit and name tags were taken away from me and I was told to wear this. I suppose my captors didn't want anyone to recognize my flight suit or emblems."

"Who was that fellow that we ran into?" Hadley Bishop, the passenger in the front asked.

"His name is Kalidasa. He was one of the captors." Excitement stirred inside the van. "No, no you don't have to worry. This isn't a set-up. He helped me escape."

"Why would he turn against his people?" Hadley wanted to know.

"He had discovered the truth about the modern Islamic movement and decided that Muslims everywhere were being deceived about the original purpose of Jihad. Their holy war. He had to leave after helping me and now he wants to try to turn around the concept of jihad."

"Why were you not injured when your fighter exploded?" Nolan Peters, the driver asked.

"I ejected just before the explosion."

"Why did it explode?" Nolan asked.

"My port engine had caught on fire and I was diving, trying to blow the flames out. When I restarted the starboard engine, the whole damn plane went up in flames."

"Captain," Adrian Chagnon asked, "who was your flight commander?"

"Col. Lowell Davis," Zack replied.

"Where were you stationed back in the States?"

"Plattsburg, New York."

"Either you are who you say you are, or you are well rehearsed. Either way we'll, for the time being, have to believe you. But if we should discover that you are lying and are an Iraqi terrorist, we shall not hesitate to throw you out of the helicopter once we are airborne," Hadley Bishop advised.

The ride to the helicopter seemed like an eternity. His nightmare of torture and lies and deception was almost over. He tried to relax and think only about going back to his home in Vermont. But his inner being wouldn't let him. He kept seeing images in his mind of that strange land he had seen in his dream and then suddenly he could remember the dream in vivid detail. Then he saw the old beggar in Riyadh and the old man who had brought him food. Somehow these two men seemed vaguely familiar, but he couldn't remember where he had known them. It wasn't as much the person themselves, but rather their philosophy, their perception and understanding. And he could almost hear the sonorous humming that he had heard in his dream. It was filling the inside of the van with its rich music. For now all he wanted was to go home. But then what? What about that strange land he had seen in his dream? Could it possibly exist somewhere, outside of his dreams? He knew then that he would have to try and find it. He was being drawn to this enchanting land, or could it be that he was being drawn back to it?

"Captain, Captain are you okay?" Peters asked.

"Yes—I was just thinking about something."

"We're here. We should board without delay," Peters added.

The doors were closed and the pilot started to lift off. "Colonel," the co-pilot said, "there is an extra man aboard."

"Peters," the colonel addressed, "who is the extra person aboard?"

"He is an American Air Force fighter pilot. We'll explain enroute. For now, we had better leave as fast as possible. I see headlights approaching."

It was a long flight back to Riyadh in a helicopter. A flight Zack had flown many times before. Col. Northrop talked with Nolan Peters at great length about Capt. Breinstein's story. "Captain," Col. Northrop asked, "isn't Breinstein a Jewish name?"

"It's Hebrew," Zack replied in a tired tone.

"I'm surprised the Iraqis didn't just shoot you on the spot."

"They thought about it, but decided to use me as a hostage for gaining the release of some of their own jailed in Israel."

It was an odd sensation to be in the air again. Zack almost asked the colonel if he could pilot the helicopter. But he knew that in his condition he was not physically fit to fly. He was too excited to sleep, so he sat watching out the window at the darkness below. The images of that land in his dreams kept coming back. And he began to wonder what he would have become, if he had not had to eject. It was obvious, even to himself, that he was not now the same person as he had been at the onset of the war. He could see things more clearly now. His understanding was more perceptive. To Intelligence, because of his perceptiveness and penetrating thoughts, he might be considered a threat. No longer would Intelligence or any other entity be able to manipulate and deceive him. He had gained an enlightened awareness which most would not understand.

He wondered if he could find the old beggar in the city. He would like to talk with him again about his ordeal. He suspected that somehow the old beggar had known what had lain ahead. No, the old beggar would not be there. Zack was certain of that. He had had the encounter with him, to help him along the way.

That was all. That was also why no other shopkeeper in the area had known of a blind beggar that Zack had met. He had been there for one sole purpose.

As they flew over Riyadh the sun was just beginning to peak over the horizon. The city was just coming alive. They made a fly-by over the once busy airbase. Zack watched with interest. "Colonel, the base is practically empty. What happened?"

Col. Northrop chuckled, "Captain, perhaps no one has told you, but we won the war. We drove the bastards out of Kuwait and sent them running back to Baghdad. When Hussein finally signed the peace agreement, the troops immediately started to ship back to the states. Only a skeleton of what had been deployed were left behind to ensure Hussein abided to the agreements."

"I guess there's a lot I don't know. Where did my squadron go?"

"Who was the wing commander?" Northrop asked.

"Col. Lowell Davis."

"He was transferred to Stuttgart, Germany. Half the squadron went with him and I think the others returned to Plattsburg," Northrop said.

Zack was still amazed how empty the base appeared. The last time he had seen it, the whole area was crawling with activity. Literally thousands of men and women had been encamped there. Every available building had been turned into sleeping quarters.

The helicopter touched down and Northrop secured the engines and rotor. Another gray military van was there to greet them, escorted by another van carrying armed guards. "In case you're wondering about the guards, Captain, these gentlemen are carrying highly classified material. Intelligence couldn't take a chance of the material falling into the wrong hands."

"You mean blueprints for the nuclear bomb?"

Everyone was astonished to learn that Zack had known of their purpose in Iraq. "You mean again," Zack scoffed. It went unanswered. But everyone there knew what Zack was referring to and they were also wondering how he knew about the mishap; the Iraqi engineers being allowed to attend the nuclear seminar in the United States.

No one left the inside of the helicopter until the armed guards were positioned outside. Col. Northrop and his co-pilot remained seated while the others climbed out. Zack waited until the Commission members were out and then he climbed down the ladder. As soon as he appeared in the doorway, all the guards trained their automatic weapons on him. He looked like an Iraqi. Coal black long hair, a beard and wearing an Iraqi black robe. What else could they have thought? Zack looked at the guards momentarily and then climbed down the ladder.

Nolan Peters walked over to the guard in charge and said, "You can call your men off, Lieutenant. He is one of us. Capt. Breinstein. He lost his F-15 returning from Baghdad and has been held hostage ever since."

"Just the same, sir, Capt. Breinstein will ride with us," the lieutenant replied.

Zack got into the van as he was directed. A guard sat on either side and their weapons loaded resting across their laps. Zack with his new enlightenment snickered at the irony of it all.

The U.N. Commission was escorted to the base commander's headquarters. The guards got out to escort the Commission and their papers into the headquarters office. "You will come with us, Captain, until we find out what to do with you."

Zack was ushered through the door and he immediately recognized the Base Commander, Col. Alfred Freedmont. He was talking with the members of the U.N. Commission and had not yet seen him. He laughed when he thought how he was dressed. Of course he wouldn't recognize him. He stood and waited with his armed escorts. When Freedmont had finished he turned to dismiss the guards and for the first time saw a man in a black robe. "What is this Lieutenant? What does this Arab want?"

"Colonel," the Lieutenant said, "He says he is Capt. Zachary Breinstein."

Col. Freedmont walked over to Zack and looked him over. Zack stood there watching and laughing to himself on the inside. "Damn it man, say something. Are you or are you not Breinstein?"

"Good morning, Col. Freedmont. It's been a long journey."

Freedmont walked around him, analyzing him from head to foot. He was amazed. He was acquainted with Capt. Breinstein and this man didn't look at all like him. "Breinstein's fighter exploded, we presumed he had been killed," Freedmont said.

"I ejected, Colonel, just before the explosion." Zack went on to inform the colonel how his port engine had caught on fire and how he had tried to blow it out. If Freedmont was not convinced before, he was now. There was no possible way for an Iraqi infiltrator to know about Breinstein's engine problem.

"Zachary, is this really you? What happened? Where have you been? And why are you dressed in that awful robe?"

The guards were dismissed and Zack told Col. Freedmont all about his ordeal. "You said Col. Rushd was taking some terrorist north to demoralize the Kurds?"

"Yes."

"Thank you, Captain. Now you probably would like to eat and sleep for awhile."

"Yes sir, but I'd like a bath and clean up and get rid of these rags."

With his hair trimmed and his beard gone Zack looked at his reflection in the mirror. For the first time he realized the effect that malnutrition had made on his body. He was skin and bone. His cheeks were hollow and he had lost all color tone in his skin. No wonder Col. Freedmont had not recognized him. His legs and shoulders were still hurting from the beatings, but his spirits were good. After eating a hearty meal he laid down to sleep. He luxuriated in the feel of clean sheets and the smell of clean air. He fell asleep for the first time since being captured, feeling good about what tomorrow might bring.

He was allowed to sleep as long as he wanted. By mid-day he crawled out of bed, showered and shaved again and then walked over to the mess hall to eat with the other airman. Without thinking he sat down to eat his meal with the enlisted men. It wasn't a contemptuous display of insolence, nor a disregard for authority, but now after his nightmarish ordeal in Baghdad, he could no longer see the pompous separation of the enlisted and the officers. They were equal, only with different jobs to perform. They both were still only pawns for Intelligence.

"Excuse me, Captain, when you have finished eating, Col. Freedmont would like to see you in his office."

"Thank you, Sergeant," Zack replied not bothering to return his salute. He simply nodded his head.

"Come in, Captain; sit down," Freedmont indicated to a chair. "There is a special flight this afternoon that'll take you to Stuttgart. You will be admitted to the hospital there for examination. And probably for a short stay until you have your health back and your leg is healed. You have a noticeable limp. Did you break it when you ejected?"

"No sir, I was often beaten with rifle butts."

"When the doctor at Stuttgart releases you, you'll be returned to Plattsburg."

"Yes, sir. Has my family been notified yet?'

"No, Captain. I have forgotten. I'll do it right away. Unless you'd prefer to speak to them yourself."

"That won't be necessary, Colonel. It would be best if someone from Plattsburg drove over to my home in Vermont and visited my wife. I don't want her told over the telephone," Zack said straight forward. And from Freedmont's expression Zack's implication was clear enough.

*   *   *   *

197

He boarded the plane and settled down in his seat and thought he'd sleep to pass the time away. Otherwise it would be a long boring flight. But he didn't sleep. Instead, he stared continuously out the window at the clouds and thought of another time and of another world.

With his eyes open and seeing only the white fluffy clouds, in his inner vision he could see the other side of the valley that he had seen earlier in his dream. Only now it was beginning to seem more real than simply a dream. He knew he had crossed the valley and had been confronted with terrible entities of some sort. He couldn't remember crossing the valley, but still he knew at some time he had. He knew he had been warned about crossing the valley and possibly encountering something of terror.

But all he could see now on the other side of the valley was serenity. A quiet place. There were no buildings and no people. Only quiet beauty and the melodious humming that filled the air. There was a purposeful connection between this serenely beautiful land and his ordeal in Iraq. But what could it be? Had his capture been structured long before it happened? A hidden reason. One where he himself was too close to see its purpose? He had changed. And he could see the changes. He could see truth more clearly now. He had learned to perceive, not merely accepting an outward appearance. In the future he would never allow another entity to manipulate him or program his thinking. Intelligence had tried and it had failed. The Iraqis tried deception and lies and they had failed. But he also knew that some where in the future there would be those who would try to dwarf the truth and control him. But they too would fail. He smiled to himself. Yes, he had changed.

*   *   *   *

When the plane landed in Stuttgart, Zack was surprised to see so many there to greet him and welcome him back. Col. Lowell

Davis was at the top of the gangway when the hatch was opened. When Zack appeared in the hatch opening, Col. Davis snapped a smart salute to honor him. "Damn! Welcome back, Captain. We all thought you had gone down with your plane. What's left of the crew are here to welcome you. You're a hero, Zack."

"Thanks, Colonel. It's good to be back. But I'm no hero."

When Zack stepped onto the gangway, Col. Davis noticed a limp in one leg and wondered if he'd make it down okay. "I'll be fine, Colonel." Davis also saw how his prolonged captivity had starved and weakened him. His clothes just hung on him. Once he was on the ground everybody rushed forward to greet him. A band played "When Johnny Comes Marching Home." Everyone wanted to shake his hand and pat him on the back and congratulate him for a job well done and for escaping from Hussein's best. No one asked how his escape was made possible or if anyone had helped him. They had a hero and that's all that seemed to matter.

Col. Davis ushered him to a car that was waiting next to the terminal. He would spend the next several days recuperating in the hospital. Dr. Reinhard was forceful. "You must stay in bed for three days and recover some lost weight and nutrition; your body is starving. You also have several fractured ribs, your left shoulder blade had been badly splintered but it has mended now. It will undoubtedly give you some problems when you are as old as I am, but until then you should be fine. Your left hip is dislocated. That has been causing the limp. I can wrap and bandage your ribs, and with rest and good food you will recover in no time." Reinhard set the x-rays down and called for an orderly to take Capt. Breinstein to his room. "Oh, Captain, one more thing, you will get the best food we can offer."

The next morning Col. Davis came to visit. They talked for hours. Davis was particularly interested with Col. Rushd's sudden interest into Northern Iraq, along Turkey's borders, where the Kurds had entrenched. He wanted to know about the attitudes of the Iraqi troops.

"They'll do anything Hussein asks," Zack replied.

"But why, when Hussein has led them into such desecration. He has sent his troops to the north to fire on the Kurds. He's killing his own people. Why do they continue to support him?"

"He's a persuasive man, Colonel. And because of their religion the Muslim people are taught submission from birth. They condone settling an argument with fighting." Zack tried to explain what he had learned about the differences between the lesser and the greater Jihad. And how through the centuries with the transition of leaders, how the lesser Jihad has commanded more attention. How it was being used as a spiritual excuse to wage war.

"How did you know about the U.N. Commission being in Ar-Ramadi? And how did you learn about the nuclear blueprints we were after?"

"Colonel," Zack scoffed, "all of Iraq knew about the commission and about Hussein's nuclear capabilities and his intention to use them against the world. The only ones that didn't know were the allied troops. After all, Colonel, isn't that the real reason we had to stop Hussein, and not the liberation of Kuwait? Intelligence, Colonel, used us, you and me, to do their dirty work. The same as Hussein deceives the Iraqis."

"It's not quite the same, Captain. It sounds as if perhaps you now think the war was wrong."

"No, Colonel. Hussein did have to be stopped. But my objection is the deception from Intelligence. The way Intelligence persuaded the Allied Forces to move against Hussein is no more condonable than the Islamic leaders using the lesser Jihad to wage their spiritual war."

Col. Davis was clearly agitated with Zack's comments about the abuse of power from Intelligence. He changed the subject. "How were you able to escape?"

"One of my captors realized the truth behind the Islamic fundamentals and Hussein's butchery and wanted to escape himself. One day I overpowered two of my captors and then

Kalidasa appeared in the doorway—well, Colonel, he helped right from that time."

"What became of him, Captain?"

Zack saw the trap before Col. Davis was through speaking. "Kalidasa said he would leave Iraq, after helping me to escape. He of course could have been executed for a traitor. He wanted to work with the Islamic movement and try to get the movement away from the lesser Jihad and back to practicing the greater. When the van door was closed, Kalidasa had already disappeared."

The conversation was changed to more pleasant subjects. Zack wanted to know about the rest of the squad. How each had come through the war. Had the squadron lost any more fighters? "No, there were no casualties, now that you're not dead." They talked about the squadron, and when the entire unit would return to Plattsburg. About hunting and fishing. About their wives and his family.

When Zack's noon meal was brought to him, Col. Davis got up, "It's time I got back to work. When you feel up to it, Captain, I'll need a full written report."

The colonel turned to leave, "Ah, Colonel?"

"Yes."

"There is one more thing you should know."

"What's that, Captain?"

"We didn't stop Hussein. Not permanently. He'll unite or try to unite all the Arab nations; sometime Sir, we'll be fighting him again."

Col. Davis didn't comment.

After the second day in bed Zack removed the bandages wrapping his broken ribs. The wrappings were too tight and he felt like he was suffocating. He was beginning to feel better already, and his skin color was taking on some tone. His face was filling out and in general he was tired of lying in bed. But whenever he tried to get out, an orderly was always there to stop him. Finally he submitted and stayed in bed. The report Col.

Davis wanted was completed, leaving him with a lot of time to think.

He thought about his roll in the war; had he fired any misguided rockets into civilian areas? Hospitals or schools? Was Hussein already rebuilding his beaten troops, for yet another avenging attack against the world? He thought about his captors and their cruel sadistic persuasions. If it had not been for Kalidasa would he be alive now? And then there was his dream that was, with each passing day, beginning to appear more reality than the awakened world around him. There he could find a greater objectivity to life with the reassurance of a serene and peaceful ambiance. He decided that once he was well and back home, he would try to find this place. He knew he had been there before, "But where do I look?"

CHAPTER ELEVEN

When Col. Davis left Zack's hospital room after their long conversation he went back to his office and told his secretary that he did not want to be disturbed. "And Sergeant you can take the afternoon off."

Lowell Davis sat at his desk with a worried look on his face. Of all the thousands of troops who had passed through the Mid-East and fought the Iraqi war, none had had the perception and understanding of the true events like Capt. Breinstein was now showing. Or had the tenacity to say or do anything about it. Here was one individual, one man who had escaped from Hussein's Talons who could now be a dangerous threat to Intelligence if he started talking. People wouldn't listen at first, but eventually someone would hear what was being said and they would ask more questions and eventually the triumph of victory and Intelligence's righteous standing would be underscored.

Could he sit by resignedly while one man, because of his perceptibility, threatened to decimate the valor and glory of a successful ploy? How had he known about Hussein's future intentions of uniting all the Arab Nations and some time in the future striking out again at the world? Had Zack only been guessing? Had he said it only because of bitter resentments for being left behind? Or had Intelligence leaked the information?

He paced back and forth in his office, smoking a chain of cigarettes. There was a smoky blue haze in the room that filtered towards the ceiling. He was beside himself with worry and anxiety. He didn't know what to do about Capt. Breinstein.

Was he worrying about Zack needlessly?

He decided finally to place a telephone call to Gen. Housman at the Pentagon. There were several transfers and eventually Housman's aide, Maj. Seams said, "Yes, how can I help you Col. Davis?"

"I need to speak with Gen. Housman."

"I'm sorry, Colonel, the General is in a meeting. Can I take a message?"

"No, Major. This is of the utmost importance and I must speak with him personally and immediately."

"Yes sir, I'll go get him."

"Who is it, Major?" Gen. Housman asked.

"Col. Davis, Sir, from Stuttgart."

Housman picked up the phone in his office. "What is it, Colonel? I was in an important conference."

"Gen. Housman, undoubtedly you must have heard of Capt. Breinstein's escape from Baghdad."

"Yes—what about it?"

"I think, Sir, he's going to be a problem."

"How do you mean?"

Col. Davis told Gen. Housman about Zack and how out of all the thousands of troops who had been in the Mid-East, he was the only one who was beginning to voice a deception by Intelligence. "Who has he been talking with, Colonel?"

"No one, except myself and the medical staff in the hospital." Davis went on to explain Zack's knowledge of the nuclear blueprints and how he had said that he believed Hussein would try to unite all the Arab Nations and attack again, sometime in the future.

It was obvious that Gen. Housman was irritated. People everywhere were still singing the hero's song and waving the flag. He didn't want some screwball to mess things up and stop the euphoria and turn the populace against the military, not just now as the majority of people were still supporting the invasion of Iraq and the liberation of Kuwait.

"Can you keep him quiet, Colonel?"

"I don't know."

"Well damn it man, give him a promotion and assign him to a new F-18 Fighter. I'll call someone in the public relations office and when he arrives back stateside, they'll arrange a parade for him in his honor. The press and TV cameras will be there. We'll do this right. He'll forget all about Intelligence's little subterfuge. That should inflate his ego enough to stop him messing with Intelligence. If that doesn't work—well we'll have to do something. I'll notify the Intelligence office, just in case. The Secretary, he may want to make some kind of a statement before Breinstein starts shooting his mouth off."

Col. Davis put the phone down and opened the top drawer of his desk and took out a new set of clover leaves. A major's insignia. He tossed them in his hand with an intense look on his face.

The next morning Col. Davis took Zack's promotion to him. "Good morning, Captain."

"Good morning, Sir," Zack said, puzzled about the early visit. He hadn't eaten breakfast yet or washed up.

"Captain, I was in touch with the Pentagon yesterday and Gen. Housman, and he has officially approved your promotion to Major. "Congratulations, Zack," Davis said and handed him the new major's insignias. "Oh, there's one more thing. You have been assigned to one of the new F-18 fighters when you return to Plattsburg."

Zack was speechless. He couldn't think what he had done to deserve a promotion and an F-18 assignment.

"How are you feeling now? Looks like you have put some weight back on."

"I feel fine—Dr. Reinhard still won't let me out of bed. My back and ribs are better."

"Good. You'll be home before you know it.

"Yes. We'll advise your family when you leave Stuttgart, so they can all be there for the hero's homecoming."

"Colonel, I'm no hero."

Davis left the room without commenting. Zack pushed his breakfast aside and laid back and stared at the ceiling. What was going on? He had done nothing to deserve a major's promotion.

The days passed and Zack regained his weight and vitality. He was allowed out of bed to exercise. He still limped but his back and ribs no longer hurt him. It was time to go home.

*   *   *   *

Dr. Reinhard discharged him from the hospital and Zack went to see Col. Davis, "Yes Major, what can I do for you?"

"I feel strong enough now to go home. I'd like to leave as soon as possible," Zack said.

Col. Davis checked with flight services and found a six o'clock flight the next evening. "There's nothing leaving before that, Colonel?"

"No, that's the best I could do. You'll stop over in Maine, at Bangor's International Airport. The plane will be refueled and you'll clear customs there. There will probably be a welcoming committee there also."

"That won't be necessary, Colonel. I only want to get back to my home."

"It's not up to me, Major. All of the returning troops have been welcomed home during their stop over in Bangor. Some Women's Christian League started it I think. From Bangor you'll fly to Newark Airport and then to Plattsburg. Oh yeah, I believe your wife and daughter are planning to join you in Newark."

The next day at 5:30 in the afternoon Zack boarded an American Airlines 747. He was given a seat in first class, not coach, by the airlines. "It's in appreciation for your part in the war," a stewardess told him. "I understand you escaped from one of Hussein's prisons. Is that right?"

"I was a hostage and I had help," Zack replied.

There were about thirty other servicemen returning state side. They rode second class coach. Once in the air, the flight captain came back and introduced himself to Zack and congratulated him for a successful and daring escape from Baghdad. The stewardess couldn't do enough to help him. All he wanted was to be left alone with his thoughts, but it was obvious he was going to be entertained all the way across the Atlantic. "Looks to me like someone doesn't want me to be alone," he said to one of the stewardesses.

"How do you mean?" she asked.

"The other thirty servicemen, are they getting the same treatment that I'm getting?"

Several hours later they landed at Bangor International Airport and before Zack walked down the long gangway he could hear the band playing in the main terminal. He was the first to disembark and when he entered the main terminal a strange lady came running towards him in tears, blessing him for helping to save the tiny country of Kuwait from that sadistic cult. She gave him a wreath made from flowers and hugged and kissed him.

Others in the main terminal seemed as eager to meet him and shake his hand. Some were saying how glad they were that he had returned safely. The other servicemen were being congratulated also, but not to the same degree. A colonel from the National Guard entered the terminal from another entrance and introduced himself to the returning men and to Zack he said, "I received a message from the Pentagon this morning from Gen. Housman. He said that you successfully escaped from Hussein's prison after eight months of captivity."

Before Zack could reply and tell the colonel the real truth about his captivity and his escape, the colonel interrupted and put his arm around Zack's shoulders while quieting the crowd. "Ladies and gentlemen, if I could have your attention please. Could I have your attention!" he said a little louder. "Ladies and gentlemen if I could have just a moment I'd like to introduce you to a real American Hero of the Gulf War. Maj.

Zachary Breinstein's plane went down over Baghdad and he was then captured by Hussein's elite guard while they were retreating from the front. He was held captive for eight months in one of Hussein's stinking prisons. Let's hear it for a conquering hero!" The whole terminal went up in cheers. Even the other servicemen joined in. Flash cameras were snapping and the television crews in the rear were busy filming the event.

Bennett closed the door behind them, shutting out the noisy crowd. "We'll stay in here until the plane is refueled and you all clear customs. The officials from customs have agreed to inspect your luggage in here away from the crowd."

"What was all that about out there, Colonel? I'm no damn hero! Who told you to fabricate that story? I've a mind to go out there and set the story straight."

"I wouldn't do that if I were you," Bennett said.

"Why not?"

"Look, Major, maybe I did stretch things a little. What harm can it do? Besides everybody needs a hero. Today you're their hero. It's my guess that your story has already gone to press anyhow. I sent my public relations man down to a press conference earlier and he gave the press guys your story. Just relax, Major, and enjoy all the attention. It'll all be over soon enough. Then everyone will have forgotten all about Maj. Breinstein and his heroic escape."

Zack sat down. Bennett was right. It was too late to do anything, at least for the moment. But he had already decided to set off a bomb shell at Newark. Gen. Housman was obviously responsible for this colorful ruse. He decided he could expect a similar reception in Newark. Only he would have his say then. For now he'd play the ruse. "I guess you're right, Colonel, what the heck, it's not going to hurt anyone."

The plane was refueled and the custom inspectors cleared the 31 servicemen. They boarded the plane and Zack decided to sit with the other men. "Sorry, Major, but you'll have to stay up here," one of the stewardesses said.

"What's the meaning of this? I only want to travel with the others."

"Sorry, Major, you'll have to stay here. They are enlisted aren't they?"

Housman had gotten to the airline, too. Who else had he contacted, and gotten to continue the subterfuge? Where would it all stop? Zack sat down and looked out the porthole. There has to be a reason why Housman didn't want him talking to people. Is he that afraid of the truth? Is Housman only an extension for Intelligence? "God what an insane world!" he said. The stewardess that he had been talking with looked at him and then went forward to the cockpit.

After the plane was airborne, Zack asked the stewardess for a pad of writing paper and a pen. He had had enough. He wasn't going to be part of a cover up any longer. He no longer needed the Air Force, Gen. Housman or Intelligence. When he finished writing his resignation he folded the pages and put them in his jacket pocket. Then reclined his seat back and dreamed of returning to that serenely beautiful world. If only he could remember where to look for it. He had been there, that he was certain of. And he'd find it again.

*   *   *   *

After the pilot had reached his flight altitude he set the automatic pilot and left the co-pilot in charge. He talked with the stewardess in the first class area briefly and then joined Zack. "How are you enjoying the flight, Major?"

"Fine, Captain," Zack supposed he had come to keep an eye on him, at Housman's direction.

"This must seem a little unusual for you, Major, after flying an F-15."

"Yes indeed, Captain. This is a Cadillac compared to a fighter."

"You must have seen some heavy combat over Iraq?"

Zack tried to sound excited and authentic, "You know if someone had told me beforehand how concentrated the anti-aircraft fire was going to be, I wouldn't have believed it. At times it seemed like we were flying into a fireworks display."

"Did you have any encounters with Iraqi fighters?"

"Before the invasion actually began my friend and I were attacked by three Mig fighters."

The captain stayed and talked with Zack until their final approach to Newark. "Better go forward now. Major—would you like to join me in the cockpit and see what it's like to land one of these babies?"

So to continue with the charade, Zack accepted the offer. He was genuinely impressed with the stateliness and its proportion. The captain brought the huge jetliner in with ease. As they were taxiing towards the main terminal Zack tried to visualize what Gen. Housman had assembled for a reception. Undoubtedly he would have gone to extremes to impress him and bolster his ego. He would have to play Housman's game a little longer. But before the day was over—. The captain interrupted his thoughts. "I've got orders to shut the engines down here and secure, away from the terminal and the crowds. The air terminal dispatcher says that the main terminal building is filled to capacity, with people and news media people, ready to welcome you home, Major."

The ground crew brought the gangway out and the door was opened. "Major," the stewardess said, "would you let the others disembark first? The captain says that Gen. Housman is coming aboard and wants to see you personally before the confusion starts. He is also bringing a surprise aboard with him."

Zack stepped aside and watched as the other servicemen disembarked and walked towards the terminal building. The crowds had broken through the security line and were rushing out to meet the men. It was a curious sight. People flocking over the men like they themselves had won the war. There was back slapping, hand shaking and a constant ring of congratulations.

When they disappeared back inside the terminal building Zack went back and sat down in the first class area.

He was deep in thought. Thinking about what he was going to do, once he was inside the terminal. And about the tomorrows. Where would he start his search for that peaceful tranquil world? He didn't know the general was aboard until he was standing next to the row of seats Zack was in. Zack turned his head to see who was there. He recognized the stars on his shoulders immediately, but not the man. He had never seen Housman before and he knew very little about him. He had rather expected to find him to be a heavy set tall man, too fat and balding. But instead he was looking at a medium build man, about his own height and weight, coal black piercing eyes and an energetic looking face.

In a smooth even voice, "Maj. Breinstein? I'm Gen. Housman."

Zack stood up and saluted. "That's not necessary, Major. After your ordeal in Iraq, it is I who should be saluting you."

"Thank you, General," Zack said trying to sound sincere.

"I came aboard so I could have a few moments alone with you before the crowds and confusion in the terminal building. Once you get inside there has been a stage erected and a podium with numerous microphones. The media would like to ask you some questions and of course take a few hundred pictures. You can cut the audience short if you wish. There will be a door to the rear of the stage and we can leave anytime you wish.

"I want to personally congratulate you, Major, for your successful escape and the valuable information you gave Col. Davis in Stuttgart. You have no idea, Major, of the remorsefulness we in the Pentagon felt when we learned from Col. Freedmont in Riyadh that you had not been killed when your F-15 exploded and the fact that you were held in prison in Baghdad without anyone knowing that you were still alive. Everyone had assumed that you were dead."

"No one is to blame Gen. Housman. It was just something

that happened from destiny. There was no way anyone could have known that I was alive. That's how my captors wanted to keep it. I was only a hostage for future use."

"I've read your personnel records. They seem quite impressive. I could use a man with your qualifications, Major. You don't have to give me an answer today, but think about it. There's a promotion that would go with the transfer."

Zack remained silent, thinking to himself. *The general was worried or he wouldn't be offering so much.* If he went to work for the Pentagon, then Housman could keep a close watch on him. That's what this is all about. Still only a ruse.

"Enough talk for now, Major. There are two people up forward who would very much like to see you. Again, Major, you have my deepest appreciation." Housman left and waited in the cockpit with Capt. Celfred while Zack was reunited with his wife and daughter.

There had been so much that had transpired since he said goodbye over a year ago, that he had seldom thought of his family. Now he was feeling guilty and tears filled his eyes as little Becky ran to her father and wrapped her arms around his legs. It was a joyous meeting for both Zack and Rachel, but it was far from being either romantic or blissful. It was a warm and affable reunion. They both had realized a long time ago that their marriage was lacking romance and vitality. They had agreed to stay together for the sake of their daughter.

When Rachel had been informed that her husband's fighter plane had exploded and that in all likelihood he had died in the explosion, she cried no tears. When Becky asked when her "Daddy" was coming home Rachel told her, that her father had gone away. A long ways from home and would not ever be coming back.

Zack picked Becky up in his arms and walked over to Rachel. They embraced and kissed and she said, "I'm glad you're okay. Becky has been so excited ever since we heard you were alive and would be coming home." They sat down in the seats,

Becky in her father's lap. They talked sociably, but not like two people in love who had been separated for months. Zack knew in his heart that there was no use in pretending. Nothing had changed between them.

Gen. Housman came back and broke up an awkward moment. "Sorry to have to rush you and your family, Major, but we can't wait any longer. Everybody is waiting for us inside the terminal."

"We're ready, General," Zack said as he looked at Rachel.

As soon as Gen. Housman appeared in the hatchway of the plane the band began to play. He led the way down the gangway and across the loading area to the terminal. Another band and an honor guard came around from behind the plane and marched behind them.

The terminal was alive with people. When Zack walked through the doors and down the passageway everybody began to applaud. Zack looked around in disbelief. He had anticipated that Intelligence would go to extremes to patronize him, but he had not expected anything so huge and eloquent. He was beginning to wish he was an actual hero. But he knew in his own conscience that he wasn't. Intelligence had gone to a lot of work and expense to continue with their charade. He began to wonder to what extent Intelligence would go to keep the masses believing what had been told to them about Kuwait, Iraq, Hussein and Hussein's nuclear capabilities. If he was considered a threat to them and their purpose, would he be endangering his family?

He laughed out loud then. Of course they would. But his death would be implemented first probably, before his wife or daughter was hurt. "What are you laughing about?" Rachel asked. "These people are here in your honor," she sounded disgusted. He didn't answer.

People were shouting "hero" and "congratulations" and Zack waved back at the people. Once on the platform that had been erected for a temporary stage, Gen. Housman seated himself at center stage, directly behind the microphone. Zack, Rachel and

Becky were on his left and on his right were two men in civilian clothes. Zack guessed they were probably U.S. Senators. The band played another rendering of the hero's song.

When they had finished Gen. Housman got up and walked up to the podium. Everybody began to applaud. Housman waited until it was quiet.

In that same smooth voice Gen. Housman addressed the audience.

"Ladies, gentlemen, friends and colleagues, I have the pleasure and great honor today to introduce you to one of the true heroes of the Gulf War. It is all too seldom that we have the opportunity to honor one of our own for exemplary service. In a lot of circumstances the individual had been killed while performing an extraordinary task and only then is he honored posthumously.

"Maj. Breinstein's F-15 was brought down over Iraq while returning from a successful mission over Baghdad, where he was instrumental in destroying Hussein's air base and taking out several of his prized Soviet Mig fighters.

"Without food or water for four days Maj. Breinstein eluded Hussein's reputed elite guard and was crossing the Iraqi desert on foot when he was captured by Col. Abdel and his retreating troops. They had abandoned their positions at the front and were returning to Baghdad.

"In Baghdad, Maj. Breinstein was thrown into a foul smelling prison. Allied bombs dropped all around him daily. He was interrogated and tortured almost daily. He had little food and almost no water. Yet he persevered, when many would have given up.

"When Hussein finally surrendered, Maj. Breinstein was secretly moved from the prison and then again relocated. He was no longer a prisoner of war, but because the Iraqis accused him of being an Israeli spy, because of his name, he was now a hostage. To be used at some future time as a trade off for Iraqi terrorists.

"Maj. Breinstein survived the numerous beatings and eventually gained the confidence of one of his captors. Working together they managed to subdue the other two Iraqi captors and successfully escaped to Ar Ramadi where they were met by the U.N. Nuclear Commission that was on inspection in Iraq.

"It is all too seldom that men of Maj. Breinstein's caliber are recognized among our fighting men and women. Maj. Breinstein never gave up hope of escape, where many of us, if in his particular situation, might have. He is certainly an inspiration to us all, and exemplifies what it means to be an American.

"Now I'm sure all of you good people didn't come here to listen to me. In a moment I'll turn the stage over to Maj. Breinstein for a few words. If the media wants to ask any questions about his ordeal, after he has had a chance to speak, I'm sure Maj. Breinstein will answer them. I only ask that you try to cut it short so that the Major can spend some time with his family." Gen. Housman turned then and addressed Zack directly, "Maj. Breinstein I want to personally thank you for your roll in the Gulf War, the President sends his deepest appreciations and wished he could have been here to greet you. The American people everywhere thank you, Major."

Zack stood up and walked forward to meet the General and shake his outstretched hand. "Thank you, General." Zack took out his resignation and handed it to Gen. Housman and then took center stage at the podium. The General sat down and put Zack's resignation in his coat pocket without opening it.

The audience stood and applauded. It was a deafening sound that vibrated through the terminal. Zack could even feel it. He stood behind the podium with his hands firmly resting on each side. He turned briefly to look at Rachel and little Becky and then turned back to address the audience. "Ladies, gentlemen and friends, thank you for this truly heart warming reception." Gen. Housman was breathing a sigh of relief. "There really isn't much more that I can say that Gen. Housman has not already addressed. Only, I certainly don't feel like a hero. The Air Force programmed me to fly an F-15 fighter and that's what I did. As I was returning from Baghdad my port engine caught on fire and while I was attempting to blow out the flames by diving, the fighter exploded. I ejected just before the explosion.

"Although I don't believe what I did or what I was subjected to as being of any heroic valor, the Air Force certainly must because I was given a Major's promotion and given an assignment to one of the new F-18 fighters.

"There isn't much more I can say, only that I thank you again for this warm reception. And it's certainly good to be home."

A news lady stood up in the front tow, "Major, are you bitter towards the Iraqis and especially towards your captors and the ones who beat you?"

"No, I'm not. I only feel compassion towards the Iraqi people because they are being misguided by illusion and a tyrant. As for my captors, two of them were killed during my escape."

Another media person, "Major, when did you first learn of your promotion?"

"While I was in the hospital at Stuttgart, Germany. Col. Lowell Davis had said that the promotion had been sanctioned by the Pentagon."

"Are you aware of any other promotions resulting from the Gulf War, Major?"

"At this time I am not, but this is only my first day back in the states. I should like to hope that I was not the only serviceman promoted."

A newsman standing in the back caught Zack's attention. "Major, we have all heard of conflicting reports coming out of Iraq of innocent people being killed in schools and hospitals. While you were in Baghdad did you see any or were you aware of any schools and hospitals being bombed?"

"I never saw any for myself, but then I never saw much of Baghdad. Col. Rushd and one of my captors said that schools and hospitals were being targeted. But no, I don't have any personal knowledge that any were bombed."

"While you were held hostage, Major, did you ever see Saddam Hussein?"

"No."

The same reporter, "Major, do you feel Hussein has been stopped from future aggression?"

"No. Even now he is rebuilding his losses and it is my opinion that once he rebuilds Iraq, he will try to unite all Muslims and all the Arab Nations and strike out again at the world."

"Will his own people overpower him and put a stop to his ideals?"

"Sadly, no. For centuries the Muslim people in the Mid East have been suppressed to the point where most of the people can no longer think for themselves. They have no imagination, they cannot act or react on their own without the fear of retribution. From birth they have been forced into submission until it has become a way of life. Submission has been ingrained so forcefully that it has literally become part of their culture. No, the Iraqis will not overthrow him."

Another woman in the front stood up. "Major, first let me thank you for taking the time to answer our questions. In light of what you have just said, do you hold the Islamic cult responsible for the savage attacks on themselves, the Jews and against others of different religious beliefs?"

"First of all, Islam, true Islam, is not a cult. If practiced according to how Muhammad interpreted God's message and wrote the principles in the Koran, then Islam is a very compassionate, forgiving and self purifying belief."

"Would you explain that further, Major? You seem to know a considerable more about Islam than do most of us?" the woman asked.

"Well," Zack began, "Jihad, the Muslim term for their holy war is in my opinion nothing more than an excuse to wage spiritual warfare against those they call infidels. Also known as the lesser Jihad. I think in the beginning Muhammad instructed his followers to fight openly against an outward attack on

Islamic beliefs. Today's Muslim leaders seem to use this concept to justify outward aggression against anyone.

"There's another holy war, called the Greater Jihad, and this is the Jihad that Muhammad stressed to his followers that should take precedence over everything else in a Muslim's life."

"Just what is this Greater Jihad, Major?" the same woman asked.

"I believe it's the purifying of one's inner self. I don't know anymore about it than that. One of my captors, Kalidasa, the one who helped me to escape and later to find the U.N. Commission was explaining what the Greater Jihad was, but there wasn't enough time for him to go into great depths. From any logical viewpoint anyone could assume that perhaps any religious prophet would stress the purifying of one's inner self over openly attacking an aggressor."

"Why did this captor, Kalidasa, I think you called him, want to help you? An American who had helped to defeat the Iraqi Army? And from your last name I would assume that you are Jewish. Doesn't that seem a little odd?" a man asked not bothering to stand up to address his questions.

"First, although my name is Hebrew, that doesn't make me Jewish unless I follow the Jewish teachings. Kalidasa decided to help me because he saw the truth behind what Hussein was doing and how he and others were openly abusing the Islamic principles. Mainly, Hussein's interpretation of his holy-war. Jihad. He wants to help Muslims everywhere to learn the importance of the Greater Jihad and stop warring against others beliefs."

Zack paused to catch his breath and to collect his thoughts. He looked around the crowd that had gathered. Scanning their expressions but not actually seeing the people themselves. That is not until he saw a familiar face in the middle of the audience. Kalidasa had indeed found his way to America. And now for a brief moment he and Zack held each others gaze and smiled.

"Major," another man asked, standing up this time to

address his questions. "You seem to be fond of the one called Kalidasa. Even though he later helped you to escape, he was still an enemy. Also, Major, what became of him when you found the U.N. Commission?"

"When I was first turned over as a captive in Baghdad, Kalidasa and two others kept me locked up in a small room. Later I was moved to another building. As time passed Kalidasa saw and understood the lies being told and taught about Islam. He helped me to escape because he had had enough of Hussein's politics," he looked at Kalidasa. He was smiling. "He wanted to help Muslims everywhere to get back to the basic concepts of Islam and to put emphasis on the Greater Jihad. When I got into the van with the U.N. Commission I turned to look at Kalidasa but he had already disappeared. He had said he would have to leave Iraq because he would be considered a traitor for helping me and in order for him to help turn around the Islamic movement, he would have to escape to another country, where his thoughts and imagination would not be suppressed.

"I haven't seen him since Ar-Ramadi. And yes I consider him a friend and I hope he succeeds with his ideas." He looked again at Kalidasa.

"Maj. Breinstein—Saddam Hussein has made repeated threats that he'll continue the war through terrorist activities. He made explicit remarks that the United States would be targeted. Do you believe he'll follow up on his threats?"

"Yes, I do. He is driven by anger and an inflated ego. He'll have to save face with his own people and the only way he can do that until he has rebuilt his country and his military strength, is through terrorist activities. It's a cowardly way to seek revenge, but he sees no shame in killing innocent people."

Gen. Housman was sitting on a knife's edge. Zack had not been too defiant yet, although Housman could read more into what he was saying than probably most of the audience. He was uneasy and wished Zack would finish now before more damaging statements were made.

A young woman in the front row directly in front of Zack stood up. She seemed too young to be a reporter and very timid. Before she was through Zack would change his opinion of her.

"Maj. Breinstein, it is a well known fact that the war with Iran had cost Saddam Hussein a great deal of money. Do you believe that his sole purpose of invading Kuwait and then annexing the country was only for the rich oil fields there?"

"I think he annexed Kuwait to show the United States that he was deadly serious about keeping Kuwait under Iraqi control. As far as the oil fields are concerned, you may be correct with your assumption. But there is one thing that you must also take into consideration. Before the interference by the British, Kuwait was an integral part of Iraq. I believe he definitely wanted the rich oil fields and he possibly considered that they actually and rightfully belonged to Iraq."

Gen. Housman was beside himself. Here it was coming. And there was nothing he could do right at the moment to prevent it. If he tried to stop Zack, the audience, the news media and the television camera crews would surely pick up on his interference and would want to know why. He sat nervously in his seat worrying about how Zack would respond.

When he made the statement about the British interference of Iraq and Kuwait there was a distinct murmur that seemed to engulf the entire audience.

The same young woman asked, "Major, would you explain what you said about the British interference? I don't recall ever hearing anything about it."

"I'm surprised," he replied, talking directly to the young woman. "I would have assumed that before writing front page articles about Iraq, Kuwait or the Gulf War, that a minimum amount of research into the history of that area would have been a prerequisite. Before the start of WWI, Germany wanted to extend the Berlin-Baghdad railroad to the port of Kuwait. Great Britain wanted to frustrate Germany's designs and declared Kuwait a protectorate. Not until 1961 did Kuwait gain independence from

Great Britain. Then in order to protect Kuwait from becoming an integral part of Iraq again, the United Nations accepted Kuwait's independence and membership into the League of Nations and Iraq's claim to Kuwait was once again frustrated."

"Why haven't we heard of this before now?" the young woman asked.

"Perhaps no one wanted you to know," Zack looked at Kalidasa again.

The young woman sat down disillusioned.

A short fat man in the front row stood up and asked Zack, "Major—in light of what you have just told us, then in your opinion was the Gulf War justified?"

Gen. Housman was sweating. There was no way he could keep Zack from answering. Not now.

"Hussein had to be stopped, there's no doubt about that. But we—all of us, should have been told the truth about what was happening over there. Instead, Intelligence fed us a bunch of lies and deceptions."

"In your opinion, Major, what were we actually fighting for in the Mid East?" the man asked.

"In my opinion?"

"Yes."

"To stop Hussein from further developing the nuclear bomb. It is also my opinion that once he had the bomb, he surely would have used it."

"Against whom?" the same man asked.

"Probably Israel."

Another man in the back row asked, "How are you so sure he had the nuclear bomb and would use it? You were a hostage of Iraq when the war ended."

"That's true I was and I was never sure when the fighting actually stopped. But everyone in Baghdad knows about the bomb Hussein was building. They also know that Hussein's engineers attended a nuclear seminar here in the United States and then they returned to Iraq with enough information to start development on the bomb."

In a quiet soft voice the young woman in the front row stood up, "Maj. Breinstein, you just said a minute ago that you were lied to and deceived by Intelligence. Are you free to tell us how that happened?"

"Yes, I can tell you," Zack turned to look at Gen. Housman. He was red with anger. But he didn't try to stop him. How could he? "Before the Allied Forces invaded Kuwait and Iraq's border, I was routinely assigned recon flights over the interior of Iraq. Repeated flights over the same area. It was obvious that Intelligence was looking for something of great importance. Finally, only days before the onset of the fighting, we were told that Intelligence had been searching for installations, laboratories where the nuclear work on the bomb was being done. At the time, Intelligence was more concerned about this than the pillage and killings occurring in Kuwait. Although the front page news stories never said anything about the nuclear facilities we were looking for. The news media were only being given the horror side of Hussein's campaign."

"But wouldn't you agree that maybe Intelligence was only protecting the reasons of your recon flights. You wouldn't expect Intelligence to openly tell Hussein what they were searching for, would you?"

"The point is Intelligence had no reason to lie about our purpose there. What we were doing flying over Iraq before the war started. I personally don't like being lied to.

"In my opinion," Zack continued, "Intelligence used Hussein's annexation of Kuwait as a justifiable reason to go after his nuclear capabilities."

There were a lot of loud whisperings and people interrupting others trying to ask Zack more questions. Some were openly defying him for what he had said. He looked again at Kalidasa and remembered something he had said back in Ar-Ramadi, "Maybe people won't want the truth."

Zack looked around him. Perhaps not. Kalidasa had

gotten up from his seat and was leaving. Gen. Housman got up and walked up behind Zack. "Major, I think we better leave." Zack looked at his wife. She too was disgusted. Becky ran to her daddy. Outside the terminal as Gen. Housman led Zack and his family to an awaiting limousine, "You just finished your military career, Major! What in hell do you think you were doing? We'll have hell to pay now, trying to quiet this!"

Zack turned around and squared off to face the General, "That's what this is all about, isn't it, General? The promotion, the assignment to a new F-18 fighter, and this pretentious hero's welcome! It's all designed to continue the cover up! To hell with the truth. And the facts mustn't underscore the grand Intelligence's scheming. General, my military career was ended when I handed you my resignation!"

"What! What are you saying?" Gen. Housman stammered. He took out the papers Zack had given him earlier and read them. There was nothing more he could say. He got in the limousine and drove off. Zack hailed a cab and took his family to a hotel in Elizabeth, New Jersey.

*   *   *   *

That night in his Pentagon office, Gen. Housman picked up his telephone and punched his special coded number. A voice answered on the other end. "Yes?"

"Mr. Secretary. This is Gen. Housman. We have serious problems."

"What kind of problems?"

"Maj. Breinstein," Housman replied.

"I've already heard."

"What do we do now, Mr. Secretary?"

"Damn it, Housman! Breinstein is one of your boys! You do whatever you have to to shut him up!"

"Mr. Secretary, he resigned his commission in the Air Force today."

"Then why in hell did you let him near the media!"

"Mr. Secretary. He handed me his resignation as he walked to the podium. I didn't have any idea that the papers would be his resignation and I put them in my pocket without reading them." Gen. Housman went on to explain why he couldn't stop him from talking with the news media there. That it would only raise more questions.

There was a long quiet pause. Finally, "Housman, do whatever is necessary to keep him quiet."

*   *   *   *

That night after Becky had fallen asleep, Rachel questioned Zack about what he had said to the news media. She found it difficult to understand or believe that the American Intelligence had deliberately deceived the people. "Why did you resign from the Air Force? I don't understand you Zack. You were promoted to Major, for Gods sake. Can't you be a little humble and accept it graciously?"

Zack tried to explain how the promotion was only another ruse, to keep him from talking. Something Intelligence was apparently good at. But she didn't want to hear it. She firmly believed that Intelligence and the military knew what they were doing and whatever was done, was done in the best interest of the people.

"What happened to you Zack in Iraq? You've always been stubborn and ready to challenge any cause or authority, but you're worse now. What happened to you, Zack?" she pleaded.

"Perhaps I can finally understand things more clearly now and see through the illusions."

They went to bed and tried to lose themselves from the subtleties of the world on the outside of their motel room, in passionate sexual bliss. Something Zack had completely forgotten all about. He tried to think when the last time he had made love to Rachel. It was before he left over a year ago, but even then he wasn't sure how long it had been before he left. They both went through the motions but there was no romance on either one's part. Their lovemaking was a disappointment to them both.

Rachel fell asleep soon after. Zack lay on his back wide awake, the events of the day running through his mind. The whole day had been staged by Intelligence. He could see it clearly now. In hopes he would be so flattered with his promotion, the F-18 and the hero's welcome home that his ego would be so inflated, he'd forget about the truth.

He thought about seeing Kalidasa at the terminal and wondered how he had managed to get there. Would he be more successful with his task?

Then he began to think about what he would do now that he had resigned from the Air Force. He wanted to tell people about the lies and deceptions of Intelligence. The television was on and he was scanning the stations with the remote control and stopped on a station that was about to broadcast the late evening news. He wanted to see if his welcome home celebration would be on the news.

It was, but when Zack had started to tell the audience about the lies and deceptions, the cameras had stopped filming. Had Intelligence intervened there, or was it just a freak coincidence?

How much better off would everyone be if they could see and understand the ultimate truth behind their everyday events? He certainly was. But would everybody? Perhaps some. But it's very likely that everyone is exactly where they are supposed to be, according to their own understanding. Then would knowing the truth be of any consequence to them or benefit? Did everyone want the truth? Probably not. That's what Kalidasa had warned him about.

He turned the television off and laid back in his bed. He decided to give up the task of telling people the truth about the Gulf War. It was evident that the country wanted heroes to come home from the war and not answers. He knew and he supposed that would have to be enough. He laid back and switched his attention to the other world he had visited in his dreams. How that world was becoming more reality than the world he was now in.

He didn't yet know where he would find this beautiful land that was so quiet and tranquil or how he would go about finding it. But he was sure that it did exist. Perhaps this world lay hidden just beyond the physical senses. A world he would have to perceive. "Who was it that had taught me to perceive? I know there was someone. Who was it?" On his inner vision he could see a familiar silhouette. The person's face and features were obscured. But there was something subtly familiar.

All night, images flashed through his mind, some alarming, some serene and pleasurable. By morning he had given up the idea of campaigning across the countryside telling people the truth about the Mid East war. He knew and that would have to be enough.

Rachel was still upset about the changes she saw in her husband. Secretly she was beginning to think about a divorce. At breakfast she ate in silence. Zack and Becky carried on an endless chatter.

After breakfast they went back to the Newark Airport and booked a flight back to New York. The drive from Plattsburg to their home in Vermont would be a welcome relief. It would mark the end to this odyssey of truth. They would be home by mid-afternoon. He would have time for a walk in the hills behind his home.

Somehow that idea was becoming more and more important, pressing him to hurry home. Could his answers be hidden there? Somewhere along the well used foot path? He wasn't sure, only that the idea kept pressing him to hurry.

CHAPTER TWELVE

At a little past mid afternoon Zack drove down his own driveway. Not much had changed during the last fourteen months. It was early September and already the foliage was beginning to change. Promising an early and cold winter ahead.

Rachel and Becky went into the house. Zack took out their luggage and carried it in. He didn't have much. Rachel had not said anything after leaving Newark and she was still silent, probably thinking about asking Zack for a divorce.

Zack went outside and unlocked the garage and then walked around the yard. It was a real joy to be standing in his own yard. Not having to worry about flying over enemy territory, the beatings from his captors or when he would eat again. All that was behind him now. He walked behind the woodshed and saw the footpath leading up into the hills. He went back in the house and told Rachel he was going for a walk before supper. "Nothing has changed, has it Zack? You spend more time walking in those hills than you do with me. Go on if that's what you want."

Zack closed the door behind him without answering. The cool September air felt refreshing as he inhaled deeply. He was still weaker than he thought, after the long months of captivity. He was limping still and had to stop often to catch his breath and to enjoy the view of the Green Mountains behind him, as he ascended the hill. There was no hurry now. No pressing urgency to find the path and climb the hill. He was here. And he was beginning to feel at home, at one with himself.

He walked on, stopping often to watch a squirrel race on

227

ahead, or to scan the countryside and enjoy what he had missed. As often as he had walked along the path, before going to the Mid East, he had never seen anyone else along the well used path. Yet, the path was already there when he and Rachel had bought the old house.

At the top of the hill he sat down on the grass and pulled his legs up under his chin. It was a beautiful day. The sky was blue and a little breeze that kept the autumn flies away. He hadn't enjoyed a day like this since he left the hilltop fourteen months ago. He sat quietly enjoying his surrounds. Then the thought came to him. He had walked through some kind of portal before, when he had noticed things were different. Would he be able to re-enter this same portal again from this side, walking along this path? Somehow he felt reassured that he would.

He got up, stretched and walked on, following the path over the top to an area where small hardwood trees lined either side of the path and formed a canopy overhead. The leaves were already a crimson yellow. He found a large rock beside the path and sat down. How he had enjoyed this particular spot in the past. Here the worries of the world didn't seem as though they could find him hidden below the crimson canopy. It was so peaceful. The only sound was that of the birds.

Beside the rock grew a cluster of wild violets. Deep varying shades of vibrant purple and the center at the base of the ovary was yellow with a black dot. Zack picked a blossom and thought how strange to find them growing in early autumn. They were usually a spring and early summer flower. The petals were unusually large, and it had a very sweet perfume scent to it.

He held the delicate flower cupped in his hands. Wondering how such a small piece of the physical world could become so intricate and exacting. A perfect specimen of the grand architectural work, surely it didn't grow to perfection by accident. Zack looked closer; how each petal was constructed. Veins from the stem extending up and spreading throughout the blossom, bringing nourishment from the ground. He was following the design of the veins through the petal. They looked like a river spreading out like a delta. He looked closer and saw how the petals were not as skin smooth as he had first thought. There was depth to the petals, a texture like soft velvet. He found himself going deeper and deeper into the violet blossom, falling downward towards the yellow patch at the ovary.

Zack was no longer aware of anything around him; the foot path, the crimson canopy, the cluster of violets growing beside the rock, or the rock he was sitting on. He was inside the blossom and acutely aware of its divinity. He let himself go free, falling towards the center of this perfect specimen of life. As he traveled further and further into the blossom he could hear the sound of a roaring river. It was the life support; nectar in the veins flowing outward to nourish each petal, each living cell.

He turned his attention once again to the yellow area at the base of the ovary. He was so deep within the blossom all he could see was the radiant yellow. It surrounded him like a shroud. The vibrant purple was gone, out of sight. He became aware of a pulsating heartbeat and knew it was only his own echoing in his ears. He traveled to the base of the ovary and stood in the radiant golden yellow cloud. The texture of the blossom here was even softer and more delicate than the vibrant purple petals. He was suspended in the middle of this, glowing yellow light, was his only description, much like standing in the middle of a fluffy cloud, if that were possible.

He looked back to see the petals again, but suddenly realized that he didn't have to turn his head or his attention. He could see the entire blossom from where he was. He was minutely aware of every detail. The glowing yellow shroud was beginning to engulf him. He struggled trying to remain above it. But he couldn't struggle. He had no legs, no arms. He didn't have a body; only the blossom.

"I am the blossom," he said firmly, "and the heartbeat is my own and also that of the violet blossom. The nectar flowing in the veins out to nourish the petals is my own! Flowing to nourish myself. I have been here before! Only then somehow I managed to travel even deeper into the flower." He stopped struggling and let himself be carried away by the essence of his own true self.

There was a faint humming. It seemed to be at a distance. He listened as he let himself be carried away. The humming was getting deeper and more euphonic. He listened intently. The sound filled the atmosphere. "It is coming from the heart of the flower. Myself!"

As his understanding grew more acute and penetrating, his fluid motion slowed to a stop. He was filled with the melodious humming and overwhelmed with blissful joy.

*   *   *   *

He was consumed with blissful joy. Overwhelmed with his rediscovery. Things began to move again. Only now he was ascending, instead of descending into the blossom. His new awareness remained with him as did the melodious humming.

He was standing on the footpath. The crimson tree canopy was gone. The rock and cluster of violets were gone. And his clothes and shoes were gone. He wore instead a saffron colored robe. Birds singing filled the air. The blue indigo sky was replaced with pastel colors. Zvi smiled. "I made it back," he said, "I found my way home. Through all the illusions, lies and deceptions, I have come home." He was back in Brahm's World. He had to see the Old One. He started walking down the path that followed the stream to his hut.

He walked along the well used path thinking of his new surroundings and what he was leaving behind in Zachary Breinstein's world. A world full of lies, deceptions and untruths. A nightmarish world indeed. Nobody there wanted to know the truth. Much like the village he had left at the other end of the enchanted valley. There his family and friends were content to know only what the Over Lords were willing to dispense to them. For fourteen months of physical time, Zvi had lived in a world full of illusions. Lies, deception and beatings could not make him submit to the will of others. Never again would he ever have to return to that world for other lessons. He was now above, what that world could offer.

As he walked along the path he couldn't help but notice that the colors seemed to be more vibrant and virtual then he had remembered. He looked at the flowers and plant life that grew along side the path and knew he was also looking at himself. He was the flowers, the grass, the trees, the water and the soil all in one. The same as the Old One was also, all of these. This is what the Old One had been teaching. And only now could he fully understand and appreciate what he had learned. He felt ecstatic with his new discovery.

He had an impetuous urge to run along the path in search of the Old One, to tell him of his ordeal in the lower world and of his new awareness. Instead, he walked amiably, enjoying his enlightenment, his freedom and his release from the physical body. It was confining and suffocating. He remembered the journey the Old One had taken him on, into the far reaches of the universe. How extraordinary that experience had been. He recalled looking back on all the celestial bodies and universes, thinking that combined, they had composed a body or object of some sort. And the Old One telling him that in time he would discover this mystery. Still, he wondered at this macro-form that contained everything in the universe, "I must know," he said aloud.

The hut was empty. Everything was as neat and tidy as it had ever been. Zvi laughed out loud at himself. He knew where to find the Old One; the atmosphere was alive with thought forms emanating from the Old One. He knew Zvi had returned and was searching for him. In his newly discovered awareness Zvi was able to interpret these electrifying impressions and turn them into visible images. The Old One was on the hilltop, awaiting his arrival. But why there?

Zvi followed the trail. Excitement of seeing his mentor and friend again, was building inside him. Would the Old One be as happy to see me? He wondered. He followed the trail around a bush that was growing beside the trail and saw the Old One standing erect on a rocky pinnacle. He walked slowly, not wanting to interrupt the Old One or startle him. But he should have known the Old One was aware of his approach.

"Hello my young friend."

Zvi smiled as he looked at the Old One. "You knew I was coming?"

"Yes, I could feel your vibrations well ahead of you. Come let us sit down and enjoy the beauty before us. And you can tell me about your adventure into the earth world." The Old One moved back aware from the pinnacle and sat upon a moss covered rock.

Zvi didn't know where to start. There were a thousand questions that needed answers. "It was—," he stopped and then tried again, "It now seems to be only a nightmare, although I know I was actually there as Capt. Breinstein. As time passes since my return here, the memories are very vivid, yet the experience also seems more like a dream."

The Old One chuckled, "You have learned another lesson my friend. To those living in the world you left behind, for them that is reality, only because they know nothing of this world. They are living more or less in a dream that they haven't yet awakened from. Your situation was a little different. Which of the two worlds, Zvi, are more real to you?"

"This world, of course. But why did I go there?"

"That will be answered for you later."

"That world actually does exist?"

"Yes," the Old One replied.

"Then I didn't follow the path that morning just by accident, did I."

"No, it was a test. You'll be told more later."

In a more serious tone Zvi asked, "Now that I am back

and that world does actually exist and it wasn't all a bad dream, then Zachary Breinstein also exists, then what becomes of him now that I have returned to this world?"

The Old One began, "In order for any of us in this world to personalize in the lower earth world, we must have a vehicle to embody. In your case it was Zachary Breinstein's body. You are well aware of the problems existing between Zack and his wife Rachel. They were both unhappy. Zack would often walk along the trail behind his house to be alone and contemplate his unhappiness. The day you entered Zack's physical body, his inner body left and came to this world for a rest. He is now back in his own earthly body and the only memories he'll have of this world will be as a fading dream. And soon that will be gone too."

"In the earth world, Old One, people there thrive on hate and fighting. That whole world exists to fight. They have invented some terrible machines of war, and the people are coarser in their understanding than we are also. They have difficulty seeing through the lies and deception, and rarely know truth. There is an entity there, called Intelligence, that controls people's thoughts and actions, the same as the Over Lords do in the village across the valley. They demand conformity of will and action and use deception and intimidation to keep the people submissive. The same as the Over Lords.

"What seemed naturally simple for me in that world, to the earth people was confusing and often misinterpreted and misunderstood."

"That's because you have learned to perceive," the Old One replied and smiled.

"There is a whole lot more that exists that lies far beyond the limits of Brahm's world, isn't there, Old One? This is only the beginning to what lies beyond. When you took me on the journey through the grand universes and we saw all, and all the celestial bodies seen together actually composed a macro body or form of some kind, and when I asked about it, you said there was no need of my knowing. There is more that lies beyond this world, isn't there? I mean there's more beyond—a greater understanding still than what can be learned here."

The Old One nodded his head approvingly, but didn't answer his questions directly. "I can clearly see that you have greatly expanded your enlightenment. Only yesterday it seems that you first crossed the valley from the village, ready to challenge openly the teachings and counsels of the Over Lords. And here you are now ready to challenge the Great Brahm. You amaze me, Zvi. I don't think that I have ever had a pupil with your zest for knowledge and truth."

Before either the Old One or Zvi could say anything further the ground began to rumble like a huge quake ready to tear open the land and spill forth its bowels. The birds stopped their singing and flew for shelter. All remained quiet except for the deep throated rumbling. In alarm Zvi asked, "What is happening, Old One?"

"There is no need of worry or concern. You are about to receive a great honor. Brahm is preparing to speak to you. He seldom or if ever speaks directly to anyone who resides in His world. There is no need to fear."

"Will I see him, Old One?"

"No, no. He doesn't appear except what you can see around you."

The Old One and Zvi both stood up and walked forward to the rocky pinnacle. The wind blew their hair. Dust clouds from the valley floor rose high in the air and then were blown away. Bolts of lightening streaked across the sky. Zvi waited in nervous anticipation. Had he said something to offend Braham? The ground stopped its rumbling. The lightening bolts flashed once more and then disappeared. The wind stopped blowing. Everything was quiet.

"Zvi!" Brahm's voice rumbled, echoing throughout the land. "You have surprised me indeed. The Old One said he had faith in your understanding and that you would find your way back to my World. I did not believe him. I thought you weak and lacking enough fortitude to help yourself!" He laughed and the ground rumbled.

"Why did you open that portal and send me to the earth world?" Zvi asked, but not demanding.

Brahm laughed again and the ground shook and rumbled until even the Old One thought the hill would collapse. "You! You puny being! You stand on that rocky pinnacle and dare challenge Me! Brahm! I can destroy you as easily as swatting a fly!"

"You sent me to that world and I was tortured and beaten, and I struggled and found my own way back. That gives me the right to now stand before you and ask, why?"

Brahm laughed again, his deep melodious voice rolling off the mountain tops to the valley floor below. "I allow you to stand before me! I allow you, because you have proven your virtue, and you are, indeed, a warrior. There are some who have crossed the valley in search of wisdom and the Old One's guidance who have not been pure of heart or courageous enough to travel beyond.

"You crossed to this side of the valley being warned beforehand of a sorcerer who lives here and the forest was enchanted. But you crossed regardless. Because your need for truth and answers outweighed the dangers. You were beset by illusions and you saw your way through them. You sought after the Old One's guidance. He taught you well!

"Yes indeed, I provided the way for your entrance into My Lower World. Earth, the lowest of all my worlds. An ashcan would be a better depiction. There, you were stripped of all memories of this land, and the Old One's teachings. It was a test to see if you had learned anything at all from the Old One's instructions. I needed proof that you could see your way clear of illusions to the truth which always lay behind the deceptions."

"I chose the crisis in the Mid East, the Jew against the Muslim and vice-versa. These two religious factions have been fighting against each other since the beginning of time and shall continue fighting until the earth world is finally destroyed. You were put into the middle of this conflict to see if you could discover the truth on your own initiative. And once you had the truth lying in your hands, to see what you would do with it. Whether you would choose the path of lies and deception and continue fighting, looking for revenge against those who had beaten you, or whether you would choose the path of truth and continue to look for the way back to your true home.

"After you had the truth you were showered with material gifts to inflate your ego and make you forget the truth. You were promoted, you were assigned to a new fighter, people everywhere called you a hero and you were offered a position working for Intelligence.

"It was a most difficult situation, but the standards for the test are set by the character and temper of the individual. I had set a trap for you, hoping to snare your ego, but you saw the lies and deception and were able to perceive the right path to follow.

"I stress the importance of seeking only after truth and accepting nothing less. Those who live in the village where you openly challenged My Over Lords are content with what I provide for them. They have no need for answers or wish to know the truth. As long as they are obedient I will continue to provide for them. But you—you were not content! You needed answers and that is the only reason you first crossed the valley.

"Are you content now puny one? With the knowledge the Old One has so graciously shared with you and the truth you found for yourself! Are you content with the answers you have now and are you prepared to stay on this side of the valley with the Old One? Before you answer, look at what I can give to you! Look at the beauty that encompasses everything. The Old One will teach you how to use your mental faculty to manifest everything of your desire. Anything you wish for can be yours by simply using your mental powers to manifest it. On this side of the valley there is always peace and joy, never any hardships or worries. For all eternity these can all be yours! Are you content with what you now have and can you exist here for eternity in peace and joy?

"Are you?" Brahm asked. The ground rumbled with vibrations of His voice.

"No— No, my Lord. I am not content with only what you can give to me. I do not mean this in a selfish way, nor do I want to appear ungrateful. But there are still many unanswered questions. There is I believe, more that still lies beyond your Worlds, My Lord. I believe there is yet a greater understanding still, than what I have found here. I want to travel to those far reaches and discover the answers to my questions."

"How dare you refuse my gifts! I! I who alone can give you everything and you refuse to accept!"

"You cannot give me the answers I need My Lord," Zvi replied.

"I can see now why you were not tempered by the illusions of gifts from the military in the earthly world. Your desire for answers and truth outweighed the severity of my test. And you now stand before me, the ruler of this world and all the worlds below this one and challenge me! You are a warrior, young Zvi. Never falter in your search for your answers. Be prepared to challenge everything you see.Do not ever accept another's belief or understandings as your own. Develop your own, and thereby will you only be satisfied with your discoveries.

"You have my permission to travel beyond My World; but do not attempt travel into the unknown alone. Go only with your guide, The Old One."

Brahm had finished speaking. He had said all there was to say. Zvi remained standing on the rocky pinnacle absorbing the words spoken by Brahm and gazing at the beauty of His world. He turned to look at the Old One, his guide and friend, he was smiling radiantly. "Come my friend," he said, "let us journey into the universes, where we traveled before. Only now with your new enlightenment you will see and recognize things that before you could not."

THE END

Other Books by Randall Probert

A Forgotten Legacy

An Eloquent Caper

Courier de Bois

Katrina's Valley

Mysteries at Matagamon Lake

A Warden's Worry

A Quandry at Knowles Corner

Paradigm

Trial at Norway Dam

A Grafton Tale

Paradigm II

Train to Barnjum

A Trapper's Legacy

Author, Randall Probert

Randall Probert lived and was raised in Strong,Maine; a small town in the western mountains of Maine. Six months after graduating from high school, he left the small town behind for Baltimore, Maryland and a Marine Engineering School, situated downtown near what was then called "The Block". Because of bad weather, the flight from Portland to New York was canceled and this made him late for the connecting flight to Baltimore. A young kid and alone from the backwoods of Maine finally found his way to Washington DC and boarded a bus from there to Baltimore. After leaving the Merchant Marines, he went to an aviation school in Lexington, Massachusetts.

During his interview for Maine Game Warden he was asked, "You have gone from the high seas to the air. . .are you sure you want to be a Game Warden?" Mr. Probert retired from Warden Service in 1997 and started writing historical novels about the history in the areas where he patrolled as a game warden, with his own experiences as a game warden as those of the wardens in his books. Mr. Probert has since expanded his purview and has written 2 science fiction books, *PARADIGM* and *PARADIGM2,* and has now written a mystical adventure, *AN ESOTERIC JOURNEY.* Mr. Probert is also currently working on another historical novel, *THE THREE DAY CLUB,* which should be available early in 2014.